The Lonely Hearts Club

The Lonely Hearts Club

BRENDA JANOWITZ

The following is a work of fiction. Names, characters, places, events and incidents are either the product of the author's imagination or used in an entirely fictitious manner. Any resemblance to actual persons, living or dead, is entirely coincidental.

ISBN: 978-1-940610-35-1
eISBN 978-1-940610-02-3

First trade paperback publication: March 2015 by Polis Books, LLC
1201 Hudson Street
Hoboken, NJ 07030
www.PolisBooks.com

POLIS BOOKS

To Ben, Davey, and Doug. Because of you, I'll never be lonely again.

ALSO BY BRENDA JANOWITZ

Scot on the Rocks
Jack With A Twist
Recipe For A Happy Life

PART ONE: FUCK AND RUN

"And whatever happened to a boyfriend"

1
Money for Nothing

"So, you're fired," he says. Just like that.

Fired.

And I'm utterly shocked. I know, no one ever expects to be fired, but I *really* didn't see this coming. My mouth is wide open as I stare back at him.

"Fired?" is all I can choke out. The room begins to spin. That may be because I was out until sunrise last night drinking vodka tonics at an underground club in Williamsburg, but I'm pretty sure that it's the news that's doing it to me, not the hangover.

"Yes. I'm sorry, Jo, but it's not working out here," he says. His skin is gleaming when he says it. His skin always gleams. He's a dermatologist, so it has to gleam in order for him to stay in business. My skin doesn't ever gleam. At the very most, it shines and turns red when I get hot or embarrassed. I feel it beginning to shine and my hand immediately flies to my cheek, which, of course, only makes it get hotter.

We are in his office when he tells me and he is sitting at his desk, his head framed by his many diplomas and awards that are hung on the wall behind him. They are, as they are always, shining brightly as if they'd been dusted and cleaned that very morning. I look at the picture he keeps framed at the edge of his desk—a photograph of his family taken at a New Year's Eve party, framed in a sterling-silver picture frame that his wife lovingly picked out for their thirtieth wedding anniversary—and then look back up at him.

"You can't fire me," I say, which I wholeheartedly believe. I really *didn't* think that he ever would or could fire me.

"I can," he says, "and I am." He begins to toy with one of the pens sitting on his desk.

"I'm your best employee!" I plead.

"You wore a 'Save CBGBs' T-shirt to work," he says.

"CBGBs was a New York institution," I say. He gives me a blank stare. I shrug in response. Is it my fault that this man has no sense of culture? Of history? "What does it matter what I wear under my assistant's coat anyway?"

"You know the dress code—scrubs or business casual," he says.

"Jeans and a concert tee *is* business casual!"

"People can see the prints on your T-shirts right through the fabric," he says. "And sometimes you wear ones with dirty words on them," he continues, whispering the "dirty words" part as if his grandmother is somehow listening from up above and would be appalled by this particular bit of information.

"Like what?" I ask. Watching him squirm is kind of fun.

"You know which one," he says. And then, in barely a whisper, "Free Pussy Riot."

"That's a band," I say, "not a dirty word." You'd think a doctor would have no problem saying the word "pussy" out loud.

"Jo, it's not just the T-shirts. You've called in the wrong prescriptions for my patients more times than I'd like to admit."

"Some of those drugs have very complicated names," I say in my own defense. And for the record, they do.

"That doesn't mean you can give a patient a more pronounceable drug without consulting me first."

"Then maybe you and your colleagues should start *prescribing* more pronounceable drugs," I argue. He furrows his brow in response. "But I'm your favorite employee!" I plead.

"You balanced the company checkbook wrong the last three out of four quarters."

"You know that I'm not an accountant." When he hired me for the job two years ago, I knew that there would be some accounting involved. What I hadn't realized at the time was that I would have to be quite so specific with the numbers. Which is a challenge for me, seeing as I'm really more of a right-brain kind of person.

"But you know how to balance your own checkbook, don't you?" he says.

For the record, I don't.

"Of course I know how to balance my own checkbook," I say and laugh, as if to say, "Doesn't everybody?" "A business checkbook is much, much different than a personal checkbook," I explain.

For the record, it's not.

"I'm your most loyal employee," I say. My last resort. I find myself alternating between staring into his solid gold, monogrammed Tiffany belt buckle and his shellacked black hair, because I can't meet his eyes.

"This is difficult for me, too, you know," he says, even though I know that it's not.

"Do you realize how embarrassing this is going to be for me?" I say. Manipulative, I know, but it's not exactly like I have anything left in my arsenal.

"I thought you don't get embarrassed," he replies, looking into my eyes, challenging me.

"I don't," I say, frowning like a little girl who hasn't gotten the piece of candy that she wanted.

"Don't take this personally, Pumpkin."

"You can't call me Pumpkin when you're firing me, Daddy."

2

I Love Rock n' Roll

"You got fired by your own father?" my best friend, Chloe, asks me.

"I know," I reply. "It's a new low. Even for me."

"What a dick move," my boyfriend, Jesse, says. Thank God I still have Jesse. I don't know what I would do without him. He understands me in a way that no one else ever has before—and I like to think that I understand him that same way, too.

Jesse is looking over Chloe's shoulder to see if the band is about to start. We are at a tiny Lower East Side club that is packed to capacity to see The Rage, one of our favorite local bands. "He could have at least had your dick brother do it."

"Andrew isn't really a full partner in the practice yet," I explain.

"You're allowed to screw the Barbie doll nurse before you're a full partner?" Chloe asks, brushing her silky black hair off her shoulders. Andrew's girlfriend—the office's head nurse—does bear a striking resemblance to a Barbie doll. But, to be fair, my brother does look quite a lot like Ken. Still, it's pretty tough talk coming from a woman who's only five-foot-two.

"At least you still have the Bumblebee," Jesse says, referring to my bright yellow VW Beetle.

"Forget the Bee, at least you still have a parking space in the garage of your building," Chloe says. "An even more elusive asset in Manhattan than an actual car."

"You're right," I say. "I guess."

"Still," Jesse says, looking into my eyes. I love it when he burns his eyes into me. Even in the dark, I can see them clearly—a light sky blue, framed by thick black lashes, just like Jakob Dylan. He has a thick black curl falling to the center of his forehead. He flips his head back quickly and it falls back in place with the masses of other curls piled on his head. "It still sucks."

"I would rather have my father fire me than my brother, I think," Chloe says to no one in particular. The waitress—who I recognize as the bassist in the band that plays the Lion's Den on Sunday nights—comes to our table. Jesse and Chloe order beers (Chloe's is a light) and I order a vodka tonic.

"Well, I'd rather not be fired at all," I say as soon as the waitress leaves.

"It'll give you more time to focus on your music, babe," Jesse says as he puts his index finger gently under my chin, angling my face upward for a kiss. It makes me smile and Chloe blush.

I did mean to get a real job. But there was always something in the way. Something more important to do. Something left that I *had* to do, like apply to schools to get my MFA in music, or some reason that I had to wait, like when my band nearly took off and we almost landed a record deal.

Life is different for people like me. Artists. I could never work for the rest of my life in an office, toiling away day and night at a job that I wasn't passionate about. I need passion in my life.

Excitement. Adrenaline. Sure, everybody says they want passion and excitement in their lives, but I really mean it.

The bug hit me when I was five years old. My parents were having a dinner party and my father encouraged me to sing a song for his guests while he accompanied me on his prized possession—his baby grand piano. He began to play "Hey, Big Spender" from the musical *Sweet Charity,* and the feeling overcame me. All eyes were on me, and it felt like magic. I opened my mouth, improvised some dance moves I'd picked up in my ballet class, and belted it out. The rest is history. I decided right at that very second that singing was what I wanted to do with my life. The only thing I wanted to do with my life.

I've been working my ass off since then to make a go of it. Nothing compares to the feeling I get when I'm on stage. The stage is my true home—it's where I come alive, where I feel the most myself, where I can do anything.

My parents encouraged me for a while. They even dragged me, Gypsy Rose Lee style, to the *American Star* auditions back when I was twelve. I made it through the entire season, leveling the competition with my killer rendition of "Hey, Big Spender." By the finals, I thought I had it in the bag. I was going against a corn-fed blonde from Kansas who had never been out of the Midwest her whole life. She had buck teeth and a flat chest—no match for my retainer and burgeoning bosom. I belted out "Hey, Big Spender" and she did a shy rendition of "Over the Rainbow" and, in so doing, stole my crown right from under me.

My parents fought for three weeks—my mother accusing my father of pushing me into a song that was "too adult," and my father accusing my mother of pushing me into a business that was full of rejection. One of my clearest childhood memories is overhearing him tell my mother that he was happy that I lost.

The irony of that little Pollyanna stealing my *American Star* crown is that the girl who beat me was Amber Fairchild. Yes, *that* Amber Fairchild. The pop sensation who flew to stardom at age fifteen, singing "I Want You to Keep Me Up All Night (All Right)." Otherwise known as the bane of my existence. I hate her brand of slutty bubble-gum pop, but what I hate more is that this girl made it and I did not. I often wonder what would have happened if I had won *American Star* instead of Amber. *I* should be the one with the record deal, production company, fan club, and slacker husband who mooches off me. Well, my current boyfriend mooches off me, so the way I figure it, I'm a quarter of the way there. The record deal has so far eluded me, but I know that it's just around the corner.

My first band—my only band, really—was on the cusp of breaking through about two years ago. We called ourselves The Lonely Hearts Club Band. Together since high school, we had it all—the talent, the drive, and even the requisite bad-boy drummer with a drug problem. We were just beginning to have a bit of a following in Manhattan—and not just among our NYU classmates, a real following. Our bass player, Kane, had a girlfriend who set up a Web site for us, and we posted photos of ourselves, my song lyrics, and our show dates. Frankie, our lead ax man, was the face. The gorgeous one who girls flocked to. He brought in the crowds. Chloe was our de facto photographer, and I wrote a blog about trying to make it in the music industry. The blog barely ever got any hits, but it made us all feel more legit.

We had a gig at the C Note in Alphabet City, and a friend of a friend of a friend's pet dog had arranged for an A&R guy from Pinnacle to come hear us play. This was it. Our big chance. The moment we'd been waiting for—wishing for—since we first got together in high school.

The night before, we all went out to play a gig at a small club in Chelsea to get ready. We were all so young then. We still felt invincible, in that way you do before anything really bad has ever happened to you, before you've really had a chance to see the way life really is. I don't remember much about that evening, but I know that I went home early to try to get some sleep before the big day. Billy, our drummer, must have stayed out at the club without the rest of the band because the next night, he didn't show up at the gig. Two days later, we got a call from New York City Hospital telling us that Billy had overdosed and died. The hospital staff told us that someone dropped him off at the entrance, left him there, and disappeared.

The record company wouldn't talk to us without him. Certainly didn't want to come and see us play anymore. Wouldn't even listen to our demo. I thought we were Blondie, but I guess even Blondie wouldn't have been signed without Chris Stein. It would be like the Doors without Krieger, the Stones without Richards. Would it be the same band? I could debate stuff like this for hours, but the point is—they wanted nothing more to do with us. And then, without Billy, we all wanted nothing to do with each other. The next Monday, I went to work for my dad.

I am currently without band. And now I find myself, six months after graduating from college, with no real job and no real prospects. And even if I did have prospects, who on earth would hire a loser who's been recently fired by her own father?

"Hey, China Doll," Chloe's flavor of the week says, pulling a chair up to our table and kissing her on the cheek. I don't even remember his name. It's never a good idea to remember their names. They're always the same—anti-establishment, angry, and unbelievably hot. I can spot 'em a mile away.

This one's wearing a T-shirt from his high school soccer team. I really hope that he's out of college like we are and just wearing the shirt ironically, but there's a good chance that he's actually still *in* high school, so I don't dare ask.

"Hey, yourself," Chloe says back. She doesn't seem to mind this ridiculous "China Doll" nickname, even though she is actually Korean.

"Hey, man," Jesse says as he puts his hand out for the flavor of the week to grab. Even though Jesse calls everyone "man," I can tell that he doesn't know this guy's name, either. After two and a half years together, I know one "man" from the other.

"She's Korean," I say to Flavor of the Week, in lieu of hello.

"Cool," he says, and leans in to Chloe for a kiss.

"You called her China Doll," I say, "but she's actually not Chinese."

Flavor of the Week breaks from the kiss for a second to regard me.

"Jo, please shut up," Chloe says, and goes back to kissing. Jesse laughs under his breath and kisses me on the head as the lights dim.

"Give me a break, Chloe," I whine. "I was fired today!"

No sympathy from the people at our table.

"By my dad!" I cry out. Heads turn. That's true star power—commanding an audience even on your worst day.

The band begins to play, and Jesse and I jump to our feet. Chloe and Flavor of the Week sit and make out, oblivious to their surroundings. Jesse and I dance, singing along to the chorus. I feel the tensions of the day fade into the music.

Four songs in, the redheaded lead singer takes a break to talk to the crowd. "Hey, we're The Rage and we just want to thank you all for being here and supporting the band," she says and the crowd goes wild. The light hits her hair and it looks like fire. "A friend of ours—a very good friend of the band—has asked us for a favor tonight. And for this guy, well, for this guy we'd do anything." More screams from the crowd. "His friend is having a pretty awful day, and the only thing that would make her life better is to sing to you lovely people tonight." The crowd goes nuts. "Can you believe that? I hope you're flattered," she says, flirting with the crowd. "Jo, are you out there? Jo Waldman?"

I turn to Jesse. "No fucking way," I say. The edges of his mouth curl slightly and he shrugs his shoulders. I put my hand around the back of his head and pull him to me and kiss him hard. "Thank you."

"It's nothing," he says. "I just wanted to do something for you today. It'll get you jump-started."

"Jump-started?"

"Yeah, now that you won't be working for your dad anymore, you can focus on your music," he says. He doesn't need to say anything else—I know where this is going. It's the same discussion we've had over and over since my band broke up junior year. I consider defending myself, telling him that I have a gig or two lined up, and that I've even been working on a new song lately, but I instead take the high road and choose not to turn this into a heated argument. I try to remember that he's doing something nice for me on a bad day.

"Thank you," I say as I walk around the table and smooth out the front of my used Levi's. I'm thankful that I'm dressed in my usual uniform of black leather motorcycle boots, ripped vintage jeans, and a fitted concert tee over a white long-sleeve T-shirt. Running my fingers through my hair to mess it up a bit, I walk to the stage. My black hair tops off the look—the bangs and layers around my face are Joan Jett, circa 1982, and the rest of it, all tangles and curls, is pure Stevie Nicks.

As I discuss song selection with the band, all I can think about is how lucky I am to have Jesse. We debate The Pretenders versus The Kinks, and I turn around to sneak a peek at him. He's staring at me. I wink at him and wonder if he can see me through the darkness.

Jesse and I met at a Battle of the Bands competition out in the suburbs of New Jersey, just a stone's throw from the George Washington Bridge. This was before Billy died, back when my band was still together, before I went to work for my dad.

It was at a dive bar called Treble that was rumored to have been owned at one time by Richie Sambora. Each July, they ran a Battle of the Bands contest, and the prize was $10,000. All of the bands that played the downtown clubs went—any band that was anything at all was there.

Jesse's band and my band were the two bands left in the finals. We won, of course, but who's keeping track? What I remember most about it was how goddamned romantic the whole thing was. I noticed Jesse on the first day of competition, tapping his drumsticks on a table in the back of the bar to Jimi Hendrix's "Fire." When he glanced up and saw me staring at him, he knocked over his beer bottle with his drumsticks, and it spilled all over the spiral notebook he was writing in. Billy caught this little exchange out of the corner of his eye and quickly ushered me away, lecturing me on messing around with the competition.

Through each of the rounds, I could see Jesse staring at me from behind his massive drum set, crystal blue eyes burning into me. Every time I was on stage, I found myself singing to him. Always to him.

"Are we the Montagues or the Capulets?" Billy asked me as we walked off the stage on the second night of competition.

"I don't know what you're talking about," I told him.

"He's in a hack band that plays weddings and bar mitzvahs every weekend," Billy said.

"Nothing wrong with making some money to support yourself," I said, even though I secretly hated bands that sold out like that.

"You're too good for him."

I started wearing tighter and tighter jeans each round, in the hope that Jesse would notice me. Any time he tried to approach me, one of my band members would be there, seemingly out of nowhere, to tear us apart and remind me that we were there to compete. On the last night of the competition, I even had my hair blown out, a fact that Chloe will never let me live down.

Right after my band was announced as the winner and we all hugged and mugged for the audience, I marched right off the stage and into Jesse's arms. It was like something out of a movie, with him waiting in the wings and everyone in the room watching us, just waiting for it to happen. I ran to him. We fell into each other's arms and kissed like no one was watching.

After that night, we spent every night together, either attending each other's gigs or meeting up late night after our respective gigs, and we haven't been apart for one night since.

Through the crowd, I see Jesse staring offstage. I turn back to The Rage as we decide upon "I Want You to Want Me" by Cheap Trick as a compromise.

I spin around to the crowd as the band begins to cue up the song. The lights hit my face and I feel the energy building up inside of me. The music penetrates my bones and I can't help but smile. This is where I belong—under the burning lights with tons of eyes focused on me—not in some doctor's office wishing the hours of my life away. I can hear Chloe and Flavor of the Week screaming my name. I can't see Jesse anymore, but I can feel his eyes on me. I can feel everyone's eyes on me. The band plays the last eight bars before the first verse and I cock my right hip, ready to go.

I adjust the mike and sing.

3
Call Me

"I am going to kill him. This time I am really going to kill him."

"Mom?" I say into the telephone. Even though it's well past 11 A.M., I'm still dead asleep. Ah, the joys of being unemployed. The morning light is pouring into the bedroom of my Soho loft. Well, my father's Soho loft—the loft he bought for a song in the '80s (parking space included) so that he could crash on the nights he taught night seminars at NYU Medical School. But I've been staying here ever since I graduated from the NYU dorms and he hasn't exactly kicked me out yet, so I sort of consider it mine.

"Your stupid father," my mother says into the telephone. "This time I am really going to kill him. The nerve that man has!"

"Mom, it's okay," I say, reaching for the glass of water that I left at my bedside the night before. "Don't worry about it. I'll be fine." I roll over and see that Jesse is already out of bed. I can smell the coffee wafting into the bedroom from the kitchen. I take a deep breath and try to figure out if he's brewing the Costa Rican dark or the Columbian medium roast.

"That man claims that you can't balance a checkbook," she says. "*Of course* you know how to balance a checkbook!"

"Babe," Jesse says, walking into the bedroom, planting a quiet kiss on my cheek, "I'm going into the studio. Can you spot me some more cash?"

"I mean," my mother continues into my ear, "who doesn't know how to balance a checkbook?!"

"Babe, I just *gave* you money for that demo last month," I whisper back, careful to put my hand over the telephone.

"You know, technically," my mom is saying into my ear, "I own half of that practice."

"Well, the band needs another demo," Jesse says, pulling on the jeans he wore last night. "Cassie's going to talk to IMC for us, and we need a new demo to give her."

"If I divorced him tomorrow," my mom says, "I could take him for half of that damn practice."

"Mom, you're not going to divorce Dad," I say to her. And then to Jesse: "Who the hell is Cassie?"

"The lead singer for The Rage," Jesse says. "You met her last night. They just signed with IMC, but it's on the down low. No one knows about it yet." He puts his fingers to his mouth to make the international sign for "shhh."

"Didn't you just meet her last night?" I ask Jesse. "Why is she telling you about their deal if it's such a big secret?"

"You don't think I would divorce that man?" my mother asks me. "Because I can divorce that man if I want—"

"I've got to get going. So, the money?" Jesse says, pulling a fresh T-shirt over his head. I cannot believe he is asking me for more money. Was he not there last night when I told everyone that my father fired me? I'm pretty sure that he was, since I distinctly recall someone calling my father a dick. And as tired as I am, I'm also pretty sure that he is the person now asking for money from said dick.

My mother is still ranting on the other end of the phone as I talk to Jesse. "I just don't think that I should be throwing money around right now," I say, and Jesse's mouth tightens into a pit.

"Throwing money around?" he says. "Is that what you call it? Don't you believe in me? In my music?"

"Yes," I say, as my mother's voice rises an octave as she details how much her friend Linda recently got in a divorce settlement. "But you were just saying how I should be focusing on my music right now. What if *I* need that money for studio time?"

"What if *you* need that money?" Jesse says. "Well, when was the last time you sat down and wrote a song? What exactly do you think you'd be recording in that studio?"

I feel my face begin to burn. "Why don't you get the money from someone else's girlfriend for a change?" I say and Jesse storms out of the apartment. As he makes his exit, I can hear him say "I didn't just meet her last night" under his breath. As if that justifies this whole prior exchange or something.

"Jo?" my mom says. "Jo?"

"Yes, Mom, I'm still here. Of course I'm listening to you."

"Well," she says, letting out a sigh, "don't think about all of this unpleasantness for a while. Have you given any thought to what you would like for your twenty-second birthday?"

"A record contract?" I say, rolling out of bed and padding toward the kitchen with the portable phone tucked between my head and my shoulder.

"I meant, more like a party or a small dinner thing, or a big present?"

"I don't know, Mom," I say, grabbing the carafe from the coffeemaker. There's no coffee left in it. Jesse must have made only enough for himself before he left for the day. I silently curse him as I empty the filter and go about making a fresh pot. "I don't really want anything. I just want the day to pass by unnoticed."

"Unnoticed?" my mother asks. I know that she is appalled that I would let the opportunity to have a party or get a huge present pass me by. She would never let any opportunity to have a party or get a huge present pass *her* by. "You only turn twenty-two once, honey."

"I know, Mom," I say. "It's just that I feel like it accentuates the fact that my life is not exactly going to plan."

"Your life is perfect. You are beautiful and talented and very, very lucky," she says. I know she doesn't mean to patronize me, but she is, as usual, totally dismissing what's important to me. We're mere minutes from the conversation turning to why I'm not pressuring my live-in boyfriend to produce an engagement ring (little does she know that said ring would probably be financed by her husband's money), so I have to clarify what the life plan is.

"I'm not where I want to be with my music," I say, missing the filter as I pour coffee beans directly onto the counter.

"There's more to life than music," she says.

"Not for me, there's not," I say, cupping the beans into my hand and putting them into the coffeemaker.

"Why don't we talk about this when you're in a better mood?" she says, and hangs up the phone just as I'm telling her that my mood is fine.

The coffee machine whizzes and whirls, grinding the beans and beginning to brew. I stare at the coffee dripping down and think about how crazy my mother is making me with the emphasis on my birthday. It's as if she doesn't have a wedding to plan, so she might as well put all of her pent-up "plan your only daughter's wedding" energy into a birthday celebration for me.

She doesn't seem to care at all that it's not what I want.

The phone rings again and I pause for a moment, deciding whether or not I should answer it at all. It would serve her right if I just didn't pick up. If she doesn't care about what I want, then I don't care about what she wants.

The answering machine picks up the call.

"Miss Waldman? Uh, I mean Jo. It's Vinnie, down at the garage—"

"Hello?" I say as I click the phone on. I silently chastise myself for forgetting to call the garage this morning to tell them that I wouldn't be using my car.

"Oh, hi. It's Vinnie, down at the garage."

"Hey, Vinnie. I'm so sorry I didn't call. I won't be needing my car today. Actually, I won't be needing it at all anymore during the week. Well, unless I have a gig. But I probably won't, so how about I just call you whenever I need it?"

"Uh," Vinnie says, "that's not what I was calling about. Manhasset Volkswagen is here to pick up your car."

"It's not going in for service today," I say as I pour myself a cup of coffee. "They must be there for someone else's car."

"Not for service," Vinnie says. "It's more like a repossession kind of deal."

"Repo—what? My car's not being repossessed," I say. "There is no way my car is being repossessed. Put them on the line."

I grab my apartment keys and race out of the loft, still holding the portable phone and wearing my PJs and no shoes. I hit the DOWN button for the elevator as a voice comes onto the line.

"Miss Waldman?" he says. "This is Matt Kassnove from Manhasset Volkswagen. How are you today?"

"You tell me," I say as I hop into the elevator. Matt begins to say something back to me, but the call gets dropped as the elevator lurches down to the basement. I burst through the doors of the garage, and a man who I can only assume is Matt Kassnove is in the driver's seat of my bright yellow Beetle, about to drive it out of the garage.

"Stop!" I scream, holding my hands out in front of me as I run to the front of the car. Vinnie is in the background, telling me he's sorry over and over.

"Miss Waldman, this is nothing personal, you understand," Matt says.

"Personal?" I say as I hop onto the hood of the car and lay down on it spread eagle. "You are taking my car, my personal car, and I am personally very upset, so this is very much 'personal' to me!"

"Miss Waldman, please get off the hood of the car," he says.

"I am not getting off the hood of this car," I say, arms and legs still splayed out as far as I can reach them. I'm grateful that the car is on and the hood is warm as the winter airs floats down into the garage from outside.

"Miss Waldman, with all due respect," Matt says, "you are not the owner of this car. Your father is. And he told me to come and pick it up. I'm just doing my job."

"My father is taking my Bumblebee?" I say, getting out of my most unladylike spread-eagle pose. I sit up on the hood and cross my legs.

"I'm sorry, Miss Waldman," Matt says.

"Wait just one minute," I say, and dial my father's office number on my portable phone. The reception is bad, since we're in the basement of the building, but we're right near the exit, so even with the static-filled connection, I can still hear.

Nurse Barbie picks up the line and I demand to speak to my father.

"This is for your own good, Pumpkin," my father explains.

"How is humiliating me in a different way every day of the

week good for me?" I ask in a whisper, trying in vain to make it so that Vinnie and Matt can't hear me. It's a losing cause, though, because they are both listening to every word as if they were in the studio audience of *The Jerry Springer Show*.

"You graduated college in May. You're turning twenty-two soon, Pumpkin. It's time to grow up. And it's my fault that you haven't. I've coddled you for too long. I gave you a job. I let you live in the loft, rent-free. I even got you a car to drive to your job. I guess I thought if I gave you all the tools, you'd make something of the opportunity. Maybe if things worked out at my office, you could have your own business one day.

"You've been standing still for the last two years and I'm enabling it. But not anymore. It's time for you to get a real job and start paying your own way. Once you do that, if you can afford it, you can have the car back."

"I can?" I ask.

"If you can afford the lease and the rent on the parking space, yes."

"I have to pay rent for the parking space, too?" I ask. No one can afford a parking space in Manhattan.

"But keep in mind, Pumpkin, you will also need to start paying me rent on the loft." He wants me to start paying for the loft? Is this the part where I lose my home and I have to move into my car, like Jewel?

I must not let this Beetle leave the lot no matter what.

"I can't afford a loft!"

"Well, then, I'd suggest you get a job quickly. I'll give you a short grace period to get on your feet, but after that, we'll be working out some sort of payment plan."

I hang up the phone without saying good-bye and get that feeling of floaty weightlessness you have when you're in a dream.

Or a nightmare.

"Are we all clear now, Miss Waldman?"

"Please just call me Jo," I say, sliding down off the hood.

"Well, then, I'm sorry, Jo," Matt says, and then drives my car out of the garage into the winter cold.

I stand there, shivering in the driveway of the garage for a few minutes, looking out to the street where Matt has just taken my car. My dad's car, I should say. That distinction has now been made clear to me by the fine folks at Manhasset Volkswagen.

"Yo, Jo, your daddy paid for your car?" Vinnie says. "Damn! How do you get a setup like that?"

"I'll let you know when I figure that out," I say and walk out of the garage to the elevator. As I walk barefoot along the garage floor, a pebble gets stuck in the middle of my foot and I have to hop back up the rest of the way to the loft.

4
Loser

I limp into my loft and hop onto the kitchen counter to clean off my dirty feet. Removing the rather large pebble that has lodged itself squarely into the center of my left foot, I begin to cry. I tell myself that I'm just crying because I'm in pain, but once I give myself permission to cry because my foot hurts, the floodgates open.

As soon as the tears start to flow, I immediately wash my hands and splash water on my face. I hate girls who cry. I'm sure that Deborah Harry never cried when she was living with her whole band in a studio apartment that only had one bed before they got their record deal. (She did have Chris Stein to keep her warm, though.)

I call Jesse's cell phone and it goes directly to voice mail. I hang up and walk over to the couch, careful to baby my left foot as I walk. Distracted by the pain, I almost walk into Jesse's drum set, and my right hip grazes his cymbal, causing it to ring out. Beck's immortal words immediately spring to mind, and I take my guitar from its stand and begin to play.

"'Soy,'" I sing, "'un perdedor. I'm a loser, baby, so why don't you kill me?'"

The phone rings and I set down my guitar and pick up the phone. I take a quick peek at the caller ID and it reads *supergood advertising*. It's safe to pick up the phone, since it's Chloe calling from her uber-hip ad agency, and not my mother calling again.

"How's unemployed life?" she asks.

"It sucks," I say, leaning back onto the couch. "My dad just had my Beetle carted away."

"No freaking way!" she says. "Well, think of it this way, now you definitely don't have to drive all the way out to Long Island anymore for a job that you hate!"

"True," I say, "but why do I feel like such a loser?"

"Because you don't have a car or a job and your daddy pays for your apartment?" she suggests, laughing. I know she's teasing me, just like she always does, but this time I take it to heart. She's right: I'm just a spoiled brat whose daddy pays for her apartment. How did I get here? I was supposed to be a rock star by now, with my *own* downtown loft, complete with parking space and car to park in it.

"Wow, that sounds even worse when you say it out loud."

"Well, at least you still have a hot boyfriend. And anyway, you'll never believe this." As Chloe segues into a story about how her expense account has been cut down, I allow myself to do something that I know isn't good for me, to indulge in an activity that I know I shouldn't: I turn on my computer and go to my old band's Web site. Now, I know there's no point in doing this and that no good will come out of revisiting my thirty seconds of glory, but at times like these, I can't help myself.

Just a few clicks of my keyboard, and I'm there. The Lonely Hearts Club Band Web site. It looks so primitive compared to what they're doing with the newer Web sites nowadays, but I like that it hasn't changed at all, a snapshot frozen in time. I click on the link for the blog and read my last entry. It's all about that last gig we were supposed to play, written the night before Billy OD'd and died. There are links to our Facebook page and Twitter account. I linger on Billy's picture a little longer than I should. A wave of sadness overcomes me, and I take a deep breath just to steady myself.

I wish I could still be that person who wrote this blog entry. Hopeful and confident, so full of possibility. Everything I wanted in life was almost within my reach, so close I could taste it. My band still intact. Like a family. Safe and sound. But they're not now. Billy is gone, and I'm not that person anymore. I don't think that I ever will be again.

I should write a blog entry now, I think. *Show the world what life is really like. Full of disappointment. Full of anger.*

"Are you even listening to me?" Chloe asks. I quickly turn off my computer, as if she'll somehow know that I'm doing something that she wouldn't approve of.

"Yes," I say. "Only thirty-five bucks for dinner when you're working late."

"Exactly," she says. "It's totally inhumane. Speaking of food, do you want to go for dinner tonight?"

"Sure," I say. "I'm tutoring Lola at six. How about eight?"

"Call me when you get back," she says, and we hang up.

Talking with Chloe cheers me up and gives me the energy I need to stay off my band's old Web site. If Chloe knew that I was on it, she'd tell me that it's unhealthy to dwell on the good old days like that.

Talking with Chloe also reminds me that I need to figure out what song I want to work on this evening with my Little Sister from the Harlem Community Center. Chloe and I first went there for a volunteer project our human services class did with them about two years ago—one of these programs where they hook you up with a child from the area who you mentor and spend quality time with. The rest of the class did the requisite one school year with their Little Siblings, but Chloe and I stuck with it, she teaching her Little Sister art, me teaching Lola about music. I hate to say it, but I think that I get more out of my relationship with Lola than she does. Getting to know her has truly been one of the brightest spots in the last few years for me. And it always puts things into perspective for me: No matter how bad I think I have it, seeing how hard Lola's mom works for her to have a better life than she had reminds me that all things considered, I really am a very, very lucky person.

What would Lola like to play today? I wonder as I flip on MTV. It's an Amber Fairchild video. Yes, *that* Amber Fairchild. Singing her latest slutty bubble-gum pop number. This one's called "Stick It (In Me)." As the video comes to a close, I see her telling an MTV VJ that the song is really about self worth and self love, and that when she's singing the song, what she's really doing is asking the Lord to stick confidence and self love and a whole host of other very Christian things in her.

As if we all can't see right through that. Everyone knows that she was sleeping with her manager before she was even legal. And with the leopard skirt she's sporting today, I'm quite certain that what he will be sticking into her after the show will not be self love.

I decide on "I'm Special," by the Pretenders, and download the sheet music off the Internet. I put my guitar in its case (I gave Lola her own acoustic guitar last year for Christmas) and fill my messenger bag with everything I'll need for the evening. I used to drive to Lola's place on my way home from working on Long Island, and I silently curse my father as I realize that I'll need to take the subway all the way uptown. Then I silently curse *myself* when I realize that I've let my MetroCard expire.

Setting down everything I'll need for later, I look around the loft and decide that today is the first day of the rest of my life. Of my new unemployed life, that is. I make a mental checklist of all the things I plan to do, all of the projects I want to tackle, in my new unemployed state. Starting in the living room, I begin to clean. As I organize and dust and arrange, I realize how therapeutic fixing up the loft is. It may be owned by my father, but as I put Jesse's and my things back in their proper spots, it still feels like it's very much mine.

It's unbelievable how even when you spend the day doing nothing, the time flies by. Maybe it's just the freedom from helping my father do pore extractions all day, but in any case, once I finish organizing the apartment, shower, and change, it's 5 P.M., time to head up to Harlem to tutor my Little Sister.

"I CAN'T believe you took the subway," Lola says to me with a laugh as she picks me up at the 6 station on Lexington and 116th Street.

"I told you not to pick me up," I say. "Why are you not at your place waiting for me, like I told you?"

"I didn't think you could survive the mean streets of Harlem all by yourself," she teases. She's eleven and already has that pseudojaded attitude that I know she thinks is cool. I know it because that's how I was when I was eleven.

"Well, I can," I say. "And I would've made my way to you just fine."

"I can't believe you even knew where the station was." As we walk from the subway to her apartment building, Lola struts and preens, checking herself out as we pass windows that she can see herself in. She's even got her guitar strapped to her back, trying to look hip, which is entirely unnecessary, since we're heading straight to her apartment anyway.

"So what do you want to play today?" I ask her as we get into her apartment, a one bedroom on 118th Street and First Avenue. Her mother, who is studying to become a nurse at night and works as a nanny to an Upper East Side family during the day, gives Lola the bedroom and sleeps on a pullout couch in the living room.

"Amber Fairchild," she says, flipping on MTV and dancing along to the "Stick It (In Me)" video, which is, for some reason, playing yet again. How can this video play twice in one day when MTV barely ever plays videos anymore?

"What did you just say?" I ask, putting down my guitar on the couch.

"'I want you,'" she sings, "'to stick it.'"

"Turn that off," I say, but she ignores me, still facing the television, gyrating along to the music.

"'Stick it in me,'" she sings. "'Stick it in me.'" I grab her hips and steady them.

"Stop it," I say. "You are not listening to this crap."

"Why not?" she asks, turning to face me. My hands fall from her hips and Lola throws her hands above her head and starts gyrating to the music again.

"She is totally antifeminist," I say, pulling her down on the couch to sit next to me. "You should like talented women, like Joan Jett and Chrissie Hynde."

"Who?" she says, now dancing in her seat, eyes back on Amber Fairchild. I click the television off.

"Or Pat Benatar," I say, grabbing Lola's guitar and tuning it for her. "I'd even accept Pat Benatar."

"Who?" she says as I line up her fingers for her to strum a few bars of "We Belong" on her guitar.

"Alicia Keys," I say as I begin to strum my own guitar. "You should like Alicia Keys."

"Why, because she's black?" Lola asks me, a tiny smirk betraying her false tough-girl front.

"No," I say, "because she is a brilliant and talented singer-songwriter who doesn't use sex to sell her records." Lola stares blankly back at me. All I can think is, *Please don't ask me any questions about sex.* "Now, let's play."

5
Suspicious Minds

"Lola wants to play Amber Fairchild music," I tell Chloe later that evening, once we are firmly ensconced at the sushi bar at Suki. Owing to my newly unemployed state, Chloe's treating me to a nice dinner, since, as she explained to me, I'll probably have to subsist on cat food and crackers from now on. I should have one nice meal before the poverty sets in.

"Is that a sign of the apocalypse?" Chloe asks with a laugh as she hands our order to the waitress. At Suki, you don't tell your waitress your order. They just hand you a piece of paper with all of the sushi choices listed and you simply mark off the ones you want and hand the sheet back to your waitress. Chloe says I'm only a pseudo-sushi eater, since I refuse to try anything but rolls. She orders a platter of sashimi while I opt for a spicy tuna roll and an eel avocado roll.

"Maybe," I say, watching the sushi chef in front of me slice through a massive piece of salmon.

"You know what else would be a sign?" Chloe asks as she breaks open her chopsticks.

"What?"

"You getting a real job," she says, tapping her chopsticks together for emphasis.

"I had a real job," I say. "I got fired."

"By your own dad," she says, rolling her eyes. "I know."

"Really sensitive, Chlo," I say, turning to face her.

"How would you like to work at supergood advertising?" she asks, turning to me. "Well, *for* supergood. You wouldn't actually be working there."

"Your agency?" I ask. "What do you mean?"

"Well," Chloe says, her smile brightening, "there's this freelance gig coming open."

"I'm listening," I say. A freelance job sounds perfect—making your own hours, working on your own time. It would give me the cash flow I now desperately need, while giving me the time to work on my music.

"Writing jingles."

"What?" I say as the waitress brings us a bowl of edamame and our bottle of sake.

"Writing jingles," Chloe says, pouring me a glass of sake twice as big as hers. "For one of our corporate clients." The fact that she's trying to get me drunk tells me that she already knows what I think of that.

"Me writing jingles for corporate America?" I say. "That really would be a sign of the apocalypse."

"Down that glass of sake and then tell me what you think," Chloe says, taking a piece of edamame. I do as I'm told. "It's freelance for now, so it's basically part-time. You'll start with one of our oldest clients—Healthy Foods. They're looking for a new image after that huge false-advertising lawsuit over their coffee, and they want us to bring in some new blood to shake things up. That's where you come in. You'd be the new blood. The designated shaker-upper."

"Still a sign of the apocalypse," I say and Chloe pours me another glass of sake. I down it, and Chloe downs hers. I take a deep breath and Chloe looks at me with hopeful eyes, waiting for me to say yes. "Actually, it's not. I'm being a brat—I need the money, and you know that I need the money—I can't believe you. You're an amazing friend. Thank you so much."

"Don't make me blush," she says, giving me a hug.

"How many people did you have to piss off for this?"

"None, actually," Chloe says as she finishes off her second glass of sake. "They thought I was a hero for suggesting it. It's a win-win." We clink our tiny sake glasses for a toast. "Cheers. To being a sellout for corporate America."

"Ah," I say, "to being a sellout for corporate America with a place to live."

"When do you have to get that first payment on the loft to your dad?" Chloe says, putting her sake glass back down on the table.

"Not for a while, I'm sure. Dinner's on me," I say. "You rule."

"It doesn't pay *that* well," Chloe says. "I'm still paying for dinner. You can just pledge your undying love and devotion to me."

"Done." We clink our glasses together again.

"Good," she says, "because you start tomorrow. We've got a client meeting with Healthy Foods at noon."

"I guess I won't sleep in," I say. "I'll set my alarm for ten."

HIGH ON sake and my newly acquired freelance gig, I get back to the loft and kick my shoes off as I walk in the door. Right next to Jesse's black Converse sneakers, there are a pair of gold stilettos that are not mine.

I make my way into the living room, where Jesse is sitting on my couch with a very familiar-looking redhead. They've already polished off a bottle of my father's 1990 Lafite-Rothschild and are laughing hysterically. Jesse knows that I was holding onto that wine for the next time my father comes over, and I can't believe he's opened it. I'm not sure what I'm more pissed off about—the fact that he's opened a bottle of wine that I was saving for my father or that he's done it with some redhead who wears gold stilettos.

"Hey, babe," Jesse says as he stands up and throws his arm around my waist. "You remember Cassie, don't you?" For the record, I don't. "From The Rage?"

"Yes, of course," I say, practically tripping over my own feet as I go to shake her hand. For some reason, I'm trying very hard to pretend that I'm not drunk. "How *are* you?"

"Great," she says. "Just great, man."

"Congratulations on your record deal," I say, and immediately recall that Jesse told me that no one was supposed to know about it. I eye the bottle of Lafite and see that it is almost completely empty.

"Thanks so much," Cassie says. "We are *psyched.*"

"You earned it," Jesse says.

"Thanks, man," she says as she gets up from the couch. "Anyway, we're recording tomorrow, so I should probably go."

"No!"

"Yeah..." Jesse and I say at the same time. I tell Cassie to stay, but Jesse maintains that she probably should go. I scramble awkwardly out of her way as she tries to gather her things to leave.

Jesse walks Cassie to the door and I fall down onto the couch. I can hear them whispering before he closes the door behind her.

I position myself just so on the couch so that I look sexy when Jesse comes back to the living room to apologize for inviting some strange woman to our apartment and drinking my father's expensive wine.

"So," Jesse says as he walks over to the couch.

"So," I say, trying to maintain my sexy pose. I'm lying on my right side with my left leg thrown lazily over my right and have my head in my right hand. I'm hoping he mistakes my drunk eyes for sexy bedroom eyes. I like to look good for arguments with Jesse, so that he can tell me that I'm right that much quicker and we can get to making up that much sooner.

"Cassie lent me money for the demo," he says, standing over me. Usually, he would plop himself right down on the ottoman, but he stands in front of the couch tonight, looking down at me.

"Why did Cassie lend you money?" I ask. It occurs to me to sit up, but I'm simply too exhausted.

"Cassie lent me money and she has none," he says, still standing over me. "You wouldn't lend me money, and you have tons."

"I don't have tons," I say, and hoist myself up to sit upright.

"Yeah, right," Jesse says, opening his arms out wide to show me the loft, as if he's one of the *Deal or No Deal* girls.

"Why did she lend you money?" I ask, as the room starts to spin. I'm not sure if it's the sake or the confusion over what is going on.

"I needed the money, Jo. You knew that," Jesse says. "I had to take the money from wherever I could."

"What are you," I say, summoning all of my energy to get up from the couch and walk toward the bedroom, "a drug addict? Getting money anywhere you can?" Jesse doesn't follow me—he stays firmly planted in the living room.

"Yes. I'm addicted," Jesse says. "I'm addicted to music."

"You're addicted to being a drama queen," I say, slamming the door to the bedroom in my wake. That was the best comeback I could think of with half a bottle of sake in my belly. I throw my clothes off in a huff and get into bed. I silently pray that Jesse will bring me a glass of water when he comes in, but he never makes it back to the bedroom. That night, he sleeps on the couch.

6
Just a Girl

"What is that thing on your chin?" Chloe asks me when we're in the bathroom after the Healthy Foods pitch meeting.

"A zit," I say. "And how about: 'Jo, you were great. That meeting went great. You were riffing like you were a hip-hop rapping genius' instead of an attack on my personal appearance?"

"Yes," Chloe says, dabbing at her shiny nose with pressed powder. "You were better than Pitbull. 'Healthy Foods puts you in the mood' was truly inspired."

"I hauled my guitar twenty blocks to the meeting and sang all of my ideas," I say. "The client ate it up."

"That part was genius," Chloe says. "They totally did eat that up. You seemed very legit."

"I blame this on Jesse," I say, jumping up onto the counter to inspect my pimple. "If he hadn't been such a prick last night, we totally would have had sex, and I wouldn't have woken up with a pimple on my chin. You never get a pimple the day after you have sex."

"Is that the kind of dermatologic advice you picked up from working for your dad?"

"It's just common knowledge, Chlo," I say, a smile creeping onto my lips. "That must be why your skin is always so clear. What time is it?"

"Funny," Chloe says. "It's almost three. Why?"

"I'm hitting the Long Island Rail Road. I've got to get a cortisone shot for this thing."

"You're going out to Long Island to have your father pop your zit?"

"Yeah," I say, waiting for her to make a snide comment about running to daddy. "Why?"

"I thought you were still mad at him for firing you?" Chloe asks.

"I am," I say, hopping off the counter, "but he's still my dermatologist." Chloe just stares back at me. "What?" I say.

"I'm coming," she says. "If your dad's giving out free dermatologic advice, I'm so there."

"Let's go," I say, grabbing my guitar. "If we leave now, we can still get an off-peak ticket."

"How very frugal of you," Chloe says. "But if you bring your guitar with you, I'll bring my sketch pad and we can take a car service and bill it to Healthy Foods."

"Done."

FORTY-FIVE MINUTES later—you don't usually hit traffic on the Long Island Expressway before 4 P.M.—we're pulling up to my father's office, and we've written three different jingles with three distinct commercial concepts storyboarded out. Chloe even brought her pencils, so the storyboards are in color.

We grab our things and walk into the Manhasset Medical Pavilion, where my father has had his office since the 1970s. Upon graduation of medical school, my father's father bought the building for him as a gift. Most of the tenants don't know that my father actually owns the entire building, since he has a management company run the day-to-day operations and make most of the management decisions for him.

The building was renovated and redecorated in the early '90s, so it still has a vague '80s feel to it. There is a small living room setup in the lobby in front of the reception desk that has two cheaply made white leather couches facing each other on a pink oriental rug with a mirrored coffee table in between them. A massive vase on the center of the coffee table is clearly meant to be the centerpiece of the setup: a pastel pink, plastic-y looking thing filled with fake flowers. The management company used to have fresh flowers brought in weekly, but the tenants banded together and agreed that they would rather pay less in rent and have fake flowers on permanent display. My mother, my father's proxy, was the sole dissenting vote in the matter.

Every time we walk into the lobby of the building, Chloe starts humming the theme song to *Miami Vice* and doing the robot.

Probably because she had so little say over the look of the building itself, my mother, who fancies herself a bit of a design whiz, is the self-appointed on-site design czar for my father's office. (She sends audition tapes to HGTV religiously each year.) Under her command, the office always looks immaculate. In its latest incarnation, it looks like a homey, welcoming living room, complete with overstuffed couches in lush fabrics and a rich blond-wood coffee table. The reception desk is the same shade of wood. I think that my mother went a bit overboard with the vanilla-colored chenille throw that is draped over the back of the couch, but even I have to admit that it does tie together the entire look of the room.

And it smells like a home, not like a doctor's office at all. My father does various on-site laser surgeries at his office, so he wants it to be a comforting environment for some of his more nervous patients. I know for a fact that potpourri is strategically hidden throughout the office so that it doesn't smell like a doctor's office, a touch my mother considers one of her more brilliant ideas. ("Martha Stewart's got nothing on me," she loves to boast. "I could be on HGTV. I just need a good scandal to get my face out there.")

Chloe is still doing the robot as the elevator doors open and we walk into the office.

"Hi, Jo," my father's receptionist says to me. I can't help but wonder if she knew that my father was going to fire me before I knew it. Or if she complained to him about me, and that was part of the reason I was fired.

"Hello, Tricia," I say. The "you little Benedict Arnold" part is implied.

"Hey, *girl*ies!" Barbie, the Barbie doll nurse, coos at us before we've even had a chance to sit down. Barbie likes to call everyone "girls," as opposed to women. Or even the less PC but more traditional "ladies." She also wears a nurse's uniform—the sort of thing one would wear on Halloween to be dressed up as a "naughty nurse"—to work every day, even though all of the other nurses wear scrubs and clogs.

"Hey, Barbie," Chloe says and I smile and give Barbie a kiss on the cheek. Barbie is the sort of "girl" (her words, not mine) who kisses everyone hello, and even kisses strangers once she's introduced to them. She's just oozing with bubbly cheer.

I should mention here that it's not just that we call Barbie "the Barbie doll nurse" because she looks like a real live Barbie doll. Make no mistake—she *does* look like a Barbie doll, from her button nose to her blonde hair to her freakishly out-of-proportion long, thin legs and large, large breasts—but also, her name happens to be Barbie. And no, that's not a nickname or an abbreviation of something like Barbara as you may be thinking. Her name is actually Barbie. It says Barbie Johnson on her driver's license and even her passport (I checked her employee file). I always thought that it was a cruel gamble for her parents to make, giving their daughter such a loaded first name, but luckily for her, she grew up to do the name justice. And then some. But I mean, what if she'd grown up to be ugly or overweight or—gasp!—a brunette! What then?

"Well, this is a surprise," my brother, Andrew, says, walking out to reception and placing his hands firmly on Barbie's shoulders. It's as if he is using her as a shield so that he won't have to have contact with Chloe and me.

"Hi," I say, leaning over Barbie and giving Andrew a kiss on the cheek.

"Hey," Chloe says, keeping her distance. She always acts shy around Andrew. It's been this way since we were young. I know for a fact that Chloe, along with every other girl in our grade, had a crush on Andrew growing up. I was never sure if it was the lure of the guy who was older than you, or if it had something to do with his Ken-like blond hair and blue eyes (inherited from my mother's side). When I was younger, I used to marvel at how Andrew's hair stayed so perfectly in place. My own black hair (inherited from my father's side) was always a holy terror, so at a certain point, I decided to let it go wherever it wanted to. When I was younger, I used to call out, "Andrew, hair number 537 is out of place. You'd better fix it" whenever I saw him, which, for some reason, always made his hand instinctively fly to his head. Chloe and our friends used to laugh at this silly quip of mine, but I would always catch them staring at him for a moment too long, under the pretext of watching him fix his hair like the Ken doll that he was.

"Hey, girlies," Barbie says, grabbing Andrew's hands as they sit on her shoulders, "guess what we're doing this weekend?"

"What?" Chloe asks. I assume she's asking to be polite, but I really have no interest in this game.

"Going to a spa!" Barbie gushes. "How fun, right?"

Andrew hates spas.

"So fun," he says, and gives a closed-mouth smile.

I know that smile. It's his "it's not a fake smile" fake smile. Andrew, for as well-kempt and immaculate as his appearance is, doesn't actually like that sort of thing—spas and grooming, in general, that is. His hair always looks perfect, but that's just because it's very thick and healthy. It doesn't move or ever get messy. Never has. In high school, he could play forward for an entire three-hour soccer game with gale force winds and his hair would still look the same as when he got on the field. All he has to do is get it cut short every three weeks. If he doesn't do that, it's a disaster, but as long as he shows up at the barbershop on time, he's golden. He may look like a metrosexual, but really, he just hops out of the shower and looks like that. No gel, no products, not even a hairbrush. It's like a slab of marble—it can be sculpted, but it never changes form.

And then there's his skin. His skin, well, just like my father, his skin is always perfect, because skin is his business. His skin *not* looking perfect is not an option. That would be like a dentist with a front tooth missing.

So I could understand a woman like Barbie assuming that a man like Andrew would be all about getting pampered for a weekend at a spa, but really, he is more the type of man who would want to go camping or rock climbing for a weekend and risk breaking a bone (he's broken twenty-six different bones in his body doing such ridiculous activities). I wonder why, after six months together, Barbie does not know that.

"Jo, you would love it," Barbie says. "Facials!" For a moment, I'm annoyed at this not-so-subtle dig at the mountain growing on my chin, but I quickly remember that Barbie is so oblivious that she wouldn't even realize that I might be sensitive about my skin because of the aforementioned blemish.

"Why don't I take a look at that for you, Jo-Jo?" Andrew says, walking over to me and tilting my face up to the light.

"I'll wait for Dad," I say, turning my face away from his scrutiny.

"Dad's doing some Botox," he says. "It'll probably be a while." He's still staring at my chin.

"Botox doesn't take that long," I say. "I can wait."

"This is why you were so bad at making appointments, Jo-Jo," he says. "You never gave anyone the proper amount of time. Botox can be *very* time consuming."

"Dad can do Botox in his sleep," I say, stepping backward so that I'm out of the strong glare of the hi-hat light above me.

"You can look at *my* face, Andrew!" Chloe pipes in, breaking the tension. She tilts her face upward, waiting for Andrew.

"I'd rather have a paying customer anyway," Andrew says, walking over to Chloe. He winks at her and she giggles like a little girl.

"Oh, she's not paying," I say, matter-of-factly. Andrew rolls his eyes and takes Chloe to an examination room.

"This is great," Barbie says, sidling up to me. "We can have more time for girl chat!"

I pick up a magazine from the coffee table and begin to flip. I'm secretly hoping that Barbie will pick up a magazine, too, and that reading fashion magazines simultaneously will take the place of girl chat.

"Does this mean you're not still mad at me, Pumpkin?" my father says, walking out into reception to greet me.

"Hi, Daddy."

"Or are you expecting to get paid for a day's work for coming here?" he says as he kisses me on the cheek.

"I have a medical emergency," I say, pointing to my chin.

"I thought you were doing some Botox, Dr. Waldman?" Barbie asks, clearly thrown by having the boss catch her sitting in the reception area reading fashion magazines. She hasn't caught on to the fact that if you're sleeping with the boss's son, chances are your job is secure.

"I can do Botox in my sleep, Barbie," he says with a gentle smile.

Ever the good patient, I stand up and position myself under a hi-hat light for my dad to take a peek at my face.

"Yes, this is clearly an emergency," my father says, bringing my face up to the light. "I can't believe you were even able to leave your house."

"Yes," I say. "I'm very brave. As a matter of fact, I was recently let go by my evil boss, but I still found the strength to get out of bed today. I'm not the type to let the bastards get me down."

"Am I the bastard in this scenario?" my father asks, now examining the other, more zit-free parts of my face.

"Well, you did also take away my car," I say.

"Okay, Norma Rae, let's go into treatment room number three."

We walk back to the examining rooms, with Barbie following closely in our wake.

"You don't have to stay," I tell Barbie as I prop myself up on the examining chair in room number three.

"Actually," Barbie says, posturing for my dad, "it's the law. A nurse must always be in the examining room with a doctor when he's in with a female patient."

"He's my dad," I say. "And I probably don't even count as a patient because I have no intention of paying for this. I think it's okay if we're alone."

"Barbie," my dad says, "would you please excuse us?"

"Of course, Dr. Waldman," Barbie says and makes a hasty exit.

"So," I say as my father goes to the counter to prepare a cotton ball with alcohol, "I got another gig. Now you don't have to worry about me starving and dying alone in Soho."

"Fantastic, Pumpkin," he says, dabbing my chin with the alcohol. "Let your mother know when it is, and we'll come into the city that night to see you play."

"No, a paying gig," I say, as he goes back to the counter to get my cortisone shot ready. "A day job."

"Already?" he says, coming back toward me. "This is even better than I had imagined! I'm so proud of you, Pumpkin! See, I knew you could do amazing things if I just gave you a little push. Tiny sting here. Aaaand, there we go. Tell me about it."

"Ow," I say as he administers the cortisone shot and then applies pressure to my chin. "It's a freelance thing at Chloe's agency. Writing jingles."

"Well, that's fantastic," he says, handing me a cotton ball to press to my chin once he's done. "That sounds really nice. A real job, so you get the health benefits and a 401(k) and all that, and you're doing what you love, writing songs. I think it's really fantastic, Pumpkin." He leans in to hug me, and my right arm, holding the cotton ball to my face, gets stuck inside the embrace. It feels a bit forced, and I wonder if it's because as he's praising me for marrying together my passion with my work, it forces him to realize that he was never able to the same thing—that he gave up his passion for the piano to instead follow his father's steady path to medicine—the sure thing. "You'll be ready to make your first payment on the loft in no time. But you should still do your 401(k), I mean, really max that thing out, don't defer on my account. I'm not going to evict you and leave you homeless, so you should do the 401(k) for all you can, and then we'll work out our payments from there." He releases me from his grip and smiles at me.

"It's freelance, Daddy," I say. "There's no 401(k), no health plan, no big salary."

"I see," he says, trying to keep an optimistic expression on his face, though he's giving me the same smile that he gave me when I told him that I didn't want to go to medical school. "It's still fantastic. It's still progress. Once they get a load of what you can do, you'll be in a corner office in no time flat."

"Thanks, Daddy," I say, as I hop off the table.

We walk out to reception, where Andrew, Barbie, and Chloe are all sitting on the overstuffed couches.

"If you two are done bilking the practice for free medical advice and committing insurance fraud, I can drive you home," Andrew says.

"Thanks!" Chloe says, her face shiny from whatever glop Andrew put on it.

"We're actually hitting some clubs downtown to see some music tonight. Not your cup of tea," I chime in, "so we'd just as soon take the Long Island Rail Road back home."

"Clubs sound like fun," Andrew says. "If I drive, will you feed me dinner first? Since I moved back to Long Island, I haven't found Suki-caliber sushi yet. Whaddya say?"

"Perfect!" Chloe says. "We love Suki!"

"We just went to Suki last night," I say.

"I love clubbing!" Barbie says.

"And we love Suki," Chloe says. "We can go to the one on West Houston tonight, since we were at Union Square last night." She shoots a meaningful glance in my direction, but I pretend to be concentrating too hard on pressing my cotton ball to my chin to notice.

"Great," Andrew says. "Then we're set."

"Girlies," Barbie says, leaning into us and grabbing both Chloe's and my hands, "we are going to have so much fun!" I wonder if she plans to change out of her naughty nurse getup before we go out. People in the West Village might actually think that she's being ironic.

Fun.

7
What Have I Done to Deserve This?

" **J**o, we need to talk." Jesse walks into the kitchen, where I'm eating a bowl of cereal. He has an "I mean business" look on his face.

"Oh, sweetness," I say, "did my hair dryer wake you up?" I've been going to the supergood offices every morning for a week now, and in my new role as a corporate American sellout, I've taken to giving my hair a few good shakes below the hair dryer before going out into the cool winter air.

Jesse shakes his head. "No, the blow-dryer was fine, but we still need to talk," he says.

"I've only got a few minutes before I have to leave," I say, glancing at the clock on the microwave oven. "Wanna meet me in Union Square for lunch?"

Jesse takes a deep breath. "I'm going on tour with the band."

"That's great!" I say, the corn flakes almost falling out of my mouth in my excitement. I'm shocked that he's telling me such monumental news with so little fanfare. "When do you leave? What cities do you hit?"

"We're leaving next week. We're starting in L.A. and working our way back."

"Jesse, that's amazing!" I say, jumping up to give him a hug. "I can meet you in L.A. when this freelancing gig is over!" But he stands still and doesn't return my embrace. He takes my hands and unwraps my arms from around his neck.

"You're not going to meet me in L.A.," he says, his hands still gripping my wrists.

"Then Nashville. Whatever. Wherever you are. I'll come meet you," I say with a smile.

"Jo," he says. "No."

"No what?" I ask. I can see over my shoulder that it's 9:02 A.M.—time for me to leave the apartment if I'm going to take the subway to work, which, considering my state of unemployment, I've really got no choice but to do.

"You're not coming with me. I'm going alone."

"Oh," I say, feeling a wave of disappointment wash over me. We never spend nights apart from each other. And now he wants to spend a whole tour apart from each other? "How long will you be away?"

"I don't know, man," Jesse says, shaking his head. I know that "man." After two and a half years together, I know each and every "man" that he's got. This is the "I'm about to disappoint you" man. He lets go of my wrists and we stand two feet apart from each other, just staring. The room begins to spin. I feel my face begin to shine and turn red.

"What don't you know, exactly?" I ask, glancing at the clock, which now reads 9:05 A.M.

"I think that this tour will be a good thing for us," Jesse says, looking down. "I think we need some time apart. You know, to think about things."

"Think about things?" I parrot back. "I don't have anything to think about. What do you need to think about?"

"Look, Jo. We're just moving in different directions lately. I'm trying to move forward and you, you're just stalled. It's like you don't even *want* to move forward anymore. You just want to wallow in the past."

"Wallow in the past?" I repeat back, sitting down on a stool at the kitchen counter.

"Then why haven't you done anything for the last two years?" he says, raising his voice.

"My band broke up," I say, my face on fire. "You know that."

"Jo," he says, "your band broke up two years ago."

"Is this about that girl?" I ask. "That redhead who was here the other night?"

"No," Jesse says, seemingly exasperated, as if he's been asked that question before. "This is not about Cassie. I mean, we're going on tour with her band—The Rage is the headliner—but *this* is not about *her*." In an instant, I realize that he *has* been asked this question before. By his band.

"Are you sleeping with her?" I spit out. I can't control my tone. I don't really want to.

"No!" he says, almost laughing at the thought of it. "No, Jo. I'm not cheating on you. Cassie and I have just gotten to be really close friends lately, and they needed an opening act for their tour, and—"

And then I realize: Jesse's either sleeping with Cassie or is about to sleep with her. I'm not sure which. He thinks he's being a stand-up guy by taking a "break" from me first, but ironically, I think that makes him even more of an asshole than if he'd just been a man and said what he really meant. I tell him this.

"I'm an asshole because I need some space?"

"No," I say. "You're just an asshole in general. How *dare* you do this to me."

Later, I will look back at this conversation and realize that I was completely on fire, but he was cool as a cucumber. I thought we still had a chance; he'd already made his decision. I was fighting for us; he was not.

"I think it will be good for us," he says, speaking in calm tones as if I were a mental patient.

"Good for us? You mean good for you. Who the fuck do you think you are? You're lucky to have me. I can't believe you're doing this to me. To us. After everything we've been through."

"We should get out of this thing for a while. See how we do when we're apart. See where it takes us."

"Get out of this *thing*? Out of what?" I ask. "Out of living in my father's apartment? Out of my doing everything for you all the time? Out of having a full-time live-in groupie?"

"I knew you were going to get like this," he says.

"Get like what, exactly?" I spit out. I look at the clock. 9:19 A.M.

"Look," he continues, "the fact of the matter is that I have an opportunity—my band has an opportunity—and I'm going to take it. Alone."

"Your band has an opportunity?" I say, barely containing myself. "You've got to be kidding me. I *paid* for your band's demo!"

"Don't be jealous of our success," he says, meeting my eyes for the first time since this conversation started.

"*Jealous?*" I say, laughing at him. The nerve he has. I may be feeling a range of emotions right now—anger, fury, rage...but jealousy is not one of them. My band was a million times better than his in its heyday. I even have the Battle of the Bands trophy to prove it. I tell him this.

"I don't know if I love you anymore."

And there it is. Just like that. He doesn't know if he loves me anymore. After two and a half years. I can barely move. I can barely speak. It literally takes my breath away for a second.

How can that be, though? We are Romeo and Juliet. David Bowie and Iman. Gwen Stefani and Gavin Rossdale. We are kindred spirits—two halves of the same whole. Except I would never do something like this to someone I loved.

"Can we please just take a little time apart to see how it is that we feel about each other? Just for the tour. That's all that I'm asking." I stare back at Jesse, not knowing what to say. Anger is coursing through my veins, and I can't formulate a thought. He wants time apart so he can go and sleep with his redhead. And I'm supposed to give him permission to do that? After he just told me that he doesn't know if he loves me anymore? "Anyway," he says, "it's almost nine thirty. Don't you have to go to work?"

"Is that why you're telling me this now?" I ask. "You goddamned coward. You fucking coward!" And then, like the coward he is, he begins his retreat to the bedroom.

"I didn't want to make it any harder than it had to be," he says over his shoulder. Why do men always say that? Why do they always pretend that they're trying to make it easier for you when what they're really doing is trying to make it easier for themselves?

"Any harder?" I say, laughing as I follow him back to the bedroom. "No, you just didn't want to have a mature conversation about it."

Jesse opens the closet door and grabs two duffel bags. I don't register it at the time, but I will realize later that the bags were already packed. He packed his bags already. Before we had this fight. He'd been thinking about this for a while—who knows how long—and he's been packed and ready to go. Just waiting for the perfect moment to tell me. A moment when I couldn't make a scene, didn't have time to fight back. Time to fight for myself.

Time to fight for us.

"I'm sorry, Jo," he says, picking up his bags. "I have to go."

I think of saying, "You'll never find another girl like me," but then I realize—he doesn't want another girl like me, otherwise he'd be with me. That's why he's leaving.

"If you walk out that door right now," I yell from the bedroom as he walks to the front door, "don't *ever* think about coming back."

And with that, he's gone.

8
You Wreck Me

Where were you? Chloe writes on a pad after I sneak into the Healthy Foods meeting a half hour late. "Artists!" Chloe's boss had self-consciously joked as I walked in. Luckily, the Healthy Foods people laughed along with him and I was able to choke out an apologetic smile as I murmured a quick "sorry" and offered a lame excuse about the subway getting stuck between stops.

Getting my heart broken at home, I write back. Chloe's face falls. I have to turn away from her—I can't take the look of pity on her face right now.

Thankfully, the rest of the meeting is short, and the Healthy Foods people do most of the talking—more strategy talk—and Chloe and I don't have to present anything. The second we are excused from the meeting, Chloe and I make a beeline to her office and slam the door.

I take a breath for the first time in what seems like ages. I tell her the whole mess in sordid detail, with Chloe punctuating the story with "that little prick" any time I let her get a word in edgewise.

"You can cry if you want," Chloe says. "No one's going to come in here."

"I'm not going to cry," I say. "I don't cry."

"I'm so sorry," Chloe says, stretching her arms out to give me a hug. "You must be so upset."

"I'm not upset," I say, gliding past her and refusing the hug. "I'm angry. I am so fucking angry."

"It's okay to be upset," Chloe says to me as I walk over to her window. Her office has an amazing view of the Empire State Building.

"Well, I'm not," I say. "I'm just mad."

My cell phone rings and I pick it up. A tiny part of me hopes that it will be Jesse, calling to apologize or tell me that I was punked. Instead, I check the caller ID, and it's the one person I want to speak to least in the world—my brother.

I pick up the phone and answer with a very bland, "Yeah?"

"Hey, Jo-Jo," he says.

"Hey," I say. He never calls me in the middle of the day, and I want him to just get to the point. "What's up?"

"Family dinner tomorrow night," he says. "Can you come out to Long Island?"

"Tomorrow night?" I ask. We never have family dinners during the week. Much less on Long Island. The most I usually manage is a dinner in the city with my father when he's lecturing at NYU Medical, or a dinner in the city with my mom when she's shopping in midtown all day. "I can't come. I don't have a car anymore."

"There's a train that gets into Manhasset at seven twenty-two P.M. I'll pick you up. Be at Penn Station at six fifty."

"I can't," I start to say, but Andrew's off the phone before I can get another word in. I look at my phone in disbelief—did he actually just hang up on me? I slam the phone into Chloe's windowsill.

"Whoa," she says, grabbing the phone from my hands. "What just happened? Was that Jesse?"

"I'm so mad at Andrew," I say, clenching my fist at my side. "He just called a family dinner and didn't even give me a minute to make an excuse for why I can't go!"

"What can I do?" Chloe says, putting her hand on my shoulder.

"You can go to this family dinner for me," I say.

"I'm not going to your family dinner for you," she says, walking to her watercooler and pouring me a glass of water.

"Men," I say, taking a sip. "This is so like them. They make a decision and you just have to go along with it. No discussion. No question—no checking in with you. 'What would you like to do? What works for you?' I mean, what if I had plans tomorrow night?"

"Do you?" Chloe asks.

"That's not the point!" I yell. "The point is—if it's a family dinner and I'm a *member* of the family, shouldn't I have been *asked* to dinner and not *told* to be at dinner?"

"Are you really this mad about the dinner?" Chloe asks.

"Yes!"

"I don't think that you are," she says.

"I think that I am," I say, finishing off my water and crumpling the paper cup into a ball in my hand.

"It's okay to be upset about Jesse," Chloe says, prying the cup from my clenched fingers.

"I'm not upset about Jesse," I say, louder, as if she hadn't heard me the first time. "I'm angry. I'm mad. He bilked me for every penny I had—every penny my dad gave me, anyway—and left me for dead."

"He left you for dead? Did he hurt you? I'll kill him if he touched a hair on your head," Chloe says, with her trademark five-foot-two tough talk. I turn around and stare back at her. "Oh, you mean dead *emotionally*," she says, whispering the word "emotionally" as if she were one of those drug and alcohol counselors from high school.

"I mean he's an asshole."

9
Scenes from an Italian Restaurant

Dominick's is an Italian restaurant about ten blocks away from the house I grew up in, and due to its proximity, my family spends an inordinate amount of time eating there. In fact, most of my childhood took place while eating at Dominick's. God forbid we travel fifteen blocks down the road to Morton's Steakhouse or twelve blocks in the other direction to that Japanese place. The one exception to this rule is Sunday nights spent at the Chinese restaurant. We *are* still a Jewish family from Long Island, after all.

When deciding where to go for dinner, the discussion always ends by my father saying, "Well, Dominick's is right here." Dominick came over to the United States from Italy when he was only sixteen years old. He opened the restaurant with the money in his pockets and a few of his grandmother's old recipes. When the restaurant grew in popularity, he brought the rest of his family over—his parents, his grandmother, and five brothers and six sisters. Every one of them worked at the restaurant. When Dominick retired, his son, Dominick Jr., took over. It was still a family place, with Dominick's family members running every aspect of the joint—his sister running the front of the house, his brother running the kitchen, and his brother-in-law taking care of the delivery and takeout orders. Growing up, any time we would walk in, Dominick Jr. would come out to greet us and shake my father's hand. Now Dominick the third runs things.

When my brother and I walk in, Dominick the third shakes my brother's hand and kisses me on both cheeks to say hello (even though he is the second generation in his family to have been born in this country).

"The Waldman kids!" Dominick says. "How's working with Pops?"

"Great," Andrew says, and quickly ushers me to our table.

We sit at our usual table—a big booth toward the back of the restaurant next to the big bay window—and my father has already ordered a bottle of 1990 Lafite.

My mother grabs me and holds me to her in a way that can only be described as clutching me to her bosom.

"You were too good for him anyway," she whispers into my ear.

"Thanks, Mom," I whisper back, and I mean it. This show of support is much better than what she was able to choke out yesterday when I told her the news. Then she immediately launched into a discussion about all I have to be thankful for, even in the wake of getting my heart broken. The conversation inexplicably segued into a discussion about the Oprah show she saw on women being sold into sex slavery. So I might be nursing a broken heart, but at least I haven't been sold into prostitution.

I'd rather hear that I was too good for him.

"Now you're here, where you belong," she says.

"I belong at Dominick's?" I say as I take my seat.

"With your *family*," she says, dragging the word "family" out to its full three syllables as if she is the matriarch of some soap opera clan.

"Some wine, Pumpkin?" my dad asks me, already pouring the wine into my glass. I stifle the urge to run up to the bar and order myself a vodka tonic, and instead gracefully accept the glass of wine my father has poured for me.

I smile back and wonder why we're gathered here today. Is my father sick? Is that why my parents have gathered all of us here? Is that why he's ordering his favorite wine? Maybe he's just found out that he's deathly ill and we're supposed to be making him comfortable and letting him do what he wants in his final moments.

But my dad's a well-known doctor who also teaches medicine. The chances of him not knowing that he was deathly ill are pretty slim to none.

Is my mother divorcing my father? She was really mad at him that other morning when we were on the phone. I mean, she's always that mad at him, threatening to divorce him, but this time she may really mean it. It would be so like her to make some big huge announcement about it. To gather her whole family around her to tell us the news.

"Sooooo," Barbie announces after we've ordered and all begun our first glasses of wine, "we have some news to share." It was Barbie who called this family dinner. Which is odd, considering she's not even part of this family. She's just Andrew's girlfriend. And a paid employee of my father.

I knew there had to be some reason I was forced to come out to Long Island for dinner on a Thursday. I tried to cancel this morning, using my breakup with Jesse as an excuse, but my mother wouldn't hear of it. First of all, she never really liked Jesse that much. She always envisioned me ending up with a smart, handsome Jewish doctor like she had, or at the very least, a rich, savvy Jewish businessman (which, actually, she had done, too).

Second of all, she seems to have this crazy notion that spending time with my family will actually make me feel better about my life.

"News?" my mother asks coyly. I can't tell whether or not she knows what Barbie is about to say.

"Yes, we do," Andrew says, wiping a bead of sweat from his forehead and taking a swig of wine.

"Excuse me," my father says to a passing waiter, "could I get a refill on my water?"

"Oh, me too, please," I say.

My mother clears her throat loudly.

"Sorry," I whisper.

"We had a wonderful time at the spa last weekend," Barbie says, slowly.

"Yes, we did," Andrew says.

"That's your news?" my father says. "Mazel tov."

"Marty!" my mother says, throwing a dirty look his way.

"Nooooo," Barbie says, smiling. She looks at Andrew and he looks back at her. They continue looking at each other and then start whispering. "You tell them," "No, *you* tell them!" to each other. They do this a couple of times until Barbie finally turns back to face my parents and me.

"We're getting married!" she squeals, throwing her left hand on the table to show us her engagement ring.

We all jump up and start hugging Barbie and Andrew. Andrew is surprisingly calm in the wake of this announcement, sort of like Johnny Cash before he walked into Folsom Prison to perform.

"I'm so happy for you, Andrew," I say on autopilot, before I can even decide if it's true.

"Thanks, Jo-Jo," he says. And I actually *am* very happy for my brother, despite the fact that my heart was recently crushed into a million pieces. But what's really fueling my cry of "mazel tov" is the fact that my mother will now have this wedding to plan, and she won't be bothering me any more about my birthday. After all, wedding trumps a non-milestone birthday any day.

"When we got to the spa, we just knew," Barbie gushes. "We just knew that we wanted to spend our whole lives together! We came home, looked for rings on Monday and Tuesday, and then he popped the question last night!"

"How romantic," my father says. I shake my head, too, and say, "So romantic."

"This calls for a toast," my mother says, and calls over a waiter to order a bottle of champagne.

"Wanna try it on?" Barbie asks me.

I do not want to try her ring on.

But she's so excited about the prospect of my wanting to try her ring on that I don't have the heart to say no. I put it on, and my mother compliments Andrew on picking out such a beautiful ring. Out of the corner of my eye, I see her wink at him as she says this and I immediately know that my mother was the one who actually picked it out.

"It's gorgeous," I say, half to my mother, half to Barbie. I give it back to Barbie and she instructs me to put it on the table first and not hand it to her directly—apparently, superstition states that if I hand it immediately back to her without setting it down on the table first, I will be an old maid. Barbie is the sort of girl who worries about such things.

"Jo," Barbie says, suddenly very serious, as she puts her ring back on her ring finger, "will you do me the honor of being one of my bridesmaids?"

A bridesmaid? Haven't I been punished enough lately? First, I lose my job. No, first, *my father fires me*. And then he takes my car away. Which is really worse than losing the job, if you think about it. Then the love of my life *leaves* me. In cold blood, no less. And now this. I will have to be a Barbie bridesmaid. No doubt the dresses will be bubble-gum pink and will fit all of her Barbie doll friends and family perfectly. I, with my crazy black hair and most un-Barbie-doll-like figure, will look more like one of those troll dolls than an actual bridesmaid.

And I can't even complain to my mother about all of this. I look up at her and can see in her face she's infuriated that Barbie has asked me to be a bridesmaid and not the maid of honor. Even though Barbie has two Barbie doll sisters of her own.

"I would love to," I say, and Barbie squeals and begins hugging the life force right out of me. She then starts bouncing as she's hugging me and saying, "I'm so happy! This is perfect!"

I immediately feel another pimple coming on.

10

How Soon Is Now?

Bad things happen in threes, so that's how I know my gig will go well tonight. I've already used up my set of three—getting fired by my dad, getting dumped by my boyfriend, and then getting enlisted in a Barbie wedding party—so nothing bad can happen to me now. I did also get my car taken away, but that should be collapsed into the getting fired thing, right? So I'm technically still at three. But if the car counts separately, then being put in the Barbie bridal party starts my next suite of three.

This show is doomed.

"You're on in five," the manager says to me as he rushes by to get up to the sound booth. I'm backstage at The Bitter End, New York City's self-proclaimed oldest rock club, for a gig featuring three other singer-songwriters. It's my favorite venue to play—small and intimate, it has the feeling of being in your living room playing for some friends. The manager here loves me, so tonight, as usual, I'm closing out the show.

I shake off the feeling that something bad is about to happen (two more bad things, to be specific) and listen to the singer-songwriter on stage. He's a guy I've seen perform before who does his whole set behind the piano, à la Billy Joel. He's singing a song about America and pounding away on his piano like he's Liberace.

"I hate this guy," Chloe says, walking over to me backstage and pointing at America guy. Backstage at The Bitter End is actually just the back of the club off the stage, so anyone can come back there.

"He's not bad," I say, putting down my guitar and really listening to America guy for a second. "He's very patriotic."

"He sucks," she says as he starts wrapping up his set.

"Thanks for coming out, guys," he says, getting up from his piano.

The stage is set up with the huge baby grand toward the back of the stage and a single stool at the front. The manager comes down from the sound booth and asks me if I want the stage changed at all, but I tell him no. It's just me and my guitar tonight, no accompaniment, so I don't need much. He goes out the back door to light a cigarette and the crisp winter air floats into the club.

I walk out on stage and sit down on the stool.

"Hi, I'm Jo Waldman," I say. "Thanks for coming out on such a cold night. The first song in my set tonight is a song I wrote recently. I hope that you like it."

My mother and father cheer from the front table, just underneath my feet, even though I've told them countless times that it distracts me when people I know are in the front row. ("We're not people *you know*," my mother says. "*We* are your parents.") I can hear Chloe screaming my name from backstage as I start to play.

> *Night in, night out, I sit and wait for you*
> *I'm here alone, it's all that I can I do*

You've got my mind, my heart and my soul
All this time, I still can't let you go

When will tomorrow be?

I do the only thing that I know how
I pray for you to come back to me somehow

Day turns to night
And winter comes
Without your love
I'm all alone

When will tomorrow be?

Another day, another thought of you
It's been a year since I've seen your eyes of blue
You've done something that can't be undone
Now I can only ask, when will tomorrow come?

I do the only thing that I know how
I pray for you to come back to me somehow

When will tomorrow be?

"Thank you," I say as the crowd begins to applaud. Since I still use the mailing list from my Lonely Hearts Club Band Web site, I recognize a few of the faces out in the crowd. I look offstage to see why Chloe isn't cheering for me, and I see that she has, rather quickly, changed her opinion of America guy. Not only does she no longer hate America guy, but she's now making out with him against the wall.

With a laugh, I start in on the next song in my set. Looking out into the crowd at the faces of people who support me and my music—people who consider themselves my fans—I can't help but think that my run of bad luck is over. Nothing else is going to happen to me; I'm not starting in on a new suite of three. I may have been having a rough time of it lately, but my luck is still better than most people's, and it's time that I stop feeling sorry for myself. As I see a girl in the back of the room mouthing the words to a song that I wrote, even though I'm singing a sad song, I can't help but smile.

"GREAT JOB," my mother says, hugging me before I'm even fully off the stage. "You were the best out of everyone."

"Thanks, Mom," I say.

"You were great, Pumpkin," my dad says. "Do you need a ride back to the loft?"

I take a look backstage, and through the darkness, see that Chloe is still entangled with America guy. "I think I'll stay and have a drink," I say. "Get home safe."

I walk my parents to the front door of the club and then make a beeline straight to the bar.

"Nice set," a guy who'd been sitting in the back of the club says to me as I walk toward the bar. I don't recognize him from any of my old gigs. He's wearing a baseball cap slung so low on his head that I can barely see his eyes.

"Thanks," I say, slinging my guitar over my shoulder.

"You're very welcome," he says, following me to the bar as I order myself a vodka tonic, my post-show drink of choice.

"Anything for your friend, Jo?" the bartender asks me.

"He's not my friend."

"I'd like to be your friend," he says. "Alan Golden." As he sticks out his hand for me to shake, I recognize his name from somewhere, but can't place him. "And this drink's on me." Drinks on him? I like Alan Golden already.

"Thank you, Alan Golden," I say and shake his hand.

"I'm a music manager," he explains, and I take a seat at the bar to listen. "I love your song lyrics. They're amazing."

"Thank you," I say, taking a sip of my drink. The first sip right after I come off stage is always the best one. I savor it as I wait for Alan's big pitch.

"I represent a wide range of clients," he says. "We should be in business together." Music to my ears. It's just like my grandmother always says—when you least expect it, your life can change in an instant.

"I'm listening," I say, stirring my drink slowly.

"I have a proposition for you," Alan says. "That song of yours—the tomorrow one—it's absolutely incredible, and I want to buy it."

"Buy it?" I say.

"For one of my clients," he says. "Can we talk about it?"

"You don't want me to perform it?" I say. "You want to buy it from me so that someone else can perform it?" I feel my face begin to burn.

"I want to introduce you to someone," he says as I get up from my bar stool.

"No, thank you," I say. "I've actually got somewhere to be."

I get a head rush as I walk to the back of the bar and process what Alan Golden has just said to me. He sat through my entire set, watched me perform, and he doesn't want to sign me. What he *does* want is to buy my lyrics for some no-talent artist who can't write so that *she* can become famous and get a record deal. My record deal. Maybe the A&R rep from Pinnacle was right two years ago—I'm nothing without my band. They wouldn't take our band without Billy, and now no manager is going to take me on my own.

When I get backstage, Chloe is still there, making out with America guy against a wall.

"Come on, we're leaving," I say to Chloe, prying her away from her prey.

"What happened?" she says, her eyes only half open, giving her guy the "one-minute" finger as she lets me pull her away.

"I don't want to talk about it," I say, and look over my shoulder. Alan is making his way backstage and has a tall blonde following in his wake, who is also wearing a baseball cap low on her head so that I can't see her eyes. I'm sure that this is the no-talent artist who can't write her own songs who he wanted me to meet, but I'm not interested.

"That's Alan Golden," Mr. America says. "He's a music manager."

"Jo, let's try to meet him!" Chloe says, grabbing my arm.

"I already did," I say, and America guy takes this as his cue to rush over to Alan to introduce himself. "Can we go?"

Alan hands America guy a business card and walks over to Chloe and me.

"Jo," he says, "this is the client of mine who I wanted you to meet. Well, she's my wife, too. She's my client *and* my wife. May I introduce you to the lovely Miss Amber Fairchild."

Yes, *that* Amber Fairchild.

She takes her baseball cap off and a cascade of huge blonde curls fall onto her shoulders. I want to tell her that the pageantry is not necessary, that I'm not a fan, but she is already grabbing for my hand before I get a chance.

"It's so nice to meet you," she says in her thick Midwestern farmer's daughter accent as she takes my hand and shakes it vigorously. She obviously doesn't remember me from *American Star*. But I remember her. Whenever I see her on MTV, her accent always seems thicker than I remember it being, and I'm sure that it's entirely put on for the cameras. But, here, now, meeting her in person, I see that it's not. This is honestly how she speaks.

"We've met before," I say. "*American Star?*"

"Good to see you again," Amber says, not skipping a beat. I can't tell whether or not she actually remembers me.

"Do you remember who I am?" I try to ask, but she's already on to the next thing.

"I love your shirt!" she says at practically the same time. I'm wearing a vintage Ramones T-shirt, one that my father bought my mother when they first began dating. That she notices it makes me start to warm to her.

"It was my mother's from the eighties," I say.

"Oh my God, no way!" she says. "I totally got the same one at Urban Outfitters today!"

"I'm out of here," I say, grabbing Chloe's arm and turning around.

"Don't you even want to discuss this?" Alan says. "We're talking about a lot of money here."

"No, Alan, I think we're done here," I say, still headed for the door.

"What is he talking about, Jo?" Chloe asks.

"Nothing," I say as I grab my guitar case. I don't even bother to put my guitar into it as I continue walking toward the door.

"A licensing deal, Jo. Royalties," he says, my back facing him.

"Don't you even want to know how much?" Chloe whispers to me, stopping in her tracks, and in so doing, stopping me in my tracks, too.

"My songs are not for sale," I say as I spin around. "I'm not a sellout."

"Getting your music out there," Alan says, "is selling out?"

"You're just going to turn it into some bland, lame, overproduced pop thing," I blurt out. "Something disposable, like the rest of your music."

Chloe gasps. Even I'm surprised at my audacity. Amber looks down to the ground and crosses one leg in front of the other.

But I'm not going to apologize for how I feel. What I'm saying is the truth about her music. And anyway, now that I have the gig at supergood, I don't have to sell out my music for money. I can wait it out until my next big break comes along, just like I know it will.

"Chloe, let's go," I say, hoping that she already exchanged numbers with America guy so that we don't have to stop again before leaving.

"One more thing," Chloe says, releasing herself from my grip and turning back to Amber before we leave. "Could I get your autograph for my Little Sister?"

THE NEXT morning, Chloe and I drag ourselves into the supergood offices for our final Healthy Foods meeting. I try not to hate her too much for asking Amber for her autograph as we walk into the conference room for the big day.

"Are you still mad at me?" Chloe asks as she sets up her easel and her storyboards.

"Why on earth would I be mad at you?" I ask as I put my guitar down on its stand.

"What?" she says. "It's not my fault that Tiffany likes her!"

"You asked for two signatures," I say as I walk toward the credenza and pour myself a cup of coffee. There is a wide assortment of things to put in your coffee in the supergood conference room—you can have three different types of artificial sweetener, two different types of sugar, agave nectar, and your choice of whole milk, skim milk, soy milk, two percent, or cream. But I take my coffee black.

"Well, she *is* Amber Fairchild," Chloe says, sitting down at the conference room table and arranging her notes. "Why do you hate her so much? She's not singing about killing kittens, for God's sake. Don't be so hard on her."

"I hate her because she creates conformist overproduced crap. She is everything that is wrong with the music industry today," I say, sipping my coffee and taking a seat next to Chloe. "She is the reason why I can't get a record deal."

"Is *she* really the reason why?" Chloe says, just as the account executive in charge of Healthy Foods walks into the conference room.

"Okay, ladies. Big day today," he says, flipping through Chloe's storyboards. "The Healthy Foods wrap-up."

Within minutes, the client has arrived and everyone takes their places at the conference room table. The account executive in charge begins the pitch meeting and Chloe passes me a note on her yellow legal pad.

Sorry, it says.

I write back: *Me too.*

Are you just saying that because I said that?

Yes, I write back.

You conformist overproduced kitten killer, she writes, *you're everything that's wrong with the music industry today.*

THE REST of the meeting flies by—the client's happy, supergood's happy, everyone's happy.

I'm happy. As we wrap the meeting, it dawns on me that I actually like working on the Healthy Foods matter. I really enjoy working at supergood. It turns out that working for The Man really isn't that bad. I don't really want to stick it to him anymore. In fact, I kind of like The Man.

"Jo," the executive in charge of the Healthy Foods account says to me after the meeting, "we will definitely contact you again when the next freelance gig comes up."

I'm all smiles as I pack up my guitar and its stand. Music to my ears—getting a paycheck for doing what I love best.

"Thanks," I say. "I really enjoyed working on this with you."

"So did we. These things don't come up that often," he says, "but when they do, you'll be the first person we call."

"When will that be," I say as we walk down the hallway toward the elevator, "do you think?"

"We'll call when the next freelance gig comes up," he says as he presses the button for the elevator. I wonder if he knows that he hasn't answered my question.

"When will that be?" I say, trying to sound confident and professional.

"First person we call," he says with a smile as the elevator doors open.

"Great!" I say.

"Great," he says. I stand there, waiting for him to say more, but he doesn't.

"So, we'll call you," he says with a smile as the elevator door closes.

When will that be?

11
Birthday

"*Surprise!*" the crowd screams as I climb up to the rooftop of the Delancey with Chloe. Even though it's the dead of winter, Chloe told me that the band we were here to see was set to perform on the roof, so I let her lure me upstairs. The retractable roof has been drawn and the heat lamps are on.

We immediately freeze in our tracks. Cameras are flashing like crazy, and somehow I know that it's not the paparazzi here to greet us. Through the flickering lights, I can barely see the crowd of people circling us.

I thought that we were coming to the Delancey, one of our favorite Lower East Side rock clubs, to see Cakewalk perform, but I now see that instead, I have been tricked into doing the one thing I do not want to do tonight—celebrate my twenty-second birthday.

"You are dead to me," I mutter to Chloe under my breath.

"I had no idea," she says without letting her lips move as my mother comes in to embrace us both.

"Surprise, honey!" my mother says, emerging from the crowd of lights like Diana Ross returning to the stage for an encore, as she pulls me to her bosom for a hug. "Are you surprised?"

"Sure am," I say.

"How about you, Chlo?" she says, hugging Chloe. "Bet you didn't think I could pull something like this off?"

"I can honestly say that I did not," she says.

"I didn't even know you wanted a party, Pumpkin," my father says as he walks over to us and hugs and kisses me. He is wearing a pair of jeans and a black leather blazer with a white button-down shirt underneath. As usual, he's got on his gold Tiffany belt buckle, but since it's the weekend, he's forgone the usual shellac in his jet-black hair, and I notice for the first time that he bears a striking resemblance to Gene Simmons.

"Me neither," I say.

"Ha!" he says back. "Your mother is something, isn't she? How are things going with the freelance job?"

"I could really use a drink," I say.

"I made sure they stocked the bar with 1990 Lafite." He produces a wineglass from out of nowhere and I take a swig, surveying the crowd. I wonder whether my parents shelled out the cash for an open bar, too. I could really use some hard alcohol right now.

A waitress walks by with a tray of mini hot dogs. Chloe, although immersed in conversation with my mom, manages to grab one and dip it into the mustard. My dad and I reach over and grab some, too.

As I look around, I see that my mother has completely redesigned the Delancey's roof deck—Chinese paper lanterns hang delicately from the ceiling, the way they used to do on the terrace of Tavern on the Green, and there are two overlapping Oriental rugs laid down on the stage, à la U2's video for

"Elevation." Right above the stage, there is a massive hot-pink neon sign announcing HAPPY 22ND BIRTHDAY, JO!

And if that wasn't enough, my mother's also had the entire thing catered. In the far left corner, where Chloe once made out with a crazy Brazilian guy, only to have his girlfriend appear and try to take a swing at her, there are mini crab cakes and chicken satay being passed around. Right in the middle of the room, where Jesse once got so drunk he threw up right on the floor, there is a caviar bar and vodka slide. People are already lined up to drink the vodka directly as it comes down the slide (which was not my mother's intention, I assure you, what with the little bamboo shot glasses she's lined up next to the slide). On the wall across from where the bands usually set up, where Chloe and I scratched our initials into the wood, there is a carving station with prime rib and roast turkey. At the prime rib station, I see Andrew loading up a plate with tons of food while Barbie stands by his side, nibbling on some celery and drinking a Diet Coke. I can tell by the look on Andrew's face that they have just been bickering. They are always quarreling with each other—I once told Andrew that they have a very Sid and Nancy-esque relationship. If only he would just get on with killing Barbie already, it might save me the misery of being a bridesmaid (she's already hinted that for the bridesmaid dresses she's leaning toward peach).

A waiter breezes by me with a tray of tuna tartare and my father and I both grab one, my father noting that for "all this money we're paying them," the least they can do is provide cocktail napkins for the hors d'oeuvres. All I can think is, *How much money did my mother pay the Delancey for this space? I will be forever known as the wannabe rocker whose mommy paid tons of cash to throw her a birthday party at the Delancey. I can never show my face on the Lower East Side again.*

Frankie, my old lead guitarist from the Lonely Hearts Club

Band, approaches us. He shakes my father's hand and gives me a hug and a kiss. We haven't even spoken since Billy died and our band broke up. He graduated right after Billy died, so I haven't even seen him in those two years.

"I'm so happy to be here, Jo," he says. "It's good to see you. Happy birthday."

"It's great to see you, Frankie," I say, and I am surprised to realize that I mean it. "How are you doing?"

"Great," he says. "Really great. I married Stacey, and we're living out in Jersey now."

"I always knew you two would get married," I say. It's kind of crazy to think that they're only two years older than me, but they seem to have everything together. "You were a great couple. Is she here tonight?"

"Right over there," he says. "She's the one accosting the waiter with the potato pancakes."

I spot Stacey across the dance floor. As she turns around and begins walking toward us, I see that she is pregnant. Very pregnant. Stacey has a massive tattoo across her stomach, which was, two years ago, incredibly sexy because she was a yoga instructor and had amazing abs. I can only imagine what that tattoo looks like now.

"Here's my baby," Frankie says, pulling her to him for a kiss.

"Here's your baby," Stacey says, stroking her tummy and laughing as she reaches over to me for a hug. "Happy birthday, Jo."

The baby talk is freaking me out a bit—this is a couple who hated last call at 4 A.M. more than any of us. It's strange to see them settled down, especially so young. As we talk, Frankie tells me that he's teaching music at a community college out in Jersey (who would have guessed that a guy with seven piercings would get a respectable teaching gig?) and Stacey's running a yoga studio in a strip mall.

"What are you up to these days?" Frankie asks.

"Still working on my music," I say. "Fighting the good fight."

"Keep on rocking in the free world," Frankie says. "Wasn't that our motto?"

"It was," I say. "So, do you ever hear from Kane?"

"Naw," Frankie says. "I haven't. Have you?"

"No," I say. "Sorry I brought it up. Have you checked out the caviar bar yet?"

"Not yet," Stacey says, rubbing her belly, "but there's sushi over there by the carving station, and it's killing me!"

"I could use a drink," Frankie says, and we part ways.

Frankie heads over to get a drink and I make my way to the caviar bar. As embarrassed as I am about the sheer spectacle of the evening, it would be a huge waste to not try the imported caviar. Walking through the crowd, I wonder how my mother even got the contact information for all of my friends if Chloe didn't help her. I survey the crowd and see several other people who I haven't spoken to in ages—even a few that I wouldn't have invited if I'd had my choice. In an instant, it hits me—she got it from the address book on my iPhone. It was synched with the computer at work, so I now blame Barbie for this whole debacle.

"The Lower East Side sure cleans up nice," Andrew says, giving me a kiss on the cheek. I wonder if that's my present from him.

"Hey, girlie!" Barbie says, hugging me as if I were her long lost sister. "Happy birthday! I got you something!"

"That was so unnecessary," I say, scooping a massive spoonful of caviar onto a blini and eating it quickly. I put down my plate, take a swig of vodka (from the bamboo shot glass, just in case my mother is watching me), and open Barbie's gift.

It's really not a gift at all. It's more like an envelope. Assuming it's a very heartfelt greeting card, I tear it open, oblivious to the red hearts adorning it. But what's inside is not a greeting card at all. The lights are low at the Delancey, so I have to position myself just so under a paper lantern to see what Barbie has given to me.

I feel my face getting shiny and red as I realize what the slip of paper actually is. I imagine steam coming out of my ears, like in a kid's cartoon. Eyes bulging out of my head. Across the top, in swirly pretty letters, it says, "Love, Inc." If I hadn't thrown it out the second Barbie turned her back on me, I would have noticed that the card was pale pink with the faint outline of tiny hearts everywhere. What I *was* able to see in the thirty seconds before I crushed it into a ball with my fist was that Barbie was giving me a subscription to an online dating service. When I thank her (disingenuously), she informs me that she thought it was the perfect gift—I can use it and have a date for her wedding. Barbie then, as is her way, grabs hold of my body and hugs me and begins bouncing up and down. I hug her back, though "hugging" might be putting it too charitably. "Strangling" is more like it.

"I'm so happy you like it, girlie!" Barbie says, just before she excuses herself to go to the "little girls' room."

"I had no idea," Andrew says under his breath. I'm not sure if he wanted me to hear him say that or not.

"What?" I say, a little too aggressively, grabbing for another blini and covering it in sour cream and then caviar.

"Nothing," he says. "Actually, I got you something, too. I thought it would be from the two of us, but..."

"You didn't have to," I say.

"I'm your brother, Jo-Jo," he says. "Of course I had to."

I freeze as I see that Andrew's present is yet another envelope.

"Trust me, you'll like this one," he says.

This envelope I open slowly, gingerly, like I've got all the time in the world. When I take out the card, I know immediately what it is—it's another gift certificate. But this one is a gift certificate for hours of studio time at my favorite recording studio. Without thinking, I jump on top of my brother and give him a huge hug.

"Thank you so much," I scream in his ear.

"Told you you'd like it," he says and lifts me a little bit in the air for effect.

"I love it," I say as he puts me back down on the ground. "Studio time is so expensive, and this is enough for me to make an entire demo."

"I know, and I know. I remember you told me that this was the place where you cut your first demo and that you loved it there, but it costs a fortune to make a demo there, so I figured that I'd help you out. Since you're unemployed and everything."

"I love it. Thank you."

"Why are you thanking him?" Barbie says, back from the bathroom. "Love, Inc. was all *my* idea!"

Andrew and I look at each other and laugh. Andrew apologizes to Barbie for trying to steal her glory as I quietly tuck Andrew's gift certificate into my pocket.

"When are they going to play some music that I've heard of?" a huge voice calls out from behind me. I turn around to see Lola and her mother.

"They're not," I say, leaning down to kiss her.

"Which is just fine," her mother says, "because we're only staying until ten."

"Mom!" Lola cries.

"When I was your age, my mother didn't ever take me to a downtown club *or* let me drink Shirley Temples. So you'd better be Mom-ing me to say, 'I'm so lucky to have a cool mother like you.'"

"If we're leaving at ten, I'm going to request some Amber Fairchild right now," Lola says, running off toward the DJ.

I look at the stage and see Cakewalk setting up. They really *are* playing. Now I *truly* can never show my face at the Delancey again. Any downtown rock club, really. How is it going to look that my parents hired a hip, new indie rock band to play my twenty-second birthday party? It's like an older, slightly more pathetic version of MTV's *My Sweet 16*.

"Cakewalk's actually performing here?" Chloe says to me, handing me a mini crab cake. "Your mother has truly outdone herself."

"I'm so embarrassed," I say.

"You don't get embarrassed," Chloe reminds me, grabbing at a stuffed mushroom that a waiter brings by on a tray.

"No, my mother's just that good," I say. "She can embarrass anyone. Even people who don't get embarrassed."

"Let's just dance," Chloe says, and pulls me up to stand right in front of where the band is almost finished setting up. We put our drinks down and begin to dance to an old Killers song that the DJ is playing.

"And now," the DJ announces, "I'm going to do one more song by special request before Cakewalk hits the stage. Lola would like to dedicate this song to the birthday girl." I smile and scan the crowd for Lola. She is jumping up and down, clapping her hands furiously, and dragging her mother out onto the dance floor. "So here's Amber Fairchild singing 'I Want You to Keep Me Up All Night (All Right).'"

Chloe and I exchange looks, and over her shoulder, I can see Barbie jumping up and down, clapping her hands furiously and dragging my brother out onto the dance floor.

"I REALLY wish I knew that you didn't want a party, Pumpkin,"

my father tells me between Cakewalk's sets, "because this party is your gift."

"How about we call it even and you just give me the loft?" I say.

"The loft?" my dad says, running his fingers through his thick black hair. "That reminds me of an old joke. A husband asks his wife what she wants for her fiftieth birthday. He says, 'You can have anything you want.' She tells him, 'I want a divorce.' The man says, 'I wasn't really planning on spending that much.'"

At around ten, the band takes a break, and we are introduced to my mother's pièce de résistance. She jumps up on stage and announces that dessert is about to be served. With a tiny wave of her wrist, waiters and waitresses come out with dozens and dozens of miniature gourmet cupcakes. Some are adorned with little music notes, and others with teeny treble clefs.

Lola and her mother come to say good-bye to me and I see that my mother has given them the party favors for the evening— the old Lonely Hearts Club Band demo CD in a red leather CD case, embossed, of course, with:

JO'S 22ND BIRTHDAY PARTY
THE DELANCEY
NEW YORK CITY

"I can't wait to put this on my phone!" Lola calls out as she walks out with her mother. I make a mental inventory of just how many of those songs are inappropriate for children.

Most of them.

"Aren't these fabulous?" my mother asks, handing me a vanilla cupcake with buttercream frosting. "I had them made specially for you from that French bakery on the Miracle Mile."

"Aren't you planning Andrew's wedding?" I ask. "Isn't that

keeping you busy enough?"

"But you're my *daughter*," she says, dragging the word "daughter" out into two words so that it almost sounds as if she has an English accent. "It's *your* birthday."

I know that what she is saying is true. I know that she loves me so much it hurts, and that she would do anything in the world for me. I *also* know that she fancies herself a real Martha Stewart, albeit more law-abiding, and would not miss an opportunity to plan an expensive, over-the-top wedding.

"Barbie's mom isn't letting you have anything to do with the wedding plans?"

"No," my mom says. "She's absolutely horrible." She looks like she's fighting back tears when she says this, and for a moment, I actually feel sorry for her.

But that doesn't last long. The next minute, I remember that I'm a loser—no job, no freelance gig, no boyfriend, no music career, and I've just turned twenty-two. I've graduated college, so there's no more excuses. I'm a loser.

"For the birthday girl," the leader of the band says, "we've got a surprise."

A surprise? Hasn't this whole night been surprise enough? I find Chloe across the room and our eyes lock.

"Dr. Waldman," he says. "Get your ass up here!" Why is the lead singer of Cakewalk directing my dad's ass to be anywhere? The crowd goes crazy, and a few of my friends from high school even start chanting my father's name. Chloe's prom date in particular—formerly the quarterback of the football team, now a three-hundred-pound electronics salesman—seems to be going wild with anticipation.

"Marty! Marty! Marty!"

My father climbs up on stage and gets behind the electric keyboard.

"I'm used to playing on a baby grand," he quips, "but this will have to do." The crowd explodes in laughter, with my mom leading the charge. She has climbed up onto one of the benches and is cheering like a groupie.

"This is dedicated to Jo," my father says. "Happy birthday, Pumpkin."

The drummer clicks his sticks together and they begin doing a cover of Tom Jones's "She's a Lady."

"Do you think your dad would hook me up with the lead singer of the band?" Chloe asks.

"I don't know," I say. "Why don't you throw your underwear up on the stage and find out?"

"I think your mother's got that one covered," she says and I look at my mother. It's impossible to stay angry with her, as cute as she looks dancing on the bench with her black leather pants and Chanel spectators on. She asked both Chloe and me, separately, of course, if she looked "downtown enough" in her little ensemble.

"I really should be more drunk for this," I say, pouring myself another shot of vodka from the slide. I consider for a moment if it would be bad form to squat in front of the vodka slide and just chug until I pass out.

"Girls! Get up here!" my mother calls out, looking at Chloe and me.

Absolutely not, I mouth back to her. And then to Chloe: "Is my humiliation not complete?"

"If you can't beat them," Chloe says, "join them."

"Never," I say. "I'm such a loser."

"Then admit defeat. If you won't do it for your mother, do it for your dad. Think about how many gigs he's come to for you over the years. He's really tearing it up."

"He is," I say, and I can't help but smile. He *is* tearing it up.

My dad is totally in his element—playing like I'd never seen him before, nailing each key and dancing along with the music. And the band actually seems to enjoy having him up there.

I grab another shot of vodka in one hand, Chloe's hand in the other, and jump up onto the bench with my mom. The three of us dance as we sing along with the lyrics.

"'She's a lady,'" we sing. "'Whoooooa, she's a lady...'"

Chloe is right. If you can't beat them, join them. After all, my actual birthday isn't until tomorrow. I can always be angry about how pathetic my life is then.

12
Owner of a Lonely Heart

Valentine's Day. February fourteenth. A day of love and romance and frills and doilies. A day filled with chocolate in heart-shaped boxes and all things pink and red.

Valentine's Day is the day on which lovers freely express their passion for each other by sending flowers, candies, and insipid love notes. Lots of love notes. According to the Greeting Card Association, approximately one *billion* Valentines are sent every year, making it the biggest card-giving holiday besides Christmas.

Dozens of red roses are sent on this day and hundreds of couples get engaged. Radio stations play love songs and bakeries bake heart-shaped cookies. February fourteenth is a day dedicated entirely to the pursuit of love.

It's also the day that five of Al Capone's men gunned down seven members of Bugs Moran's gang with tommy guns in a garage on Chicago's north side in 1929. But people usually don't send cards for that.

It being Valentine's Day, and me being alone, I do what any respectable single woman who's utterly alone would do—I open a bottle of Stoli and order in some fried food from my local Italian place.

"That'll be $32.15," the hostess says after she's tallied up my dinner delivery order.

"But I get the same thing every time," I say, pouring my first vodka tonic of the evening. I pour way too much vodka into the glass, making it stronger than I intend it to be, but I'm not exactly drinking it for the taste this evening. "Isn't it $18 and change?"

"Oh," she says, "yeah, normally it is, but there's an extra charge on all of the menu items for Valentine's Day."

"What?" I say, since I must have misheard her. There's no way in hell this girl just told me that even though I'm ordering in for one, she's charging me extra because it's Valentine's Day. In fact, since I'm ordering for one and it's Valentine's Day, shouldn't I get a *discount* instead of a price increase? The whole situation really brings out my Irish. Being a Jewish girl from Long Island, I don't really have much Irish in me, but it brings it out nonetheless.

"Oh," she says. "I was just saying that there's an extra charge on all of the menu items for Valentine's Day."

"But I ordered for one," I say, pacing around my kitchen with my glass as I speak. "Clearly I'm alone and it's Valentine's Day."

"Yeah," she says. "I know. It's just that there's an extra charge on all of the menu items for Valentine's Day."

"I heard you," I say. I take a big gulp of vodka.

"Okay, yeah, so it should be there in about twenty minutes," she says, trying to get me off the phone.

"I ordered for one."

Dead silence on the line.

"I'd like to speak to a manager," I say, polishing off my first glass in just one large gulp.

"Um, okay," she says. "Hold on."

"Hi there," the manager's cheery voice announces, as I'm

pouring vodka tonic number two. To call this one a vodka tonic would be a bit of a misnomer. Glass number two is more like a vodka with a splash of tonic. "I'm Greg. I'm the manager here."

"Hi, Greg," I say as I sit at the kitchen counter and swirl the glass to mix my drink. "I understand that it's Valentine's Day and that means that you have to gouge the eyes out of all the lovesick puppies who come into your restaurant tonight. I would do the exact same thing, Greg. The same thing. I mean, fuck them, okay? Fuck 'em, Greg. But I am home—alone—ordering for one. How *dare* you charge me extra for my goddamned Caesar salad and chicken parm. Tonight of all nights. I mean, what the fuck, Greg? What the fuck?"

"You are absolutely right, miss," Manager Greg says to me as I down the second glass of vodka. "I'm so sorry."

My Caesar salad and chicken parm arrive hot on my doorstep twenty minutes later, and the delivery guy presents me with the bill. I glance at the bill, ready to pay, but then I notice something. It's not a bill for the usual amount—it's a bill for the jacked-up Valentine's Day price.

"I'm not paying this," I say, handing back the bill to the delivery guy.

"Um," he says, shifting his weight from foot to foot. "Whaddya mean?"

"I mean you can tell Manager Greg to go fuck himself," I say.

"Um, wait? What?"

I hand the delivery guy a tip. "This is for you. You can tell Manager Greg I'm not paying for this. If he has a problem with that, he can come up here himself." I grab the bag of food just before I slam the door.

I barely even taste the chicken parm. Minutes later, I realize that I must have eaten—the takeout container's empty—but it's like I didn't even have a bite. Anger coursing through my veins, my face getting hotter by the second, barely processing a thought. Just seeing red. Blinding red. I look down at the takeout container and realize I'm still hungry.

But I don't want to eat. I want to rage.

Put it into a song, I tell myself. *Get it out with your music.*

But the words don't come. There's no structure, no rhyme or reason—I just want to scream at the top of my lungs for a while. To blow off steam.

A tear comes to my eye as I think about everything that's happened to me in the past few months. All the things that I've lost, all the things that were totally out of my control. The job, the guy, the freelance gig, the wedding.

The guy. My eyes burn as I force the tears back, refuse to let them out.

I look at my computer across the room, its black cursor against the pale white screen flashing in the dark. Talking to me. Beckoning to me. Write. Get it all out.

So I do.

PART TWO: DOG DAYS ARE OVER
"You can't carry it with you if you want to survive"

13
Love Stinks

'm sleeping on the couch, one too many Valentine's Day vodka tonics heavy in my belly, when I hear my answering machine across the room.

"This is some seriously antisocial stuff, Jo-Jo," Andrew says in the distance. "If you're not out killing people at random, call me back."

I don't know if I'm dreaming it or if he's really just left me a message, but I'm too tired to even try to figure it out. As I determine that it doesn't really matter whether or not Andrew left me a message, the phone rings again, leading me to the undeniable conclusion that I'm actually half awake.

"Why are you so angry at Walt Disney?" Chloe says into my answering machine.

"What?" I say, grabbing at the portable phone that's on my coffee table and turning it on.

"'FUCK DISNEY.' That's what you said," Chloe says. "You said, 'WE GREW UP ON WALT DISNEY, BELIEVING HIM WHEN HE ASSURED US THAT "SOMEDAY" OUR PRINCE WOULD COME. HE

MADE US THINK THAT LOVE WAS THAT ONE KISS THAT COULD BRING YOU BACK TO LIFE, WHEN IN REALITY, LOVE MAKES YOU FEEL JUST LIKE BAMBI, AFTER HIS MOTHER GETS SHOT.' Kind of harsh, don't you think?"

"What are you talking about?" I say, rubbing the sleep out of my eyes and sitting up on the couch. My laptop is still turned on, sitting on my coffee table, staring at me like a one-night stand you'd really wish would just leave your apartment already. "When did I say that?"

"Just now," Chloe says, "on your blog. Well, on your old band's blog anyway. And on Facebook. And Twitter. And Instagram, probably, but I haven't checked that yet. I thought I told you that it wasn't healthy to try to revisit the past like that?" As Chloe is still talking, I flip through my computer's index of Web sites recently visited. "You said, 'THERE WAS A MAN I LOVED. A MAN I LOVED MORE THAN ANYTHING IN THE WORLD. MORE THAN ANYONE I'VE EVER LOVED BEFORE. AFTER TWO AND A HALF YEARS TOGETHER, THAT MAN TORE MY HEART OUT AND DIDN'T LOOK BACK. AND THE WORST PART IS THAT I DIDN'T EVEN SEE IT COMING. I THOUGHT THAT I HAD LOVE, BUT I NOW REALIZE THAT THERE'S JUST NO SUCH THING.' No such thing as love? Jo, are you even listening to me?"

"I'm listening," I say, as I hop onto my band's old Web site. It takes a few seconds to load, but I'm soon on the blog page, clicking around. My words are staring me right back in the face. My drunken, angry thoughts that were meant to be kept to myself are there on the screen, apparently there for all the world to see.

I was never particularly computer savvy, so when I wrote all of my deepest, darkest secrets on the blog, I just assumed that since the site wasn't really active anymore, they'd just stay there for me, password protected. But in my vodka-tonic-induced haze, I must have somehow posted it so that anyone who hopped on the site could see it. "I'm just trying to figure out how I posted this stupid thing and how to unpost it. I didn't mean for it to be public. Anyway, they're the drunken ramblings of a lonely idiot who's alone on Valentine's Day."

"'I SEE COUPLES,'" Chloe parrots back to me. "'EVERYWHERE I LOOK, EVERYWHERE I GO. HAPPY COUPLES IN LOVE. THE CITY'S JUST LOUSY WITH THEM. THE ONLY CONSOLATION I HAVE WHEN I SEE THESE LOVESICK PUPPIES IS THAT THEY ARE JUST MERE MOMENTS FROM BEING AS HOPELESS AND ANGRY AS I AM. THEY ARE ONE GOLD STILETTO, ONE BOTTLE OF WINE AWAY FROM HAVING THEIR WORLDS CAVE IN ON THEM. FROM BEING BURIED ALIVE IN THEIR OWN MISERY. BECAUSE I KNOW SOMETHING THAT THEY DON'T YET KNOW: IT WON'T LAST. IT NEVER DOES.'"

"Yes," I say, still typing away furiously, trying to take down what I wrote. "Enough. I can read. But how did you even know that there was something new on there?"

"You linked to it on Facebook. And Twitter."

"I don't even know how to tweet," I say.

"Apparently you do," Chloe says. "Oh God, whatever you do, don't check Instagram."

"Why not?"

"No reason. Anyway, I also got an e-mail from your mailing list," she said. "Remember how the blog was set up to e-mail your entire mailing list when a new post went up?"

I immediately sober up. What have I done?

"No," I say, slowly backing away from my computer. "I did not remember that at all."

What have I done?

What. Have. I. Done. This is not possible. This is just not possible.

My face heats up. Somehow in my Valentine's Day–induced rage, I thought it would be a good idea to send this rant to everyone on the Lonely Hearts mailing list, Twitter feed, and Facebook page. Which means that the same messages that Chloe received were also sent to more than 2,500 people throughout the tristate area. In one fit of fury, I have completely humiliated myself, my friends, and, quite possibly, my family.

My only hope is that the e-mail gets caught in everyone's spam filters since the site was set up such a long time ago.

All 2,500 spam filters.

And that no one checks Facebook. Or Twitter. Or, apparently, Instagram.

"My God, Jo, how drunk *were* you?"

"Very, I guess," I say as I read more of what I wrote on the blog.

"My favorite part is where you start attacking the grandmothers," Chloe says, "it has to be someone's fault, right? Why not blame the grandmothers? Here we go: 'ALL MEN SUCK. ALL MEN WILL LIE TO YOU AND LET YOU DOWN. THERE IS NO SUCH THING AS A GOOD MAN—ONLY A MAN WHO IS TEMPORARILY BEING NICE TO YOU BECAUSE HE WANTS YOU TO HAVE SEX WITH HIM OR TO GIVE HIM MONEY. GRANDMOTHERS—I KNOW WHAT YOU'RE THINKING. SHE OBVIOUSLY HASN'T MET MY GRANDSON. BUT, NO, THIS GOES FOR YOU, TOO. YOUR GRANDSONS SUCK. THEY LIE. THEY ARE ASSHOLES. THEY CANNOT COMMIT.'" Chloe laughs. "I love that part."

"I didn't mean to attack grandmothers," I say.

"I posted a comment," she says. I quickly click on the link for guest comments. This is going from bad to worse.

"'AMEN, SISTER'?" I say, skimming over Chloe's entry quickly. "Since when do you say things like 'Amen, sister'?"

"Isn't that the problem with a blog?" Chloe asks. "You end up writing stuff you would never say out loud. Actually, maybe that's the beauty of a blog. That's why you did it, right?"

"No," I say. I don't really know why I did it. "It was just to let off steam, I guess."

"Do you feel better now?"

"No," I say. "Not really." And I *don't* feel any better. The rage is still coursing through my body. My face feels hot and there's nothing I can do to cool it down. I'm still angry—I still feel like opening my window and screaming at the world. The rage quickly turns to sadness as I read the rest of Chloe's entry:

> *Love is selfish. Love is a lie. Love is waking up in the middle of the night to a phone call saying that the love of your life OD'd after he's been promising you for months on end that he's been sober. Love is having to call your boyfriend's parents right before Christmas to tell them that their son is dead and you don't know why and you don't know how because you weren't even there.*
>
> *Love tears your heart out. Love kills your soul.*

"Oh, Chlo. I'm so sorry," I say. "I didn't mean to upset you."

"Thinking about Billy always upsets me," she says. "Nothing unusual about that."

"I really didn't know it was going out to my whole mailing list," I say, taking the throw blanket that's draped over the back of the couch and putting it across my shoulders. "You know I would never do anything to hurt you, right?"

"You didn't hurt me," she says. "Billy hurt me. When he cared more about drugs than he cared about me, that hurt me. And he hurt you, too, right? The band broke up after he died. But you? You didn't hurt me. You know, I always think of him on Valentine's Day. Getting that all out on your blog actually made me feel better, you know?"

"I'm glad it made you feel better," I say, wondering why I didn't feel any better after I vented all of *my* feelings. "Anyway, what are you doing on the Internet when you have a Valentine's Day date? Did you get rid of him already?"

"I sent him home," she says. "He took me out for drinks. Who does drinks on Valentine's Day? No matter how casual you are with a guy, on Valentine's Day, a girl deserves dinner. Don't you think?"

"Do you want to talk about it?" I ask.

"I wasn't going to date him past this weekend anyway, so there's really nothing to say."

"I meant, do you want to talk about Billy?" I ask, drawing the blanket over my head and lying back on the couch.

"Didn't I say enough?" she asks, laughing. I'm happy that I got her to laugh, but then I remember that for Chloe, she really has to cry it all out until she feels better.

"There's no limit on how much you can cry to your best friend," I say.

"You said it best, Jo: 'We're believing in a lie. True love isn't really out there; it's a myth. It's no different than Santa Claus or the Tooth Fairy. So, I say—let's just grow up already and call a spade a spade. Let's just stop deluding ourselves and admit that there's no such thing as love.' That's what you said. Didn't you mean it?"

"I guess," I say as I read the rest of what I wrote: *I'm done with love. I'm giving up on love before it breaks my heart again. And I'd suggest that you do the same thing, too.* "I just didn't mean for that—for how angry I feel—to upset you," I say.

"Everything you wrote, everything you said, is exactly how I feel," she says. "How I felt, I mean. I think I'm still mad at Billy for dying. I keep thinking that I'm over it, that I'm ready to move on, but then the tiniest thing will happen—like I'll hear some song he loved, or some song he hated—and everything just comes flooding back to me, you know?"

"I know," I say.

"And I'm still on the mailing list for the goddamned Guitar Center," she says. "Why is that place still sending me mailers when I haven't even shopped there in over two years? I just got one yesterday."

"That sucks," I say, making a mental note to call Guitar Center tomorrow.

"I just wish I could stop thinking about him, you know?" she says. "When do you think I'll stop thinking about him?"

I try to formulate a response, but I can't. I don't think that she will ever stop thinking of him, much in the way my father never stops thinking about his own father, who died when I was only three years old.

"It's okay to think about him," I say. "You loved him, he loved you. He was brilliant, and an amazing musician and songwriter. Hugely talented. Can't we remember him for that?"

"I guess so," Chloe says. "Hey, this is weird."

"What's weird?" I say, blanket still over my head.

"Check out the comment section."

"What is it?" I say as I sit up and look at the computer screen.

"The number keeps going up," Chloe says. I look at the number of guest comments and Chloe's right. The number keeps going higher and higher, faster and faster, right before my eyes.

"Something must be broken," I say, hitting whatever keys on my computer that I can. "It says it has ninety-seven comments."

"Hey, look," Chloe says. "This one says 'AMEN, SISTER,' too!"

"People are actually posting comments?"

I click back to the link for guest comments and Chloe is right—this is not a mistake. The blog has already gotten ninety-seven comments and the count is growing by the second.

Ninety-eight, ninety-nine, one hundred, one hundred and one, one hundred and two...

14
Wanna Be Startin' Something?

"**D**o you like pizza?" I ask Max, the number-one IT guy at Chloe's ad agency. He's at the loft since Chloe begged him to come by and fix my computer after it crashed this morning. Apparently it wasn't equipped to deal with the volume of responses I downloaded from my blog. I'm supposed to be making him lunch for his services, which is fair, since he's doing it for me on his lunch break.

When Max walked in, I almost laughed out loud. He looked like he came straight from Central Casting for the role of dorky computer guy: sandy long hair half pulled back into a ponytail with the sides falling over his overgrown sideburns, black horn-rimmed glasses, and a short-sleeved button-down shirt and khakis. You can tell these are his "I work in an office" khakis that he only wears Monday through Friday, from the hours of 9 A.M. to 5 P.M.

Totally not my type. Which doesn't matter at all, since I'm not looking for anyone new right now. *Especially* now. Now that I've sworn off love and encouraged 2,500 people in the tristate area to do likewise.

But still, I find myself wondering why Chloe never dated Max, because there's something about him that I instantly like.

"Who doesn't like pizza?" he says with a laugh. "But you know, I was promised a homemade lunch for my services."

"Oh, don't worry. They'll make it from scratch over at Mario's," I tell him with a sly smile. The phone rings and I pick it up.

"Is this some sort of a joke, Jo?" my father says.

"Hi, Daddy," I murmur into the phone as I turn my back to Max.

"This computer thing you've written, is it a joke?" he asks. "Why are you so angry?"

I'm wondering how my dad even saw the blog. He barely knows how to operate a computer. I ask him as much.

"Barbie printed it out for me," he says. *How very helpful of her,* I think. "She's worried about you."

"No," I say. "She's just worried about having a deranged bridesmaid walk down her aisle."

My father is not amused. "It really doesn't matter why *she* printed it for me," he says. "What matters is why *you* wrote it."

"I don't know why I wrote it," I whisper into the phone, hoping, for some reason, that Max cannot hear me. "But you don't have to worry about me. I'm fine."

"This is not the sort of behavior a person who is 'fine' exhibits," he says. "Maybe you should come home to Long Island for a few days. Just to relax."

I think of telling him that spending a few days on Long Island with my parents will have the opposite effect from relaxing me, but think better of it. "I'm fine here in the city."

"Well, then I'll come into the city," he says. "Meet me at Balthazar at seven."

I try to voice my dissent, but he's already hung up the phone.

Now I know where Andrew learned that trick. I set the phone back in its cradle a little too harshly and it makes an audible crash.

"I'm just about done here," Max says, pretending not to have heard this exchange with my father.

"Can I get you anything to drink?" I ask.

"Whatever you're having is fine with me," he says.

I've been drinking water all morning in an attempt to flush out all of the vodka tonics I drank last night, but there's something that seems wrong about giving a guest a glass of water. Alcohol would be too festive for the occasion, so I compromise and bring two iced teas over to the couch.

"Thanks," he says, and turns my laptop to me.

"Thank *you*," I say. "How does it look?"

"All better," he says, taking a sip of his iced tea. He leans over and shows me around the Web site, demonstrating all of the changes he's made to accommodate the massive amount of traffic the site is getting. With his arm brushing mine, I'm suddenly very aware of the wife beater and pajama bottoms I'm still wearing. And that I'm not wearing a bra. "You know, you could make a ton of money with this Web site on advertising. You've obviously hit a nerve here. This is what people want to read, how they feel. You've tapped into something special. Are you tracking how many people have tweeted at you? Have you seen what some of these people have written to you? You've practically started a movement."

"A movement is not exactly a bunch of people from your mailing list writing comments on your blog post."

"You have more than 50,000 people on your mailing list?"

"2,500," I say, not quite believing my ears. "Did you say 5,000?"

"Fifty," he says. "50,000."

"That's not possible," I say, inching away from Max. He smells like soap and lemon and sweat.

"I know people who have quit their day jobs on a lot less," he says, nodding at me. "With the traffic you got in just one night, I'd imagine that you could start selling ad space on this thing as soon as today. I can help you out with that, if you wanted."

"You'd help me?" I ask as my mind begins to race. I could do this. I could actually do this. Work on my music during the day and update the blog at night. This could actually be the start of something.

"Yeah," he says. "I could be like a consultant to your site or something like that. I could even help you with a redesign, since it's sort of dated. We could create a brand that goes across your blog, your Facebook page, and your Twitter page. Make it relate more to your blog, less to the band."

"I want it to still relate to the band," I say and Max looks back at me. "I'm not ready to let go of the band yet."

"Okay," he says, furrowing his brow, "but the real money's in the high-traffic area—the blog."

"I could use the money," I say, and immediately realize that we are sitting in a 3,000-square-foot loft in Soho. "This place is my dad's and he wants me to start paying rent on it."

"The nerve," Max says and we both laugh, me nervously, and him…I'm not sure why. As I look at him, I notice that his sideburns are a much darker shade of dirty blond than the rest of his hair.

"Hey, so do you really believe all this stuff?"

"What stuff?" I say, still laughing as I sip my iced tea.

"The stuff you wrote on your blog. About love being evil and killing your soul and all that?" he asks as he puts his iced tea down on the coffee table. I'm charmed by the fact that he first locates a coaster before setting it down. Jesse never once thought to use a coaster. Or to take care of the loft in any way at all. Or me, for that matter.

"I didn't write the 'killing your soul' part," I say as I quickly take another swig of iced tea.

"About swearing off love?"

"Um, yes," I say, holding my glass between my hands. "I guess I do. I mean I did. What I meant was—"

Fortunately for me, the buzzer interrupts my fumbling and I get up to answer the door.

I try not to look Max in the eyes as we sit at the kitchen counter to eat our pizza.

"Thank you for coming over to fix my computer," I say, taking out a piece of pizza and putting it onto a plate for him.

"I didn't mean to get too personal," Max says in between bites. "I'm sorry about that."

"You didn't," I say. "It's fine. After all, it's out there in cyberspace, right?"

"Right," he says. There's a long spell of silence as we both chew our pizza. Whenever it seems like one of us is done chewing, the other takes a sip of iced tea so as to not have to talk more.

It goes like that for a while. Sip, bite, sip, bite. Glance over at the other person—quick sip to avoid talking. Finally, Max breaks the silence: "So, is Jo short for anything?"

"No," I say, but it's a lie. I never tell anyone the truth about my name anymore. That my given name is actually Jodi.

I always lie. Right to their faces. Jodi just sounds so ordinary and commonplace. Anyone can be a Jodi. Anyone. But not just anyone can be a Jo. I've been going by Jo since I was in the second grade. Even the second-grade me was cool enough to know that I could never be one of the legions of Ashleys, Jessicas, and Brittanys we had running around our school.

Also, there was another girl in our class named Jodi who

everyone hated and made fun of. They would taunt her in the halls by singing, "Jodi is grody, Jodi is grody..."

"That's a strange name for a kid," he says. "Did they tease you as a child?" I can see in his eyes that he is dying for me to say yes—that he was tormented as a child, himself—and that he wants to make that connection with me.

But then I think about my broken heart and my vow to never let that happen again.

"No."

I look into his eyes (dark green? hazel?) and he looks like I just killed his pet dog. He wipes his mouth and gets up from the counter.

"Thanks for lunch, Jo," he says, putting his plate into the sink. "I'd better get back to work now."

"Thanks for fixing my computer," I say, watching him as he walks toward the door and fumbles with his coat. I want to say more, but I don't know if I should. Did I really mean what I said about giving up on love?

"Good luck with everything," he says as he throws his scarf around his neck hastily.

"You know what?" I say, jumping up from my seat as he reaches for the door. "I think I might want some help with the Web site after all. Are you free tomorrow night?"

15
You Really Got Me

Facebook status update from Rachel Gray:
Have you guys seen The Lonely Hearts Club Web site lately? Jo Waldman is reading my mind. Love sucks—the sooner we all figure that out, the better. #LonelyHeartsClub

Tweet from @juliamusic:
Jo Waldman has got it right over on @LonelyHeartsClub. I vow to be done with love, too!

E-mail from Allsnotfairinloveandmusic:
Dear Jo,
You don't know me, but your post struck a chord. You see, I've been married for a while now, and we're no longer happy. We're growing apart. I know that I vowed to the Lord to stay married till death do us part, but it's becoming harder by the

day. But I can't leave. I have nowhere to go. What should I do?

INSTAGRAM FROM CHLOCHLO: PICTURE OF A DEAD BIRD IN THE STREET
This is what love does to you. #LonelyHeartsClub

It never stops. The computer keeps chirping, telling me that more and more people are reaching out to me. Don't they know that all I want to do is get under the covers and hide?

I don't even recognize most of the screen names—not on the blog comments, not on Twitter, Facebook, or Instagram. Who are these people? I have no idea how they even found me. Could the reach of my crazy rant be even wider than I thought? I check the site—more than 300,000 unique views. That can't possibly be right. I'll have to have Max check that for me when he comes over later. 300,000. There's just no way.

The idea of it terrifies me. I flip on the television and tune to *The Today Show*. Nothing like bland morning TV to clear one's mind. Which I now have the luxury of doing every morning since I'm presently sans job.

Amber Fairchild pops onto the screen. She is seemingly everywhere. Why can't I ever get away from her? She's there to do a live version of one of her disposable pop numbers, she tells Matt Lauer. Except she doesn't say it that way, of course. She says, in her throaty farmer's daughter accent, "I'd love to perform for you." Even Matt Lauer can't control the chuckle that escapes his lips as she says this. Does she realize that everything she says is a double entendre? Did someone from her camp tell her that this is actually clever? A way to get respect as an artist?

The music pulses and throbs and she takes her sequin-bedazzled ass over to the mike. She shimmies her hips and throws her hands above her head—her signature dance move—

and begins to sing.

Correction: Her lips are moving, but no sound is coming out. It takes me a second to process what's happening, but the studio audience knows it immediately.

"Hey," an audience member calls out. "What's going on?"

Amber's face twists into a question mark. She has no idea what to do, so she does what she's always done since she was fifteen years old: She keeps singing. Or pretending to sing, to put it more accurately.

I can't believe my eyes. She's lip-synching. She's actually lip-synching! There's no greater crime in pop stardom than lip-synching. You might as well put a disclaimer on your album cover: The artist cannot actually sing. All songs have been auto-tuned so that no trace of her actual singing voice remains. A huge laugh escapes my lips just as I hear my computer dinging again.

This thing has got to stop ringing. Or at least I'll need a better sound if this thing's going to be exploding all day and all night. I guess I should call Max about that. He's been over just about every night since Valentine's Day, but I can't help it. I keep finding new things to ask him about. And as much as I haven't admitted it to myself yet, it's sort of nice having someone around. Having *him* around.

"Do you subsist entirely on pizza?" he asks me as I order in yet again from Mario's.

"I happen to think that red wine and a pepperoni pizza is as close to perfection as you can get," I say.

"Good point," he says, and takes a big swig of wine and another bite of pizza. "I think you may be onto something."

"Anyway, I can't really order in from my Italian place anymore," I say. "I sort of had an incident."

"I don't even want to know," Max says. "But there's more to

life than just Italian food. Riesling goes really well with Chinese food or Thai. Do you have any whites in that collection of yours?"

"That's my dad's collection," I say, looking at the massive wine fridge that's parked in the kitchen. "I've got a few bottles of my own in the fridge."

"So I don't rate for the fancy collection," Max says, pushing his dirty-blond hair behind his ears. "I think I see what's going on here."

"*I* don't rate for the fancy collection," I say, flipping my hair back off my shoulders.

"Well, if I had a fancy-wine collection," Max says, leaning into me, as if he about to tell me a secret, "I would let you share it with me."

"Thank you."

"You know, there's a Thai restaurant just down the block that's pretty good," Max says, eyes still looking at the computer. "Maybe we could hit it one night, drink some Riesling."

I don't know how to respond. Did he just ask me out on a date? Surely he knows by now that I don't believe in love, that I'm not interested in dating.

"Thai food?" I manage to eke out. Max keeps his eyes planted on the computer screen, fingers still typing away.

"Or not," he says. "Whatever."

"Okay, whatever," I say. And he doesn't bring it up again the rest of the week.

INSTAGRAM FROM CHLOCHLO: PICTURE OF A YOUNG COUPLE KISSING, SUNLIGHT STREAMING THROUGH FROM BETWEEN THEIR FACES.

Suckers. These people are just minutes away from having their hearts totally ripped apart.

BLOG COMMENT FROM ROCKBOY1983:

I know how you feel. Love can suck the soul right out of you. It used to be the thing I lived for—finding love, falling in love, being in love. Love was my oxygen. But it's all different now. I don't know if it's different because I'm an adult or because I'm with the wrong girl, but I'm now stuck with my girlfriend, since she recently announced that she is pregnant. This doesn't feel like love. This feels like my duty. I'm not going to run away from it, but this isn't how I imagined how my life would turn out.

Love steals your life away.

16
Heat of the Moment

This is it. I can feel it. It's the start of a new chapter. A new me. I may have been standing still for the last two years, but that's over. Now is the time that I do something.

It's been three weeks since my Valentine's Day rant went viral, but it's taken me that long to come up with the next thing I wanted to say. I considered getting liquored up and writing again in the middle of the night, while in a rage, but having Max around all the time doesn't engender the sort of rage I had coursing through my veins when I was with Jesse.

Instead, I go back to what I know: I get out my old Moleskine notebook, the one I used to carry with me everywhere to jot song lyrics in. The blog post I come up with is entirely different from the first—it's a series of observations, stories from my past, and even anecdotes from friends. But the message is the same: Love breaks your heart. Love makes you weak.

And it's just as well received as the first. Maybe more so. Comments are flying in, and I'm getting mentioned on Facebook and retweeted so much that I can barely keep up. And I should probably post something on Instagram. If only to get Chloe off my back about Instagram. She has not shut up for the last three days about Instagram. (An argument for having Chloe take over Instagram duties?)

Max is over working on the Web site when the computer chirps. Yet again. He's changed the sound of the chirp to an old-fashioned telephone sound, but that's no less annoying than the default setting.

"We've gotta change that sound," I say.

"It's retro," Max says. "You look like the sort of girl who likes retro."

I smile, and a tiny giggle escapes my lips. I have no idea if he's flirting with me—is that flirting? But it seems like he is. And even though I've sworn off love, I like it. I like it a lot.

"Are you flirting with me?" I ask. I've been thinking about the Thai food offer all week, but just haven't known how to bring it up again. Is there an organic way to say: *Ask me out again. This time, I'll say yes.*

Max gives me a look I can't really register. "No," he says. I'm about to tell him that it's okay if he was, when the computer chirps again. That damned noise.

"This one any better?" he asks. It's the sound of screeching tires.

"No," I say, and lean over his shoulder to turn down the sound.

"Hey," he says. "I need to hear that if I'm going to change it."

He plays another clip for me. It sounds like an '80s video game. Chomp, chomp, chomp.

"No," I say.

"You don't like video games?" Max asks.

I shake my head *no*.

"Oh, man," Max says. "You're going to want to read this." He turns the computer screen my way. He's showing me an e-mail. Doesn't he know how many e-mails I get a day? An e-mail isn't exactly going to get me excited. I can barely keep up as it is.

But this one is different. Max is right—I do want to see it. It's exactly what he promised me the first day we met: an advertiser. It's an offer to pay me to put an ad up on the blog.

"This is from Love, Inc. They want to put an ad up for a dating site," I say to Max. "That makes no sense."

"Maybe they think that you guys are all talk about this whole anti-love thing," Max says.

"I'm not all talk," I say.

"Oh, I know that," Max says and puts his head back down into my computer. And then, under his breath, "I didn't mean to offend you."

"You didn't offend me," I say. "I'm just telling you that I'm not all talk. So, do you think I should let this Love, Inc. thing put up an ad on the site?" I don't mention the fact that I recently got a gift certificate from Love, Inc. and promptly threw it in the garbage. But if I write back to them, I plan to put that in the e-mail.

"Of course you should," Max says. "It's a no-brainer."

"But it's the opposite of the message I'm trying to convey with the site," I say. "You realize that, right?"

"I disagree. The site's about love. It happens to be about rejecting love, yes, but it's still about love. This ad would be right in your wheelhouse."

"This ad makes me a sellout," I say.

"This ad makes you money," he says. "And this loft looks expensive."

"This loft *is* expensive," I say. "And it belongs to my father. Who's now charging me rent that I can't afford."

"And you're really questioning whether or not to take the

ad?" Max says, laughter in his voice. "You'll be the homeless girl with really high principles."

"Let's write back then," I say. I sit down right next to Max, close—too close, really—and start to type.

E-MAIL FROM JO@LONELYHEARTSCLUB.COM:

I'm interested in your offer. But there are some rules you'll have to follow if you want your ad to be on my site. First and foremost, you'll have to change your logo. I can't have something pink and red and all girly on my site. You can keep the graphic, but you've got to make it edgier. And the color scheme has to go. You can only use the colors black, white, and gray. And I reserve the right to put any tagline on the ad that I choose. You don't get final approval. I recently got a gift certificate to your site and threw it in the garbage, so it will probably be something along those lines. If you want to meet these terms, double your ask and we'll get your ad up tomorrow.

Rock and roll,

Jo Waldman

"You're a tough cookie," Max says.

"Oh yeah?" I ask, and it comes out a little flirtier than I'd originally thought. Did I mean to be flirting?

Max looks away.

"I should get back to work," he says, and takes the computer over to my kitchen counter.

"You do?" I ask. "I thought we were talking."

"Girls who look like you never would have talked to a guy

like me when I was in high school," he says, and I challenge him with a look. "I get it. Would you have ever talked to a guy who wore glasses and played D&D?"

"D&D?" I ask, silently praying that he's not asking me about some sort of sexual fetish.

"Dungeons and Dragons," he says.

"Oh," I say. "When I was younger, I wasn't really into video games."

"It's not a video game," he says and laughs. "It's a role-playing game."

"Oh," I say, unsure if that meant that it *is*, in fact, some sort of sex fetish thing.

"The point is," he continues, "girls like you never talk to me. I get it, Jo. You don't have to apologize. You don't have to worry about making me feel bad. I've met girls like you before."

There's really only one thing you can do when someone challenges you like that. And that is to show them how wrong they are.

I lean into him. Lingering only for a brief instant, I kiss him. Our lips touch and I realize that I'd wanted to do that from the first minute he walked into my loft.

Max barely moves. I pull away from him and look into his eyes. Was that wrong? Did I overstep my boundaries? Worse, did I just sexually harass the only person who's actually helping me with this thing? Was the Thai food not an offer for a date?

Then something changes in his eyes. Max grabs my shoulders and pulls me to him. We're kissing, his lips are all over mine, and I can't remember the last time I was kissed like this. If I was *ever* kissed like this. His lips are soft and I melt into him. He's got his hands tangled up in my hair and I run my own hands down his arms. His arms are strong, stronger than I would have thought, based on what he looks like in his work shirt, and I feel my face getting hot. But I don't care. I just want him to kiss me more, harder, stronger, and I don't want him to stop.

We stumble out of the kitchen, arms entwined, lips locked, and fall onto the couch.

"Should we go into the bedroom?" I murmur.

"Slow down, there," he whispers. "I want to enjoy you."

He kisses my neck, my shoulders, my collarbone. Then he lifts my shirt up and plants kisses all over my belly.

"Don't stop," I say, and he says, "I won't."

We're kissing and we're kissing and our bodies fit perfectly with each other. It's like my body was created just to nestle into his. Every move he makes drives me crazy and I tell him so.

"You're making me crazy, too," he whispers in my ear. And then he kisses it. He brushes my hair to the side and kisses my neck. Slowly. Deliberately. Like it's the only thing he has to do all day.

We kiss again and I pull at his shirt, try to pull it over his head, but he says, "Stop."

"What's wrong?" I ask.

"I like to go slow," he says. His hand caresses my cheek as he says it. "There's no rush, is there? I want to get to know you."

"Is that what the kids are calling this these days?" I say. I smile at him.

"Is this going to be a problem?" Max asks.

"Is what?" I say, wondering why he's talking and not kissing me.

"Your new role as the poster girl for the anti-love movement currently taking place in Manhattan," Max says. "This sort of seems the opposite of all that. Can we be doing *this* when you stand for *that*?"

"Yes," I say, a little too quickly. "Of course we can. It's not going to be a problem."

At this point, I'll do anything to get the talking to stop and the kissing to start up again. I'll say anything. Anything he wants right now.

But he's right. It *is* going to be a problem. I know it will. Of course it will. How can you be the symbol of all things anti-love if you're falling for someone you just met?

17
More, More, More

TWEET FROM @DISCOSUX:
Viva #LonelyHeartsClub!

BLOG COMMENT FROM NEWYORKDOLL:
I'm so glad I found this site. I've been broken-hearted for over six months now, and it seems like no one understands how I feel. My friends are sick of hearing me talk about it, my family wants me to move on, but it's all I think about all day at work. At home. In between. Sometimes I can't even sleep at night.

A friend of mine said that I should just repeat this mantra over and over again in my head: How can you love someone who would treat your heart like that?

So that's what I tell myself. How do the rest of you deal with it?

RESPONSE FROM CHI-TOWN GIRL:
Don't be reckless with other people's hearts. Don't put up with people who are reckless with yours.
—Mary Schmich

RESPONSE FROM FREEPUSSYRIOT:
Listen to Jo: Love sucks!

18

What's the Matter Here?

"**W**hat is this?" I say, barging into Lola's apartment.

"Did you print that out?" Lola asks, referring to the print-out of my latest blog post that I'm holding. "God, you are so 2002."

"Is this your comment?" I ask, pointing to the one in question, the comment with the tag WhateverLolaWants. I won't let the veiled insult about my age get me off track. Though, seriously, I'm only twenty-two years old—how old does Lola think I am?

"Yeah, it's mine," Lola says. "What of it?"

"I don't want you on the blog."

"Everyone's on the blog," she says. "Why can't I be?"

And she's right. The Lonely Hearts movement is everywhere—it's all over Facebook, Twitter, and Instagram, but the blog itself is where the real stuff happens. It's where people pour their hearts out, where people confess their true feelings. Two months after my first post, and it's grown exponentially.

Lola opens her laptop and shows me that it's not just her—all of her friends are leaving comments. I'm not sure what I'm more shocked about: that the blog is catching on with kids so young or that I can't tell the preteen comments from the adult ones.

But hey, even eleven-year-olds need to get out their anger and rage, don't they? I mean, maybe there'd be less Ritalin prescribed if kids were encouraged to write down their feelings more often.

"You just can't be," I say. I realize I sound like one of my parents: Why not? Because I said so! But now, talking to Lola, I feel like "Because I said so" is a very reasonable response to "Why not?"

Lola responds with a look, and my phone begins to ring.

"Hi, Pumpkin," my dad says.

"Hey, Dad."

"The first of the month is coming up," he says.

Is this man about to evict me over the phone?

"Yes," I say. "It is."

"Any job leads?"

"You know, Dad," I say, "I'm with my Little Sister right now. Can I call you back a bit later?"

"That's not a paid job, is it?" he asks.

"No," I say. "It's not. But I have some advertising money coming in."

"Well, that's great, kiddo!" my dad says. "Keep me posted."

What I don't tell my dad is this: even with the ad on my blog, it won't pay for the loft. I have no other ad prospects on the horizon, no other job prospects. No matter what I tell him, or myself for that matter, by the first of the month, I'll be packing up and moving out. I have no idea where I'll go—real estate in Manhattan is outrageously expensive, no matter what neighborhood you look at, no matter how small of a place. Even Brooklyn's completely out of reach for me. If you want to live in New York, you need to have a job. One that pays a lot.

Lola breaks my train of thought—she's reading all of the

Lonely Hearts blog comments aloud, guessing at the age of each one.

"This lady sounds really bitter," she says. "I bet she's old."

I refrain from asking her how old she thinks "old" is.

"Listen to this one," she says. "'The love of my life left me for my best friend. How do I get him back?' I think she's missed the point of your blog. This is the sort of person who's gonna bite for Love, Inc. This is why they put an ad on your site."

"Are you ready to play?" I ask Lola. I settle myself on the couch and take out my guitar.

"Have you ever thought about getting all these people together to meet?" she asks.

"No," I say, tuning my guitar. "That's not really the point of this whole thing. I think that people like the idea of saying what they really feel, but staying anonymous. Isn't that the point of the entire Internet?"

"I don't know about that," Lola says, and she turns her laptop toward me.

And she's right. There's no mistaking what's happening:

FACEBOOK COMMENT FROM REBECCAFINE:
We should all meet.

BLOG COMMENT FROM ROCKSTAR1993:
Yeah, let's meet.

TWEET FROM @FREE2BU&ME:
Jo, you need to do this!

BLOG COMMENT FROM ANDERS7886:
We want to meet.

E-MAIL FROM HMANNING@GMAIL.COM:
We want to meet.

TWEET FROM @BLONDIEISMYSPIRITANIMAL:
We want to meet. #LonelyHeartsClub

FACEBOOK COMMENT FROM SETHRONALD:
We want to meet.

INSTAGRAM PICTURE FROM RAGEISTHENEWBLACK: A GRITTY PICTURE, AN AERIAL SHOT, OF A BAR FILLED WITH HIP-LOOKING PEOPLE, ALL DRESSED IN BLACK.
This should be us. #LonelyHeartsClub

9,087 likes. 9,088. 9,089...

19
I Started Something I Couldn't Finish

"I told you that Riesling went well with Thai food," Max says. But I'm barely eating. Sure, the food's great, but all I can think about is kissing Max. We're nestled in a corner table at Kittichai, with a perfect view of the reflecting pool.

"It does," I say, and take a sip of my wine. Max's leg brushes against mine and it sets my entire body on fire.

I look at him and he smiles at me. I smile back, but I get the sudden feeling that someone's looking at me. Watching me. Judging me. After all, aren't I the girl who swore off love? Who's now running a Web site (or "media empire," as my mother is telling her friends) dedicated to all things anti-love?

Even my outfit's all wrong. Gone is my usual uniform of ripped jeans, concert tee, and motorcycle boots. Tonight, I'm wearing black skinny jeans with a black tank. Hardly revolutionary compared to what all of the other women at the restaurant are wearing—and hardly as dressy—but a big change for me. I even borrowed a pair of heels from my mom's collection. I told myself that I only wore them because they made me taller and Max towers over me at six foot four, but I know that a tiny part of me also liked the way the heels made my body look. Liked the way they made me walk differently.

"Try this," Max says, and puts some pad thai onto his fork for me to taste. I am not the sort of girl who likes to be fed by one of her dates. I can feed myself quite well, thank you very much. But when I look into Max's eyes, something inside of me just melts. Everything changes. My shoulders loosen, my legs turn to jelly, and it feels like I can breathe again, after being stuck underwater for a very long time.

"Delicious," I say, and I'm not sure if I'm referring to the company or the food. I polish off my third glass of wine and decide that it doesn't really matter.

We walk a few blocks to the rock club where we're watching a new band play, and I remember why I hate wearing heels. For starters, my feet are killing me by the time we get to the club. The balls of my feet ache, and something's been rubbing the side of my big toe. And then I remember the narrow flight of stairs I need to walk down to get to the club.

"You've never heard of Daft Punk?" Max asks me as we settle into a spot at the bar.

"I've heard of them," I say and laugh. "I just prefer real instruments."

"They use real instruments," Max says. "How else would they make the music?"

"It's electronic," I say, laughing. Usually when nonmusic people try to talk to me about music, I get really annoyed. But on Max, it's kind of adorable. "They use computers to create their sound."

"What's wrong with computers?" Max asks, faking an indignant look.

"Music should be grittier," I say. "It should be real."

"Computers are real," Max says. The crowd is beginning to fill in and he has to lean over and yell into my ear just so that I can hear him.

"No, they're not," I say back. I hope he can hear my flirty tone, even though I'm yelling while standing on my tippy toes to reach his ear.

He kisses me. "There's more than just one way to create music," he says. "Isn't that a good thing? All different people like different things."

All I can think is: *Please don't say you like Amber Fairchild. Please don't say Amber Fairchild.*

"I'm glad I'm introducing you to some real music," I say.

"I'm going to get you to love Daft Punk," he says back. "Different is good, too."

A blinding light shines in our faces and it takes a second to figure out what's going on. No one else in the crowd reacts. That's what I love about the rock club scene downtown. Nothing surprises anyone. Ever.

I see a NY1 reporter doing some test shots by the stage. She catches my eye before I have a chance to look away.

"I know you," she says, moments later, as she taps me on my shoulder. I drop my hand from Max's and turn around.

"You do?" I ask, but I already know where this is going.

"I'm Mindy McGreening, and you're Jo Waldman from the Lonely Hearts Club."

"Lonely Hearts Club *Band*," I correct.

"We're here to do a segment on the band playing tonight, but maybe I can do a quickie on you before we get started? People want to know about this movement you've created."

Before I can say no, she's given the head nod to her cameraman, who's now coming our way. I turn to look at Max, and he smiles back at me. I nod my head toward the bar, and he knows what I'm asking him to do. He smiles slyly and then turns away, pretending he doesn't even know who I am.

"We're here with Jo Waldman," Mindy begins. The camera light is blinding, and it takes effort for me to stop squinting. "The poster child for lonely hearts everywhere. She's started an underground cult movement for all things anti-love. How did this start, Jo?"

"It's not really underground," I manage to eke out. "It's on Facebook and Twitter, and I've got a blog and stuff."

Mindy motions to the cameraman to turn the camera off.

"First time on camera?" she asks.

"Um, yes," I say. I've been on stage hundreds—thousands—of times and I'm embarrassed that she's calling me out for my lack of experience in front of an audience.

"This is a one-minute human interest piece," she explains. "I want to quickly tell the story of how this whole Lonely Hearts thing came to be and what's going on with it."

"The Lonely Hearts Club was my band," I say. "*Is* my band," I then correct.

"No one cares about that," she says. She sees my face fall and softens it: "I mean for this story. We've got only a minute here, so let's keep it to how you started the blog. We're going to tell the viewers a story. Just look at me and pretend that we're just two friends having a friendly conversation. That fair?"

I'm about to say something, explain that I don't really want to be on camera, that this whole thing was really just a mistake, when the cameraman starts counting down: "And in three, two—"

"We're here with Jo Waldman," Mindy begins again, "the poster child for lonely hearts everywhere. She's started an underground cult movement for all things anti-love. How did this start, Jo?"

I'm suddenly very aware of how much my feet hurt. I reach back to the bar to grab my drink. Surely some vodka will help ease the pain.

"With a lot of vodka," I say, and take a gulp of my drink.

Mindy laughs. "I'm sure the viewers can relate. How many of your best-laid plans got started with too much vodka?" she asks the camera.

I keep my gaze set on Mindy, like she told me to. "It was Valentine's Day, and I'd just been broken up with, and I needed to rage. To get out all the anger. I wrote that first blog post, and I didn't really mean to send it out to the whole world."

"But the vodka," Mindy says.

"Yes," I say. "The vodka."

"Don't drink and blog, people!" Mindy cautions with a big smile. "Or maybe do! How many readers do you have, Jo?"

"I'd estimate about 500,000 now," I say. Max keeps telling me that I need to know my numbers cold if I want to attract bigger advertisers to the blog, but I can barely keep up with the comments and tweets, much less my numbers.

"Wow," Mindy says. "That's a lot."

"It's growing every day," I say for the benefit of any advertisers who may be watching.

"Tell us," she says, "what's the next step in the Lonely Hearts movement?"

"Movement?"

"What are your next plans? What's the next phase? What are you and all of the other anti-love activists going to do next?"

"Some people have expressed an interest in meeting up," I offer.

"A party?"

"I guess," I say.

"You heard it here, first, folks," Mindy says. "The Lonely

Hearts Club Ball. Coming to you soon!"

I smile at the camera, just like I'm supposed to, but inside, all I can think is: *What have I just done?*

20
Moving Out

Chloe's keys dangle from a keychain with a miniature statue of David. Seeing it always makes me smile. I know she got it while on her semester abroad in Florence. She bought the same one for me.

I let myself into her apartment and throw my duffel down. I packed in a hurry—most of the stuff in my dad's loft belonged to him, anyway—as if I couldn't wait a minute longer to get out. But when your father is throwing you out of his apartment, it's best to leave in haste, isn't it?

Chloe's not around, since she's on an extended business trip to San Francisco. Her firm's opening a new office, and she and her boss were sent over to supervise the art department. It's cool that she's so respected at work that her boss saw fit to bring her, out of all of the other associates, but I miss her. Life's been a total whirlwind since the Lonely Hearts Club Web site took off, and I could really use my best friend. But Chloe said that it would work out perfectly—I could crash at her place while she was away and get acclimated to my new adult life. One where I don't rely on the kindness of Daddy to get me by, and have to make some actual money to survive.

I suppose she did have to leave town after making a remark like that to me.

It's so weird to be in Chloe's space without her. Even though we've been the best of friends since the second grade, it still feels incredibly intimate to be at her apartment without her here. Sure, I know everything about Chloe's life, every detail, really, but there's just something about being among all of her stuff without her.

I flip on the TV for a little background noise—it's too quiet here without Chlo—and Amber Fairchild is on VH1. Seriously, is that girl *everywhere*? I change the channel to NY1, a safe haven from bubble-gum pop, and head to the refrigerator. Empty. I get the feeling Chloe took out all of its contents just to prove her point: In adulthood, you stock your own fridge.

I text her as much.

She texts back: *LOL! Nah, I just figured that you'd let the milk spoil and the cheese go bad and I'd come home to a stinky apartment.*

My eyes narrow as I text her back: *Try not to have an affair with your boss, okay?*

She quickly replies: *Oh, silly girl. You know I'd never fool around with someone I had to see every day!*

I have to stifle a giggle. I check my wallet for cash and then make my way toward the front door to hit a supermarket.

When I return to the apartment a half hour later, my computer's buzzing—someone's inviting me to a video chat.

"Hey, Chloe!" I say, as I sit down and get myself comfortable on the couch.

"Hey," she says. "I had to check and see if you were starving to death in my apartment. I really don't want to come home to a dead body. That'd be stinkier than the moldy cheese."

"I'm still alive," I say. It's so good to see Chloe. I know I saw her yesterday before her flight, but I still miss her like crazy. "Thank you for asking."

"I wasn't sure if you'd figure out how to feed yourself without Daddy's credit cards," she says.

"I have a little money coming in from the ad," I say. "We can't all graduate and get a perfect job we love."

"Yes," she says. "But most people do get *a* job."

"I get it," I say. "You're disappointed in me. My father's disappointed in me. Even the checkout guy at the Food Emporium is disappointed in me."

"The checkout guy?"

"Is it part of the adult experience to be humiliated at the checkout line as you figure out how many items you can afford to buy?" I ask.

"Yes, definitely," Chloe says.

"Okay, good," I say. "Just checking."

Chloe fills me in on the deal so far in San Francisco—great music scene she plans to check out, not so great extended-stay hotel room she plans to never be in, and totally great restaurants she's already begun to explore.

"Are you ready to come back yet?" I ask.

"No, not yet," Chloe says and laughs. "Hopefully, it'll be just a few weeks, not a few months."

I hadn't realized a few months were on the table. I figured she'd be home after just a few weeks.

"Well, hurry back," I say.

"I will," she says. "Now make yourself at home."

So I do. I grab my duffel and look for a closet to ditch my stuff. Even though I'll be staying in her bedroom, I feel like taking over her closet would be rude.

I open the entryway closet and move her jackets into her bedroom closet. As I'm about to unpack, I see a few old posters rolled up toward the back of the closet.

Well, she did say to make myself at home, I think. Nothing like a few concert posters on the wall to cozy the place up.

I unroll the first poster and it's a Lonely Hearts Club Band poster. The ones she designed a few years ago when we were doing Battle of the Bands. I remember how proud she was of the design she created—it looked like that iconic Ramones band logo. She'd written the name of our band around the circle, where the names of the band members were on the Ramones logo, and instead of a bald eagle inside of the circle, there was an electric guitar. It was such a clever idea. Since then, she's come up with about a million more clever ideas like that for her company, but at the time, it completely blew all of our minds.

As I roll the poster up, ready to put it back where I found it, I see a box. And I can't help myself. I pull it out of the closet and look inside. There are hundreds, thousands maybe, of photographs. I remember this phase in college, when Chloe toted around an enormous professional camera from her photography lab and documented every second of our lives. There are pictures of everything—our old college dorm, some of the rock shows we used to do at the downtown clubs, and Billy. So many pictures of Billy. Pictures of him alone, pictures of him with her, pictures of him behind his drum kit. A set of his old drumsticks are at the bottom of the box. It's like a shrine to him. I had no idea that Chloe kept all of this stuff.

My first instinct is to throw it all away—I feel my eyes tearing up just looking at this stuff, so I can only imagine the impact it must have on Chloe. But then I have no idea what I'd say to Chloe once she realized it was gone. I dab at my eyes with the tip of my finger.

You are not the sort of girl who cries, I tell myself, and I take a deep breath. That's usually all it takes to keep the tears at bay.

I know I should stop looking. I know I should. But every time I tell myself to put everything away, stuff it back where I found it, I find another reason to look. Another thing I want to see one more time.

I look through the pictures a bit longer—it's like a car crash I can't take my eyes off—and then I repack the posters, drumsticks, and the box, just as I found them, and shove them back to the bottom of the closet.

21
All She Wants Is

"What's this?" I ask Max. It's been only a few months, but already we've fallen into a sort of pattern. Well, not a pattern so much as he comes over to Chloe's place every night. But isn't it like that when you're discovering someone new? Everything about them is fascinating, and you seemingly can't get enough. Why see them once a week when you can see them twice? Why see them twice when you can see them three times? Four times?

Every night.

"It's an article about Daft Punk," he says, throwing down a bag and melting into the couch.

"I thought we'd settled this," I say. "Didn't you like the band we saw?"

"I would've liked it more if I didn't have to pretend I didn't know you."

"I can't be seen out on a date if I'm the symbol for all things anti-love," I say.

"I thought you said that this wouldn't be a problem," he says.

"It's not," I say.

"It's not?"

"You know I couldn't have that reporter see us together and risk exposing myself as a total liar," I explain. "She seemed very interested in all things Lonely Hearts Club."

"I'm interested in all things Lonely Hearts Club," Max says, pulling me onto the couch.

"I'm not reading this article," I say, and grab Max for a kiss.

"It's about how they use instruments to make their sound," he says in between kisses. "I thought you'd like the bit about Nile Rodgers."

"No way," I say, pushing him off to read the article.

As I read, Max picks up my guitar and pretends to play. He has no idea what he's doing, but still, he manages to hit a few chords here and there. The article's fascinating, and I make a mental note to download Daft Punk's latest album, the one featuring Nile Rodgers on guitar.

Max continues his attempt at my guitar. I take his second finger, and put it on the third fret of the sixth string. Then I take his first finger and put it on the second fret of the fifth string. And then finally, his third finger on the third fret of the first string.

He strums and it sounds beautiful.

"A perfect G major," I say. "That's your first lesson."

"I always wanted to play guitar," he says.

"Oh yeah?" I ask, adjusting his fingers into a C major. "Why didn't you?"

"I don't know," he says. "Got into other things, I guess."

"Like G and G?"

"D&D," he corrects. "Yes, that. And computers."

"I can't imagine doing anything besides music," I say.

"Then why don't you book more gigs?" he asks. "Get your band back together?"

"I *am* doing my music," I say quickly, but we both know it's a lie. The only things I've put in my notebook lately are notes on what to write for the next Lonely Hearts Club blog post.

All I do all day is write about how love breaks your heart. And then all I do all night is fall deeper into it.

"I just want you to be happy. You know that, right?" Max says.

"Then come over here," I say.

His lips touch mine and I forget to breathe. He moves down to my neck and I feel myself breathing again, only they're short, tight breaths. I close my eyes as I wait to see what he'll do next. His hands run up and down my arms and I grab onto him.

And then our clothes are off and we tumble onto the ground. His hands are all over my body; my hands are all over his. It's like we can't get close enough to each other. And then we do, and with his body over mine, inside of mine, I feel like we are meant to be together. Like we were made for each other. This is what I long for, all day, and I can never get enough of him.

"Oh my God," I say, breathless, sweaty, and spent.

"I love…" Max begins to say, but then thinks better of it. "I love being with you."

"Me too," I say.

"We didn't even make it to the bed," Max says, as we lay on the floor, side by side.

"No, we did not," I say. I grab his undershirt and put it on. I love the way it smells, like sweat and lemon and sweetness. "Hand me my guitar."

"You're going to play for me?" he asks as he reaches up for my guitar.

"I am," I say, and tune the strings.

I start to play without really knowing what song I want to sing to him. Just random chords, warming myself up, figuring out what's next. Then it comes to me. "'Don't get me wrong. If

I'm looking kind of dazzled,'" I sing slowly. "'I see neon lights. Whenever you walk by.'"

I strum along to the Pretenders' melody and Max watches me as I play. The way my fingers move over my guitar, the way I tap my foot to keep time, the way my lips move.

"'I'm thinking about the fireworks,'" I sing, "'that go off when you smile.'"

Max smiles back at me, on cue, and I continue the song: "But don't get me wrong."

MAX FALLS asleep, but I'm wide awake.

The computer is on, always on, beckoning me, asking me to hop on and see what's happening with the site. My Twitter feed is on fire—#LonelyHeartsClub is trending after my last post. I hear the sound of a record scratch—the new sound of messages and comments that Max installed for me—and I click over to the blog. The comments are the ones I'm used to seeing by now. Allsfairinloveandmusic doesn't know how to leave her husband, even though they've completely grown apart. RockBoy1983's girlfriend is pregnant and now he feels forced to marry her. Chloe's even figured out how to put her Instagram pictures onto the blog as comments. The latest one is a picture of Marilyn Monroe and President Kennedy with the caption: Love kills you.

But one comment in particular stands out to me.

BLOG COMMENT FROM PIANOSOUNDSLIKEACARNIVAL:
You don't really believe all this negative stuff about love, do you?
I quickly respond to the comment: *Yes, of course I do. Love makes you weak. Vulnerable. It crushes*

you whole.

I wait for a response from Pianosoundslikeacarnival, but it doesn't come. Instead, hundreds of blog followers get into the game.

RESPONSE FROM LOVESTINKS:
Are you accusing Jo of lying? You think she's a hypocrite?!

RESPONSE FROM YOUREALLYGOTMENOW:
How dare you question Jo? She's the one who started this whole thing. She wouldn't lie to us.

RESPONSE FROM ROCKER92:
Jo says what she means. How could you question that?

I look back at Max, asleep in my bed, and I feel a sinking feeling in my stomach. I should never have started this. I tell myself that I need to break it off with him. It's not fair to him. It's not fair to the blog followers. It's not fair to the 200,000 people who tweet at me, "like" me on Facebook, and follow the Lonely Hearts Instagram account that Chloe sent up. I'm living a lie.

I walk back into the bedroom and Max half opens one sleepy eye.

"Get over here," he says. He pats his hand on the bed, at the space where I'm supposed to be sleeping. I stand for a moment, just staring at him. His eyes begin to close again.

"Hey," he says, eyes still closed. "I see neon lights whenever you walk by, too, you know."

I get into bed and curl next to him. Like I had any other choice.

22
Koka Kola

The Love, Inc. ad was just the beginning. Apparently, my tagline of "I got a gift certificate to this site and I threw it in the garbage" worked well for them. They love being a part of the Lonely Hearts Club site, and even bought a big banner ad to go on top.

The ads, as Max promised, keep rolling in. The Italian restaurant that started this whole thing contacted us next. They couldn't even afford a tiny side ad, the cheapest type we offer, but Max gave them a discount. He thought their ad, with my tagline "This restaurant tried to charge me an inflated Valentine's Day rate when I was ordering for one, but I told them where they could put their inflated Valentine's Day prices" would do well. He was correct. Manager Greg e-mailed me a week later to say that they could barely keep up with the new demand the ad generated.

A bunch of the downtown clubs where I play also asked Max for a discount. He obliged—I told him that the site needed some street cred, and it was important to have them on there.

Next came the chocolate. Godiva—Godiva!—booked an ad that said, "Who needs love when you have chocolate?"

Even Guitar Center got into the game. Their ad ("Jo called us up about our mailing list and ripped us a new one—we loved it.") actually pays us by clicks, so we're making money off them every day.

It's a lot of money. Just not Soho-loft money. I'm starting to save up for the first month's rent, so that I can move back into the loft, but the problem is, then I'll need a second month's rent, and then a third month, and then…Well, you get the point. The Soho loft costs a fortune. I understand that it's not fair to expect my dad to keep it sitting there empty when he could be making thousands of dollars a month by renting it, but at this rate, I wonder if I'll *ever* be able to move back in.

"I guess you'll just have to move in with me," Max says, and I laugh. "What's so funny?" he asks. "I wasn't joking."

"It's only been a few months," I say. "I'm not going to move in with you."

But my body language tells a different story. My legs are twisted toward him, my shoulders squarely facing him. I've even developed the very un-me habit of twirling my hair in my fingers.

"You'd rather be homeless than live with me?" he asks.

I laugh, and then realize that I do want to move in with him. I really do. We spend all of our free time together, so it would make sense, wouldn't it? But it seems crazy to move in with someone so soon. Especially since I was just living with someone else who recently moved out.

Well, Jesse and I weren't technically living together. He *technically* lived with three of his bandmates and slept on the couch. But he spent all of his free time with me and all of his stuff was at my place, so you can draw your own conclusions from that.

But still. Moving in together? It sounds so formal, so definite. And I'm only twenty-two years old.

"I'm not going to be homeless," I explain. "I'll just keep crashing with Chloe until I figure something out."

"What happens when Chloe gets back from California?"

"I'll just move on to the couch," I say.

"Ouch," he says, and grips his chest dramatically, as if I've just shot him in the heart, at close range.

"Want me to kiss that and make it better?" I ask.

"Does Chloe know about us?" he asks. I don't know how to respond. The truth is, Chloe does not know about us; no one does. Not even my parents, who I usually tell everything. But it feels like telling Max that might hurt his feelings. And I don't want to do that.

"I haven't really told anyone yet," I say. "But it's not because you don't mean something to me. You do."

"You mean something to me, too."

"This is a really weird time for me," I say. "With the site and everything..."

"I know," he says. "No pressure. You should do whatever feels right."

I nod my head in agreement, but all I can think is: *This* feels right. Maybe I should seriously consider moving in with Max. But what would that mean for the Lonely Hearts Club?

"You may not have to move out after all," Max says as another e-mail pops up.

"What?" I ask. His eyes are glued to the computer screen and I edge over, close to him, to take a look.

"I knew it was just a matter of time until someone like this came along," he says, and we both read the e-mail in silence.

"Cobra Vodka?" I say. "Never heard of them before."

"Who cares?" Max says. "Look at what they offer to do an ad."

The number's big. So big, in fact, that I have to read it three times before I can process it. This would take me one step closer to staying in the loft. This would definitely cover the first month's rent. Maybe even the second. But does this mean that the discussion with Max about moving in is over?

"Let's do it," I say. I'm not entirely sure what I'm suggesting— the ad or the offer to move in with Max?

"Do you want to do the honors?" he asks and turns the computer my way.

I write an e-mail back to Cobra, explaining my usual stipulations for having an ad on the blog—they have to match the color scheme of the blog (or lack thereof, I should say), they have to allow me to create my own tagline, and they don't get final approval. I click SEND.

"Then that's it," Max says.

"I guess so."

23
Hide Your Heart

We're kissing and we're kissing and it's like we don't even notice that a band is here to play.

I feel a pair of eyes on me and I look across the room.

"What's wrong?" Max murmurs into my ear. Chills go down my spine and I have to close my eyes for a second just to take it all in.

"I think that guy's staring at me," I say, and then bury my face in Max's chest. It's like I'm a child, making myself invisible by simply closing my eyes.

"Which guy?" Max asks and turns around. But by then, the guy's right next to us.

"Hey," he says to me. "Do I know you?"

"I don't think so, man," Max says and turns his back on him.

But he doesn't walk away. "Are you Jo Waldman?" the guy asks and puts his hand on my arm.

"No," I say. "You must have me confused with someone else."

Max grabs my hand and we make our way to the bar. Out of the corner of my eye, I can see the guy typing away on his cell phone.

"Hey, you are!" he says, walking over to the bar. "You're the Lonely Hearts Club girl! I'm VelvetUnderground98." He's holding his cell phone up so I can see—it's the Lonely Hearts Club Web site.

I turn back to the bar as quickly as I can. Max puts his arm protectively around me as we wait for the bartender to get our drinks. Max throws a bill down on the bar as the bartender slides two beers our way.

But I feel like I can't turn around. I don't want to be questioned again. And I can sense that Max feels it, too. Like we're being watched. Like someone knows something that we don't know. I have to get out of there.

The guy calls out to me and I turn around. He's now got a bunch of Google images up on his phone. They're of me. All me.

I grab Max's hand and we make our way toward the back of the club. I push open the door, the secret one that most people don't know about. I push it open and Max and I run through. We hold hands as we run up the steps—a tiny, narrow iron staircase—and make it up to the rooftop.

"Are you okay?" Max asks, once we're out in the damp night air.

"I just needed to breathe," I say.

"I know what you mean," he says.

We walk to the edge of the roof and look out at the city skyline. It's beautiful up here, looking uptown at the city—a mess of light and sound and energy. Max takes my hand and I give it a squeeze.

"Hey," he says. "Do I know you from somewhere?"

"What?"

"Yeah," he says. "You're that girl. That girl from that Web site."

"You must have me mistaken with someone else," I say,

catching on.

"No," he says. "It's definitely you. You're the one who's sworn off love."

"Why yes," I say, as prim and proper as I can muster. "You've caught me. I'm the anti-love girl."

"That's too bad," he says. "Because I really want to kiss you."

"Well, I really want to kiss you, too."

"Too bad you've sworn off love."

"Too bad."

"Do you think maybe I could convince you otherwise?" he asks, leaning into me.

"Oh," I say. "I don't know. I really, really meant it when I said that I didn't want love."

"Well, that's a problem," he says. "Because I really, really meant it when I said that I wanted to kiss you."

"Then we seem to be at an impasse," I say. Our faces are inches apart and I can feel his warm breath on my face.

"Indeed."

I can't help but smile and Max smiles back at me. I wonder for a second who's going to break character first—if he's going to give in and just kiss me, or if it will be me who can't take it anymore. But then he puts his hand on my cheek and we both lean in at the same time to kiss. I melt into him and memorize the moment. His smell, the sounds of the city, the way he presses my body into his. Is there anything sexier than kissing on a Manhattan rooftop?

I really don't think so.

24
Constant Craving

"Didn't I tell you to answer my landline?"

"I didn't even know people still used landlines," I say. "Chloe, you are totally retro."

"When I get back I'm going to have, like, a million messages!" Chloe says. "I thought you were going to text me my messages? That was part of the payment for letting you stay there rent-free, you know."

I send Chloe a text: *Telemarketer. You may be a winner!*

"Cute," Chloe says. "I wanted to check in on you."

"I'm fine," I say, watching Max get settled in, putting the Chinese food on the kitchen counter, looking for plates. "How are you?"

"I'm more worried about you," Chloe says. "Have you burned my apartment down in a rage yet?"

"Not yet," I say, watching Max as he uncorks a cheap bottle of wine. Will I ever tire of just staring at Max?

"Well," Chloe says, "that's good to know. Are you listening to me? Earth to Jo. You sound like you're somewhere else."

I was. If only I could tell her about it. I make myself more present for our call. "How's California?" I ask. And then, not waiting for an answer, "How's your boss? Please tell me you're not sleeping with your boss."

"My boss?" Chloe asks. "Ew, gross. No, I'm not sleeping with him. We're working our asses off here, trying to get things set up so we can come home."

"I miss you," I say.

"I miss you, too," she says.

Neither of us says anything for a second. We both let it sink in. It sucks having your best friend across the country. Even if you still haven't told her the single most important thing that's been happening to you lately, a girl still needs her best friend.

"The music scene out here is sick," Chloe finally says.

"That's cool," I say. "See any bands I've heard of?"

"Nope," she says. "Totally different from the scene we're used to. It's kind of cool to go to a rock club and feel completely anonymous, you know?"

And I do know what she's talking about. She once told me that anytime she walks into a downtown rock club, she thinks everyone is staring at her, whispering behind her back that she's the girlfriend of that drummer who OD'd and died. No matter how many times I tell her that that's not the case, there's no convincing her. It's hard to prove a negative.

"It's great to lose yourself in music," I say, and Chloe agrees with me. "Do you bring the people from your office?"

"No," she says, reading my mind like she always does, "I don't bring my *boss* to hear music. I am *not* sleeping with my boss."

"I wasn't trying to infer you were," I say, but I'm lying. I was totally trying to figure out if she was going to seedy clubs (read: places with flowing alcohol) with her married boss.

"Liar," she says.

I look at Max, and he's got plates and wineglasses set up and ready to go. He holds a wineglass out for me to take. I smile back at him and say to Chloe, "You have no idea."

25
Helter Skelter

FACEBOOK COMMENT FROM SEXMACHINE:
Saw you on NY1—make this happen! #LonelyHeartsClubBall

RESPONSE FROM SEATTLESCENE:
I didn't see it—what's happening?!

RESPONSE FROM SEXMACHINE:
Jo's planning a huge party to get all of us together! #LonelyHeartsClubBall

FACEBOOK COMMENT FROM PIANOSOUNDSLIKEACARNIVAL:
A party? See, Jo, I knew you weren't serious. I'm almost relieved.

26
White Wedding

The day's a total blur. I can't tell the difference between the Plaza, the Pierre, or the St. Regis—they've all melted into one uber-glamorous memory. It doesn't help that I'm totally sleep deprived. Tending to the blog all day, and then seeing Max all night, has turned out to be very tiring.

But I can't give either one up.

Barbie's on total overdrive. It's like wedding planning is her crack. She's bouncing and smiling and squealing all day long. More so than usual, I mean. Which is amazing, seeing as she visited all of these venues already with her own parents. She's only showing my parents again today as a sort of accommodation. Clearly, Andrew's told her how left out my mother feels where the wedding plans are concerned.

We talk to all of the wedding planners, tour the ballrooms and bridal suites, and even taste the food at the St. Regis, but I can tell by the look on my mother's face that it's not enough. She knows that she's been excluded, and that this is all just for show. She knows that even though she and my father will be paying the tab for half the wedding, Barbie's mother will be deciding everything. They won't be asked their opinion on anything, not in a way that actually matters, anyway. They'll just be handed a bill. A very, very large bill.

I grab my mother's hand as we leave the last hotel (the Plaza? the Pierre? Who can remember at this point?) and walk toward the car. She squeezes back, and I know that she needed that.

"Do you want to come with us for dinner?" my mother asks.

I do not want to come for dinner. I want to get back to the loft and meet up with Max, which was my plan. It was the thing that got me through the day, knowing that he'd be waiting for me. I have no desire to drive all the way out to Long Island for a long, drawn-out dinner where I'll have to hear Barbie squeal about the curtains at the Plaza versus the plush carpeting at the Pierre. Or the elevators at the St. Regis.

"I'm sure she has plans," my father says.

"Right," my mother says. "You probably have plans. You don't want to come all the way out to Long Island."

But watching my mother smile, even though I know she really wants to break down and cry, is really more than I can bear.

"No plans," I say, and my mother smiles. For real this time.

"I'M CONCERNED about you channeling all of your creative energy into something so negative," my father says. We're at Dominick's for dinner after a very long day of shopping various New York City hotels for Andrew and Barbie's wedding. Has he been waiting all day to say this to me? Is this what I have to look forward to for the duration of the meal? I take a bite of an onion roll as I consider my father's statement.

"Forget about that," my mother says. "Who's going to want to marry you if you stand for the opposite of love?"

"I'm not really all that interested in getting married," I explain.

My mother shakes her head no, as if she's not buying this. Not at all. Not for even one minute. "You were never one of those little girls who went through an 'I hate boys' stage," my mother says. "Never thought that they had cooties or that they were gross. You were always pretty boy-crazy, even when you were in the crib. When men would come by and look at you, you'd always coo and smile at them."

"I don't think that boys have cooties now, Mom," I say. "I just think all men are evil."

"Now is not really the time to go through such a phase," my mother says to me. "Now is the time to be concentrating on things like getting married. Not obsessing over why men are evil."

"I don't care about getting married," I say, starting the same conversation we've had thousands of times before. "What I want is—"

"Mad, burning, passionate love," she finishes for me. "I've heard the speech before."

"There's nothing wrong with what I want for myself," I say.

"Can you register at Tiffany's for mad, burning, passionate love?" she asks.

"This isn't the issue," my father interjects, putting his wineglass down on the table. "The issue is you putting all of your energy into this uncontrolled rage. Something so negative. We're worried about you, Pumpkin."

"You don't have to worry about me," I say, putting down my wineglass and calling the waiter over to order myself a vodka tonic.

"Do you really believe all this stuff you're saying?" he asks.

"Yes," I say, but I can't meet my father's eyes. "Of course I do. Why would I write it if I didn't really believe it?"

"How's the rent money coming, Pumpkin?" my dad asks.

"It's not," I say. "I mean, I'm making some nice money from all the ads, but it's not enough to pay for the loft just yet."

"What are your plans?" he asks.

"Well, I'm hoping to get a few more advertisers," I explain. "I should be able to have the money soon."

"By the end of the week soon?" my dad asks, and I know what he's saying. It's either pay rent or he'll let the month-to-month renter he's presently got in the loft sign a year-long lease. It's been long enough. He's been telling his month-to-month renter that he can't sign a year-long lease in the hopes I'd be able to return, but that's all over. This month, he's not going to do it again. This month, he wants the money.

"No," I say. "I'll bring the rest of my stuff over to Chloe's."

"You can stay with me!" Barbie exclaims with glee. "We'll be doing so much with wedding planning that it actually makes sense!"

Barbie can never express a thought without saying it emphatically.

"I think I'll stay at Chloe's," I explain.

"But she'll be back from California soon," Barbie pleads.

"Thank you so much for the offer," I say. "Really appreciate that."

Barbie's face falls. But then, like a baby with something shiny, she remembers that she was discussing floral arrangements, and she starts talking again.

"I really wanted calla lilies, but then my friend who read this book about the meanings of flowers told me that calla lilies represent death. So I can't use those now, can I?" She laughs, as if this is a very funny joke, so the rest of us begin laughing, too.

My mother tries to say something about calla lilies, but Barbie's already onto her next tangent.

"And I really love hydrangea, but they can fall the second you cut them, and what if my bridal bouquet gets all limp? How bad would that look? And anyway, I really need a flower that I can dry out so I can keep my bridal bouquet. Jo," she says solemnly, as if she were about to bestow upon me the secret of the universe or the key to a city or something, "you may be in charge of taking the bouquet and drying it out. Do you think you could do that? If you can't, I'm sure one of my sorority sisters could do it. But I really want you to feel included, so I want to give you little jobs that you think you might be able to do."

I can barely hear Barbie talking any more. All I can think is: If this moron's planning an entire fancy wedding, how hard could it be to plan a party for 10,000 anti-love New Yorkers? Surely they won't care about floral arrangements. I can just take a peek at Barbie's binder filled with wedding plans and figure out what needs to be done to plan a large-scale party.

As Barbie dissects the difference between red and pink roses (red conveys passion, pink says joy and appreciation), I snag her wedding binder. I half expect to see a Photoshopped picture of her and Ryan Gosling on the cover, that's how juvenile the whole thing is, but I get past the lace and tulle pasted to the front and open it up.

The thing is an organizational marvel. She should be the one running my dad's office. No wonder I got fired. It's divided into sections with color-coded tabs: venue, entertainment, décor, food, attire.

I can probably find a venue. I've played all of the downtown rock clubs before, and all of the owners know each other. I can probably get a huge discount, too, based on the amount of alcohol I'd assume an anti-love crowd would consume.

Between Chloe and me, we've got entertainment covered. We've got so many connections in the music industry combined that it will be more about whittling down our options so as not to offend friends, rather than finding musical acts. That one's easy.

My mother can help out with the décor. She can get out her own feelings of rage about Barbie and Andrew's wedding by creating the ultimate shrine to lonely hearts everywhere. The anti-Barbie wedding, if you will.

As for food, I'm not really sure what one would serve at a party dedicated to all things anti-love. Pigs in blankets seem like they'd be more festive than the occasion merits. In my mind, I mentally change this tab to instead read: drink. We'll need an open bar with copious amounts of alcohol. Who needs to eat?

Attire. That one's simple: Everyone wears black from head to toe, or you don't get in.

"What do you think, Jo?" Barbie asks me, and I have no idea what she was just saying. I nod yes and think to myself, *Yes. I could do this. I could actually do this. The Lonely Hearts Club Ball.*

27
Can't Get You Out of My Head

"It's just like a sleepover," Chloe says, "the sort we had when we were younger."

Chloe's back from California. And we're celebrating. I've got the apartment decorated—streamers and balloons that I bought at the party store down the street—and a bottle of prosecco chilling in the fridge.

I'm so happy Chloe's back. My best friend is finally home. But now, of course, I have to give up the bedroom and move onto the pullout couch. And I have to hide my relationship with Max. Or maybe I just tell her? But what would I say? *Hey, Chloe, I know I've been dedicating my life to this anti-love movement, encouraging you to do the same and drudging up memories of the biggest heartbreak of your life, but hey! Guess what? I'm dating Max now, so that's all an act!*

Maybe not.

"Didn't we have balloons like this at that slumber party your mom threw us when everyone at school was invited to Debbie Berman's sleepover party except us?"

"I don't really remember that," I say.

"How could you not remember that?" she asks. "We spent half the night crying about what losers we were. How we were completely invisible and no one would even notice that we weren't there."

"I guess," I say.

"This slumber party is going to be much, much better than that one," she says, opening the bottle of prosecco.

"And much longer," I say. "Or was that your subtle way of telling me you're kicking me out after tonight?"

"I am not kicking you out," she says. "That was my way of telling you that I'm psyched you're here. This is going to be so much fun."

Chloe fiddles with the computer to get some music playing and I send a text to Max—there's no way I'll be sneaking out of Chloe's place tonight. Chloe spins around and clinks her glass to mine, a toast.

"So we're really doing this?" Chloe asks. "The Lonely Hearts Club Ball? The Web site was not enough for you?"

"We're doing this," I say. "Haven't you been reading the site? People want this. People want to meet."

"How on earth are we going to do this?"

"Easy," I say, and present Chloe with my answer to Barbie's wedding binder—it's my Lonely Hearts Club Ball binder. A black binder from Staples like Barbie's, not decorated but with the same tabs Barbie had in hers: venue, entertainment, décor, ~~food~~ drink, attire.

My tabs are not color coded.

"This seems like a lot to do," Chloe says, flipping through the pages.

"We have a long time to do it," I say. "We're throwing the party on Valentine's Day."

"That's genius," she says.

"Thanks."

It feels good to be throwing ideas around with Chloe. Working with her on the Lonely Hearts Club Ball reminds me of our short time working together at supergood. We make a great team. I remember, for a second, how we used to collaborate together on art for the Lonely Hearts Club Band demo covers, but then I quickly force myself to stop thinking about that, like I always do.

"Overall concept?" Chloe asks.

"Anti-love, all the way," I say.

"That's a good start," Chloe says, "but we need more. What, are we just going to hang some black drapes and call it a day?"

"No," I say, even though I hadn't really thought of anything past "anti-love." I think about how Barbie plans to manifest her theme of "summer in the South of France" throughout the wedding. One of her ideas was to have tiny jars of sand on the tables (my mother quickly nixed that idea). "We can have smashed Valentine's Day candies in little mason jars on the tables."

"Needs to be bigger," Chloe says. She pulls out a sketch pad and begins to draw.

"I'm going to bring my mom in to help us decorate," I say. "Maybe she can come up with something."

"Your mother's going to help us?"

"Yes," I say.

"I'll believe that when I see it," Chloe says, with laughter in her voice. "How's this: unhappy couples throughout history. Think Sid and Nancy, Tina and Ike Turner, Jack White and Karen Elson."

"That's kind of dark," I say. "Don't you think?"

"Isn't that the point?" Chloe asks, her brow furrowed. "I'm sorry, isn't this—"

"Yeah, sorry," I say. "You're right. Love that idea."

"We can get a local artist to mock up faux portraits of the unhappy couples. And then, on the bottom, where the plate would read the name of the painting or the name of the artist, we can instead have anti-love quotes from our users."

"Genius," I say, as Chloe shows me a rough drawing she's just created of Sid and Nancy.

"'I've only been in love with a beer bottle and a mirror,'" I read from the bottom of the drawing.

"Sid said that once."

"Perfect," I say. "That might be better than quotes from our users."

"Good point," Chloe says, drawing again. "So let's have quotes from the unhappy couples under their portraits, but instead, we can have the quotes from our users etched on the walls. Or tucked into cookies or something. Or set up like a tree, and when you come closer, you see that it's not a tree at all, but actually little pieces of paper that look like a tree. Each piece of paper can be a quote from a user."

"That's perfect," I say.

"This is fun," Chloe says.

"Ooh, I have an idea," I say. "At midnight, let's stage a reenactment of the Saint Valentine's Day Massacre. We can get fake tommy guns and everything. Maybe hire some actors to dress up as mobsters?"

"Love it," Chloe says, and goes back to her sketch pad. I do a quick Google search on the Valentine's Day Massacre, and Chloe interrupts my train of thought. "Are you humming?" she asks. "What are you humming?"

"I'm not humming," I say, quickly. A little too quickly.

"As I live and breathe," she says, "Jo Waldman, you are humming a pop song."

"No, I'm not."

Chloe hums a few bars herself. "Yes!" she says. "You were just humming that Faith Hill song!"

"It was playing in your elevator on my way up tonight," I explain.

"A pop song turned into Musak, no less!" Chloe says. "Alert the press!"

"It's just an annoying melody that got stuck in my head."

"'This kiss, this kiss,'" Chloe sings out loud. She grabs my arms and holds me close for a slow dance. "'Unstoppable! This kiss, this kiss!'"

"Okay, enough," I say, and sit back down.

"Are you getting soft on me?"

"No," I say. "But I *am* rather disturbed that you seem to know the lyrics to that song."

"Well, there *is* this guy," she says. With Chloe, there's always a guy.

"What's his name?" I ask. "Actually, don't even bother telling me. By the time I remember it, there will be a new one."

"I don't know his name," she says, with a devilish look in her eye.

"The plot thickens," I say. "Do tell."

"I've been having flirtatious e-mail contact with Rockboy1983," she says. "The whole time I was in California, he kept me company. Online, that is."

"You love the rocker boys!" I say. "I'm confused, is that the name of his band or something?"

"That's his username on the Lonely Hearts Club blog," she says. "You don't remember him? Girlfriend's pregnant, he's stuck?"

"I knew that sounded familiar," I say. "But if he has a girlfriend, why are you e-mailing him?"

"He doesn't love her," she says.

"Chloe, stay away from this guy," I say.

"We haven't even met yet," she says. "Relax."

"But now we're planning a party where the two of you can meet."

"Isn't that the point of this party?" Chloe asks. "We're all venting about love, but all we really want to do is find it, right?"

"This is not love. He's just another guy in a band who's not going to love you the way he should," I say, and Chloe's eyes fill with tears.

"Chloe, wait," I say. "I didn't mean it like that."

"I'm not crying because you said it," she says. "I'm crying because it's true. Billy didn't love me. Not really, anyway."

"Of course he loved you," I say. "Of course he did. Just because his demons overtook him doesn't mean he didn't love you."

"What's the point of all this?" Chloe asks, blotting her eyes with a tissue. "Do we want love or do we hate love? I can't even tell anymore."

"Neither can I," I say. And I really mean it.

28
Brilliant Disguise

always thought I'd be in the *New York Times* one day, but I thought it would be the Arts section, not the Styles. And I thought it would be for my music, and not as some trend piece. But here I am, on the front page of the Styles section, the poster girl for the anti-love movement currently taking place in Manhattan.

"Above the fold," Max says. "Nice."

Max tosses me the *Times* and then brings me a cup of coffee in bed. He's got a great apartment on the Upper West Side—a prewar place filled with light and far enough away from Chloe's to avoid being caught. He hops back into bed with his own cup of coffee and my cell phone buzzes.

It's a text from Chloe: *Where ru? Never came home last nite?!*

I text back: *Didn't think u were making it home—what happened to rockboy?*

Chloe: *Never showed. U were right. Brunch?*

I text back: *Crashed with some old college friends - meet u l8r?*

Chloe: *I'll be in the park drawing.*

I should have known Chloe would be in the park drawing. The second the weather heats up, that's where you can always find her—at Bethesda Fountain, with her sketch pad and charcoals. And it's already summer, so the weather's perfect for it. But there's no way I'm leaving Max's bed anytime soon.

"Lemme see," Max says, and grabs the Style pages from my hands. "'Manhattanite Jo Waldman has started something. In just a few short months, she's become the spokesperson for all things anti-love, a movement that's 875,000 people strong and growing.'"

"I can't listen," I say. "Don't read anymore."

"Aren't you closer to 900,000 these days?"

"I don't know," I say.

"You don't know?" he asks. "I check every half hour to see if we've hit a million yet. I can't believe you're not checking this thing more often."

"That's why I employ a super-handsome IT guy to take care of that stuff for me. And maintain all of the fabulous ads he's procured."

"Employ? You're paying me for my time?"

"No," I say, twirling a lock of seriously mussed hair around my finger. "But you still must do as I say."

"Yes, mistress," Max says, and puts his coffee mug down on the bedside table. "Anything you say."

My cell phone rings. "Please hold for Bee Maran."

"Hello?" I say.

"Hi, Jo?" a voice I can only presume belongs to Bee Maran says. "I'm the booker for *The Today Show*. I just read your Styles piece and we want to book you."

"I don't understand," I say, and put my phone onto speaker mode. Max and I huddle over the phone as Bee explains.

"We want to do a story on this anti-love movement you've

started," she says. "Usually summer is when we talk about fun outdoor dates or how to meet people in the Hamptons, but this summer is looking like it's going to be dominated by punk rock and black roses. All because of you."

"Black roses actually symbolize death," I say.

"Is that a no?" Bee asks.

"She'll do it," Max says, and Bee thanks him. He grabs my phone away from me and takes out a notepad to write down all of the information Bee gives him. I'm glad he has the presence of mind to think about jotting this stuff down. I'm sort of awestruck by the whole thing—a mix of excitement and fear overcome me. By the time I'm cognizant enough to speak clearly again, Max has already made all of the arrangements with Bee.

"I can't believe you just did that!" I say to Max as he shuts my phone off.

"You aren't getting this whole 'advertisers bringing you money' thing," he says. "Don't you ever want to move back into the loft? Or get a place of your own? Or move off Chloe's couch?"

"Yes," I say. "I do. Of course I do."

"Well, this will get us even bigger advertisers," he says. "And maybe we could even line up some investors, start getting ready to sell the site when interest peaks."

"Sell the site?" I say. "It's my band's Web site."

"It's the Lonely Hearts Club now," he says. "And the way to make real money off this thing is to sell it when it's hot. Lesser Web sites have made millions off sales like these."

I don't know what to say. How could I sell the Lonely Hearts Club Web site? That would mean that I'm giving up on the band forever. Sure, we haven't played together in years, but other bands have been apart for years and then come back together. Wasn't that always the plan?

Only, I'm not sure what the plan is anymore.

29
Today

Backstage at a downtown rock club is a dark and dirty place where the dried-up alcohol on the floor sticks to your boots and you're ill-advised to sit down. The green room at *The Today Show* is an entirely different sort of place. It's beautifully appointed, with welcoming couches and a water and coffee setup. There's even a tray of delicious-looking mini muffins.

"You're going to do great," my mother says, and smiles warmly at me. My father refused to come ("I won't encourage this negativity" were the words he used), but my mother stands proudly as I nervously stuff mini muffins into my mouth. "We should live tweet the green room."

"What do you know about live tweeting?" I ask my mother.

"It's a thing," she says. I suspect she's not entirely sure what Twitter even is. "I heard one of the other guests talking about it in the ladies' room. They said they were going to live tweet the green-room experience so that by the time their segment went on, they'd be going viral."

"That's actually kind of brilliant," I say.

"Do you want me to live tweet for you?"

"Do you know how to use Twitter?" I ask.

"No," she says. "But how hard could it possibly be?"

My mother has a point. I quickly hand over my phone, and give her a brief explanation of 140 characters and what a hashtag is.

"Can you tweet a photo?" she asks, holding my phone up to my face to take a quick shot.

"Sure," I say, and then take the phone back to show her how. It's then that I see what her proposed first tweet is:

Jo looking gorgeous as she gets ready to chat up Matt Lauer. #LonelyHeartsClub

"Mom," I say. "You cannot tweet this."

"Why not?" she pouts. "You look fabulous. I told you that black leather jeans were the way to go."

"You just can't tweet that," I say.

My mother's about to object again, something about how the Twitterverse would want to see how beautiful I look, when we're interrupted by Matt Lauer. I don't even have a chance to question my mother on how she knows what the Twitterverse is.

"Jo?" Matt Lauer says as he comes to greet me. "Hey there, just wanted to say hello before we went on the air."

"Hi," I say, shaking his hand. I'm hoping that mine isn't too sweaty. It's easy to look cool, but my hands always betray me. "Nice to meet you."

"I'm Jo's mother," my mom says, grabbing Matt Lauer's hand. "Nancy Waldman. You can call me Nan."

"Nice to meet you, too," Matt says. "Jo, did Bee tell you how it's going to go today?"

"Yes," I say. "We'll talk about how the whole thing started, how social media plays into it, what my plans for the site are."

"Exactly," he says. "I saw your NY1 interview. It was great. Do the same thing—look at me, not the camera. We're just having a conversation. Nothing to be nervous about."

"Oh, she's not nervous," my mother interjects. "She's been on stage since she was five years old."

"Great," Matt says. "Then we're all set."

"YOU HAVE a glow about you," Matt Lauer tells me. We're on air, and I'm trying to act natural, just like he said. Trying to pretend we're just two friends having a regular conversation. But it's not easy. My face feels like it's on fire and I could really use a glass of water. "If I didn't know any better, I'd say you were in love."

I laugh nervously. I don't really know how to respond. Do I deny it? Do I admit everything? Do I accuse him of being glib?

"Love?" I say, and Matt smiles back.

"But I'm guessing that's not it, since you're the face of the anti-love movement taking place in Manhattan right now," he says. "Tell us about that."

I take a deep breath. I can do this.

"It all started on Valentine's Day. I was broken-hearted, alone, and drunk. Not a very good combination."

"No, it's not," Matt says and laughs.

"I decided to get out all of my feelings, all of my frustrations, on my blog. Little did I know, I was actually broadcasting these feelings—my deepest, darkest thoughts—to 2,500 of my closest friends."

"Your band's old mailing list," Matt says.

"Right. But it turned out to be a good thing. Because now I know I'm not alone. There are other people like me. People who've had their hearts broken. People who have been betrayed by love. People who want to vent their pain and anger. And we're the Lonely Hearts Club."

I look off camera, and I see my mother frantically taking pictures of me. I can't help but smile, and I take another deep breath.

"And for those of you who don't know where to find them," Matt says, "we've got the Web address right there at the bottom of your screens right now. Tell us, Jo, what's next for the Lonely Hearts Club?"

"Okay, lonely hearts: mark your calendars. Get ready for the Lonely Hearts Club Ball—this year on Valentine's Day. Now you don't have to sit at home drinking vodka and eating cheap drugstore candy. You can be with people like you—others who have sworn off love and just want to rage."

"I assume information about the party will be on your Web site?"

"It's there now," I say. "Tickets go on sale in October."

"You heard it here, folks," Matt says. "Go to the Lonely Hearts Web site and check out the information about the Lonely Hearts Club Ball. Now, Jo, before you go, I'd be remiss if I didn't ask you one last thing. Are you sure you've sworn off love? There isn't anyone out there who could convince you otherwise?"

"No, Matt," I say, looking into the camera. "I'm done with it. No more love for me."

30

You Drive Me Wild

"Well, if I show you how to do that, you won't need me," Max says. But it's not true. I will need him, still. I *do* need him. I tell him so.

He smiles widely and shows me how to make the changes to the site I was talking about. He has it set up in a very user-friendly way, since when he first created it, he imagined that he'd be setting it up for me and then walking away. He didn't intend on staying around quite as long as he did.

"Thanks," I say, and he tells me that I am very welcome.

Everything he says to me seems like an unqualified invitation to sex. "You're very welcome" means "Let's have sex." "What do you want for dinner tonight?" means "Let's have sex before the food comes." "Whose place are we meeting at?" means "Do you want to have sex at your place or mine?"

I'm in a particularly good mood today because the Amber Fairchild lip-synching scandal is on full tilt. Her fake celebrity friends have all shunned her, and there's even talk that her squirrely husband has moved out. I have to Google the word "schadenfreude" to explain to Max how I feel about it.

"Well, that's not very nice," he says, furrowing his brow.

"Maybe I'm not a nice girl," I say, an attempt at flirtation. I edge closer to him, but Max doesn't respond.

"No, seriously," he says. "Why would you revel in someone else's misfortune?"

"I should have had her life," I say, anger I didn't know was there bubbling in my voice. I feel the folds of my forehead deepening, my hands balling into fists. "I should have had her career."

"You don't want her life, do you really? Married to a man she doesn't seem to really love, making music that you think is overproduced and awful, tethered to an image you think is deplorable, and surrounded by sycophants, not real friends."

"Well, no," I say. "I don't want those things. But I do want a record deal. I want a career in music."

"You will get a record deal," he says, taking my hands in his. He takes one hand and raises it to his lips. He kisses it gently and it sends a chill down my spine. "Jo, you're enormously talented. If only you could see what I could see. It just takes the right person to see what you have, and you'll get what you want."

Is it any wonder we end up in bed?

BLOG COMMENT FROM PIANOSOUNDSLIKEACARNIVAL:
I know you don't believe in all this negativity, Jo. Love exists!

RESPONSE FROM WANNABESTARTINSOMETHING:
Jo rocks. If you don't agree with that, you shouldn't be on this site in the first place.

RESPONSE FROM NYDOLLS:
What are you doing on this site if you don't want to rage? Get off the Lonely Hearts Club blog if you aren't on board.

RESPONSE FROM LONDONCALLING:
Easy to sit behind a computer and criticize. Lonely Hearts Club forever!!

AN HOUR later, we're back to it, working on my site together. Sitting side by side with an amazing guy, I can't help but think that Max was right. I may not have the music career that Amber has, but I have someone wonderful in my life, and I'm surrounded by friends and family. I may not have a place to live other than Chloe's couch at the moment, but that's only temporary. I'm doing pretty well for myself.

Could it be that the rather large shove my dad gave me out of the nest was actually a good thing?

"What should we do for dinner tonight?" he asks.

"I don't know," I say. "What do you want?"

"I was asking you what *you* wanted."

"Oh, me?" I say, feigning innocence. "You know me, I'm so predictable. I always want the same thing."

"You do?"

"Yeah."

He grabs me and kisses me.

"Hey, what are you doing for Thanksgiving?" he asks.

"Thanksgiving?"

"Yeah, I was going to head up to my parents' place for the

long weekend," he says. "I was thinking that maybe you'd like to come?"

"To meet your parents?" I say. A million thoughts flood my mind:

My parents don't even know about Max.

No one knows about Max.

How can we keep this secret if his parents know about us?

Where would I tell my parents that I'm going?

What would I tell Chloe?

"Don't look so terrified," Max says, laughing. But I can tell it's a fake laugh. I know that I've disappointed him.

"I'm sorry," I quickly say. "It's just that I haven't even told my parents about us yet. I haven't told anyone."

"What, are you afraid my parents will rat you out to the Lonely Hearts Club community?" Max jokes. But I don't respond. That's exactly what I'm afraid of. "Oh man, that *is* what you're afraid of. Do you really think my family would do that to you? And anyway, what would be so bad about that? What would be so bad about letting people know about us?"

"Nothing would be bad about it," I say. "In fact, it would be great. It's just that if I do that, the Lonely Hearts Club Web site would cease to exist. You can't run a Web site that stands for the opposite of love if you're busy falling into it."

"You're falling into it?" he asks.

"You know that I am."

"I am, too," he says.

"But that's not enough for you?" I ask.

"For now it is," he says. "I guess. But it won't always be."

"After the Lonely Hearts Club Ball, we can go public, I promise," I say. "I've got so many people working so hard on it, I don't have the heart to destroy everything we've built up so far."

"I understand," he says. "You'll probably want to sell the Web site around then, too, so we should keep planning for that."

I shake my head in agreement, but the truth is, the thing I don't really want Max to know, haven't told him yet, is that I don't want to sell the Web site. It's my band's Web site, not my own really, and I can't let go. Not yet, anyway. But there's no way Max will understand that, so I keep it to myself.

I've been doing a lot of that lately.

31
Stop! In the Name of Love

When you book an event at the Chalice, an old abandoned bank in Chinatown, now newly renovated into a humongous party space, you get the services of a complimentary party planner. My mother, who gleefully accepted the responsibility of the Lonely Hearts Club Ball décor, is not pleased with this development.

"And what exactly is your experience in planning a party on this large of a scale?" she asks the planner.

Our party planner, Kitty, comes from the Barbie Johnson school of enthusiasm.

"Well, I'm coming from the corporate side," she explains. She's about one glaringly large smile away from bouncing up and down like Barbie. "I worked at the USTA? Tennis? You know, the US Open? I planned all of their corporate events. I even got to meet Michelle Obama once!"

"Well, for this event, discretion will be important," my mother says. "This is an altogether different crowd from the tennis people you've worked with, and you'll need to turn a blind eye to some of the things you'll be seeing here."

I find it hilarious that my mother is trying to tough-talk this poor party planner with her tweed suit and three-inch Chanel spectators on.

"Will we have full access to the vaults?" Chloe asks, and Kitty tells us that yes, our guests can use the old vault spaces.

The ballroom is massive—the ceilings are triple height, the windows are enormous, and there's not one, but four, separate chandeliers dangling from the ceiling. There are catwalks all along the ballroom, with tiny alcoves that look down. When this operated as a bank, those served as the offices. Now they are set up like miniature lounge areas. Some lonely hearts are not going to be lonely for long with those things.

Then it's time to see the vaults. We go through a corridor toward a cavernous space. The massive vault door is now left permanently open ("Don't want any party guests getting locked up!" Kitty nervously laughs), but there are five different vaults inside, one bigger than the next. Chloe goes off to the first one, and I just stand still, taking it all in. My mother has stayed back in the ballroom, where she is trying, in vain, to get a measurement on the windows for draperies.

"This area would be great for dressing rooms, if you and Chloe were planning on having hair and makeup done here," Kitty says.

"We weren't," I say.

"I hope you won't hold this against me," Kitty confides, "but I recently got engaged! We're planning to have the wedding here, and I'll be using this area as my bridal suite."

"Congratulations!" I say. "That's wonderful news!"

I give Kitty a warm hug, but she's holding back. "I wasn't expecting that reaction," she says.

"What were you expecting?" I ask.

"I was just hoping you wouldn't fire me when you found out!" she says with a laugh. She tries to play it off like a joke, but I know that she's serious. She really thought we would fire her because she was engaged.

"I wouldn't fire you for that," I say. "In fact, I'm happy for you!"

"Happy for what?" Chloe asks, emerging from the third vault.

"Kitty just got engaged," I say, grabbing her hand to look at the ring.

"You're fired," Chloe deadpans.

"Chloe!" I chastise. And then to Kitty: "You're not fired."

Kitty laughs.

"I'm pretty sure she gets the joke," Chloe says. "But the real question is, why don't you?"

I ignore Chloe. "Have you decided on a theme yet?" I ask Kitty. I now know, after listening to Barbie, that without a good theme, your wedding will be a total and utter failure. It might even make the marriage a disaster.

"What's with all the questions?" Chloe asks me as we make our way back to the ballroom.

"What do you mean?"

"All those questions you were asking Kitty about her engagement. What's with that? You hate love," Chloe says. "Don't you?"

MY MOTHER is on a two-story ladder, tape measure in hand.

"Oh, hi, girls!" she says.

"Get down from there!" I say. "You're going to kill yourself!"

"I'm going to coordinate décor and drinks with your mother," Kitty says calmly, but her legs betray her. She runs to my mother as quickly as her high heels will allow. She steadies the ladder, and then talks my mother down from it.

"What's with you?" Chloe asks me.

"What do you mean?"

"First you're humming pop songs, and now you're asking some stranger about her wedding plans. Who are you, and what have you done with my friend Jo?"

"I'm just trying to be nice," I say.

"Nice is saying congrats and then looking at the ring," Chloe says. "You're about to become an invited guest."

"I am not."

"And throw her a bachelorette party."

"Stop it."

"Seriously," Chloe says. "What is with you lately? If I didn't know any better, I'd say there's a guy in the picture."

I look down at the floor. I can't bring my eyes up to meet Chloe's.

"Oh my God," Chloe says. "There *is* a guy! And you haven't told me about it. Wow. Is Jesse back? Did he come crawling?"

"No," I say. "Jesse did not come back."

"Well, then where are you every night? You don't have *that* many friends who I don't know. NYU and Columbia weren't exactly that far apart from each other. Where have you been?"

"Okay, okay," I say. "I *have* been seeing someone."

"Who?"

"Max," I say, and Chloe's face explodes with a million expressions at once: shock, surprise, but most of all, joy.

"Max?" is all she can say in response.

"Yes, Max." Just saying his name makes my pulse start to race.

"Max from my office Max?"

"Yes!" I say. "Why are you so surprised?"

"I didn't see that one coming," she says. "He is total boyfriend material, though. Very good guy."

"He's not my boyfriend," I say quickly. "We're just sleeping together. No feelings, just sex. That's all it is."

"Really?" Chloe says. "He doesn't seem like that type of guy. He seems intense. Like he doesn't do surface. Like the kind of guy you fall in love with."

"Well, he's not," I say. "He's a rebound guy. Nothing more."

"Oh."

"Yeah."

"Then good for you," Chloe says. "If you're happy."

I nod my head in response.

"You are happy, right?"

If she only knew.

32
(You Gotta) Fight for Your Right (To Party)

TWEET FROM @LATRANSPLANT:
Will I see you at the Lonely Hearts Club Ball?
#LonelyHeartsClub #almosthere

TWEET FROM @MISFITS91:
It's all happening soon. #LonelyHeartsClub
#LonelyHeartsClubBall

TWEET FROM @GREENDAYOFFICIAL:
Come see us perform at the #LonelyHeartsClubBall.
Order tix here: http://tinyurl.com/q2zsoxm

TWEET FROM @JOHNNYROTTENLIVES:
It's going to be the night of the year.
#LonelyHeartsClubBall

TWEET FROM @BLONDIEISMYSPRIRITANIMAL:
The goddess is coming! The goddess is coming!
Blondie's performing at #LonelyHeartsClubBall
#dreamcometrue

33
Hanging on the Telephone

The music takes care of itself. The acts practically book themselves—as we plan the party, managers call us, hoping to get their acts on the roster. Everyone wants to be a part of it—every punk rock band I've ever admired—but there's something missing. Something I can't put my finger on.

We've got the bands I've been listening to lately ready to go: Green Day, Blink-182, and Fall Out Boy. We've got the bands I've always loved, like No Doubt, Panic! at the Disco, and Garbage. And we've got the bands I grew up on, like Joan Jett and the Blackhearts and the Violent Femmes. Even Blondie herself, Debbie Harry, is set to make an appearance on the Lonely Hearts stage.

But there's still something I have to do. A feeling I just can't shake. This high-profile event, this enormous thing I'm planning, this party that will garner more press than anyone could ever dream of—my band should be playing. The Lonely Hearts Club Band.

My band hasn't played together in two years—hell, we haven't even spoken in as long, with the exception of a hello and good-bye at my ill-conceived birthday bash. And I can't do it. I just can't do it. It's been months that I've been thinking about getting my band back together, but I can't bring myself to make the call. I can't make any of the calls.

I hop onto Twitter and see that the Lonely Hearts Club Ball is trending. People are getting excited about the bands we've booked, and the band themselves are thrilled to be a part of it. I send a few retweets and compose one of my own:

Where will you be on February 14th? If you're a Lonely Heart like me, you need to be at the #LonelyHeartsClubBall so we can rage.

I hit SEND and immediately get retweeted hundreds of times.

@Iloverockandroll tweets, mentioning me and my tweet: *What are you waiting for? Get your tix now!*

I think to myself, *What am I waiting for?* I pick up my cell and dial. I don't have to look up the number. This one, I know by heart.

"Hi, Frankie?"

MY CELL rings, and even though I usually screen all my calls, I pick up. I'm still so jazzed about making that first call to Frankie, the Lonely Hearts Club Band's lead guitarist. Next on my list is a call to Kane. I try not to think about the fact that I'll need to find a new drummer. Someone to fill Billy's place.

"Jo Waldman?"

"Yes," I say, not recognizing the voice, and instantly wishing I'd let the call go to voice mail.

"I wanted to talk to you about the Lonely Hearts Club Web site," he says, after a long introduction about who he is. I instantly forget about ninety percent of what he's said. He's speaking quickly, and I can barely process what he's saying. "We've been following your site for a while, and we'd like to make you an offer to sell the site."

"Sell?" I say. This, I can understand. I may not fully understand who this guy is, but now I get what he wants: He wants me to sell my band's Web site. "I'm sorry, the site's not for sale."

I don't know why I'm so surprised to be getting this call—it's what Max has been building toward this entire time. A big sale, a nest egg, the chance to get the loft back. But even with all that he's prepared me, I'm still shocked that someone's offering to buy.

"Why don't we meet in person?" he says.

"I'm not meeting you in person," I say. "I have no idea who you are."

"I run a number of Web sites, and we think your site would be a great addition to our brand."

"What's your brand?"

"Relationships," he says. "Love."

"Love is not my brand," I say. "In fact, it's the exact opposite of my brand."

"I represent some Web sites that are very well known."

"Like what?" I ask.

"The one I think you're most familiar with is Love, Inc. We're their parent company," he says. "They're the biggest advertiser on your site."

"Not the biggest," I say. "We've got bigger." But I know that all this is beside the point. I know that I'm just stalling for time. It doesn't matter who the biggest advertiser is on the site. What matters is that he wants to make me an offer.

"Why don't I take you for lunch, tell you a little about who we are and what we do? I can give you a full proposal at that time."

"Not interested," I say. "Sorry."

"Tell you what, I can give you my contact information and when you change your mind, you give me a call?"

"I'm not going to change my mind," I say. "I never do."

"It's a lot of money, Jo."

"The Lonely Hearts Club site is *not* for sale."

34
Surrender

"The peach really brings out your eyes," Barbie says.

I'm in a dressing room at Vera Wang, trying to wrangle myself into a duchess satin floor-length gown. The material has no give to it, and once I'm able to (finally) pull it up, I notice that there's a humongous bow up top that will cover my breasts.

"My eyes are brown," I say.

"The peach brings it out," Barbie says.

I frown as I look at my reflection in the three-way mirror. Does anyone ever really want a color that helps to bring out the brown in their eyes?

"The bow is so chic," Barbie's sister says.

"So chic," her other sister says. "It reminds me of that black-and-white Valentino from last year."

They're both wearing the same dress as me, and I must admit, on them, it does look impossibly chic. On me, it's a mess. I've got bulges everywhere, the peach drains every ounce of color from my face, and I can barely walk.

"Should we try the chiffon?" Barbie says. She's sitting on a couch, sipping a champagne cocktail. I suggest that perhaps she should be the one modeling the dresses, since her figure's so perfect, but she doesn't fall for it.

I retreat to my fitting room (at least I don't have to share one with Barbie's sisters) and look at what the salesperson has pulled for me. There's a peach chiffon dress, all whispers and lightness, and next to it, there's a black dress that I know Barbie didn't pick out. I pull back the curtain to see which dress Barbie's sisters have on, and the salesperson catches my eye. She winks at me and motions for me to go try the dress on.

As I take the dress off the hanger, I realize that it's midnight blue, not black. A navy so dark it almost looks black, it's edgier than the ones that Barbie's been picking out. Fabric drapes everywhere, and there are pieces of fabric falling every which way. It looks like something Gwen Stefani would wear, if Gwen Stefani ever had to serve as a bridesmaid.

I give it a twirl, and as much as I hate to admit it, I really like the way I look in it. Love the way I feel in it. I'm already imagining myself at the wedding, dancing with Max in it.

"How's the fit?" I hear the salesperson call out to me.

"I think it's good," I say. "But I can't get the zipper up."

"May I?"

"Come on in," I say, and she pulls back the curtain to enter my dressing room.

"Oh, this is great on you," she says. And then, in a whisper, "I'm wishyouwerehere. Love your site."

I smile back at her. "Thanks," I say. "This is great."

"What's great?" Barbie says.

"I just pulled this for your fiancé's sister," the salesperson says. "Sometimes you just look at someone and know what will work."

"That's not peach," Barbie says, hands on her hips, pout

beginning to form on her perfectly full lips.

"I know," the salesperson says apologetically. "You're right. I just thought—"

"I said peach," Barbie says, her voice an unmistakable whine. I'm not sure which she's about to do first: start yelling or start crying. "We all like peach, right?" I half expect her to start stomping her feet.

Barbie's sisters quickly agree, but I can see them all eyeing the dress I've got on. Even with gorgeous blonde hair, perfect figures, and blue eyes, is peach really anyone's favorite color when it comes to formal dresses?

"Sorry about that," the salesperson says. "Peach is fabulous. But you know, Shana Slade had her bridesmaids in midnight blue, so I just thought—"

"From the *Real Housewives of Long Island*?" Barbie says. "Oh my God, I love that show!"

Her sisters are a Greek chorus of "I love it, too!" and "That's the best show on TV!" and "Shana Slade is my favorite housewife!"

"Yes," the salesperson continues. "I love the show, too. Shana had a ten-person bridal party, just like you. Vera did each girl in a different dress, each one wearing midnight blue, the color Jo is wearing."

"We'll take it," Barbie says.

The salesperson and I share a tiny smile as my cell phone rings.

"Hey, Dad," I say.

"Hi, Pumpkin," he says. "I was calling to rescue you from bridesmaid dress shopping. Should I make some excuse for you to leave? A bridal bouquet-drying emergency, perhaps? Or we can pretend I signed you up for a class in flower drying, to really sell it."

"I'm actually fine," I say, as I see Barbie's sisters retreating to their fitting rooms, arms filled with midnight blue.

"Fine?" my dad says. "You're at Vera Wang. Trying on bridesmaid dresses. I figured by now you'd be broken out in hives."

"We actually found something I really like."

"You found a peach dress that you like?"

"I think the color scheme is changing," I say. "And yes, I like it." I twirl again and watch the dress as it floats around me.

"Do I need to come over there and take your temperature? You must be ill," he says.

"I think we're doing navy dresses now," I whisper into the phone.

"How did you swing that?"

"I don't know, really," I say, with a touch of laughter in my voice. I really don't know what just happened or how I accomplished it, but I'm happy either way.

"Well, let's meet at Balthazar for lunch," my dad says. "You can tell me all about it then."

"The girls are all going out for lunch," I say. "And I think some of Barbie's sorority sisters are meeting us."

Dead silence on the line.

"Dad?"

More silence.

"Hello?"

"I'm sorry," my dad says. "I thought I just heard you say that you're going for lunch with Barbie and her sisters and her *sorority* sisters, too, no less. We must have a bad connection."

"No, you heard me correctly," I say and laugh.

"Something's different with you lately," he says. "What is it?"

"Nothing's different," I say. "Same girl as before."

"Are you?" my dad asks. And as I twirl in front of the mirror in a glamorous Vera Wang gown, I have to admit: I'm not really sure I am.

35
Is This Love?

"There's a lot of chatter about this pianosoundslikeacarnival guy," Max says. "Do you want me to do something about it?"

"Want you to do something about it?" I ask. "You sound like you're in some mafia movie or something. What are you going to do? Take the guy out for posting negative comments?"

"No," Max says, laughing. "But I can block him from commenting."

"Oh," I say. "I didn't know you could do that."

"I can do anything you want."

"Now that sounds interesting," I say, smiling. "Tell me more about this 'anything I want' thing."

Max crawls across the couch to where I'm sitting. He kisses my ear. His kisses are always so gentle, and I can feel my face lighting on fire just from his touch. Then he moves to my neck, and I lean back and run my fingers through his hair. My cell phone rings, and he asks me if I need to get it. I grab my phone from the coffee table and look at the caller ID.

"I don't have to answer," I murmur.

"Who was that?" he asks.

"No one important," I say. "Just these guys who wanted to buy the Web site."

Max pops up and regards me. "That's amazing. What did they offer?"

"It doesn't matter," I say, climbing over to him. "I turned it down anyway."

"What do you mean you turned it down?" Max asks me. He stands up from the couch and begins to pace.

"I said no."

"No? You don't just say no. That's not how these things happen," Max says. He's panicking, grasping at straws. "They have the lawyers draw something up, they send you a proposal. You don't just turn it down. You *can't* just turn it down."

"I told them I wasn't interested," I explain. "Look, Max, it's not a big deal. It's not what I wanted. It doesn't matter."

"It's not what you wanted?" he asks. "I thought it's been what we've been building up to this entire time?"

"I'm not ready to let it go yet," I say, almost under my breath. I don't want him to hear me say it out loud—that I don't want to let the band go, I don't want to let my old dream go. I can't let it go. I just can't.

"How much money was it?"

"The Lonely Hearts Club Band Web site is not for sale," I say. "I thought I'd explained that to you."

Max exhales deeply. "How much money was it?"

"A lot."

"I don't understand," Max says. "Why'd you just say no outright? Why wouldn't you at least entertain the offer? What does it hurt to hear what they have to offer?"

"I don't want to be a sellout," I say.

"This again," he says. He rubs his hand across his forehead, as if I'm a toddler and I'm giving him a headache with my ridiculous logic. "You don't want to sell out. You don't want to make money. Are you scared of being a success or something? I've heard about this—people being scared of their own success so they sabotage it. Self-sabotage, it's called. Is this what it's all about?"

"How is selling my Web site being a success?"

"Well, let's see," Max says, pacing the floor. "You create something. You build it up. And then you sell it. For a lot of money. That money enables you to do whatever you want. Like move back into the loft, for example. Or find your own place. Or book expensive studio time. You can make the music you want. On your own terms."

"I didn't think of it that way."

"Do you want to move off Chloe's couch?" Max asks. "Or do you want to just keep our relationship secret for the rest of our lives?"

"This is about *us* now?"

"Is this a relationship?" he asks.

"Of course it is."

"Okay, then why are we keeping it a secret? It's been almost a year. You haven't told your family. You haven't even told your best friend."

"You know why," I say. "You know I can't."

"Lemme guess," he says, standing up from the couch to pace around the living room. "You don't want to be a sellout."

"No," I say. "Yes. I mean, the site is important to me. I thought you knew that."

"I *do* know that," he says, running his hand through his hair. "What I'm trying to figure out here is if *I'm* important to you."

"Of course you are," I say, grabbing his hands and pulling him back down onto the couch. "You know you are."

"Did you really mean what you said on *The Today Show*?"

I can't even recall what he's talking about. There have been so many interviews, so many magazine stories, so much coverage that I can't even remember what I said anymore.

"What I said?" I ask.

"That you're done," he says, looking down at my hands. "No more love for you."

"No," I say.

"No?"

"No, I didn't mean it."

"Jo, I love you," he says. He takes my face in his hand and gently kisses my lips. "I love you.

"I love you, too," I say. And then I kiss him back.

36
Dance the Night Away

It's here. It's finally here. It's Valentine's Day and anyone who is anyone is at the Lonely Hearts Club Ball. The Chalice has the entrance lit up in various shades of black, gray, and white (my mother's brainstorm) and there's a gray step-and-repeat setup at the red carpet. Which is actually a black carpet (Kitty's idea).

My mother is far too busy bossing around Kitty to make an appearance on the black carpet, but Barbie insists that she and Andrew get photographed. When the photogs ask her who they are, she says, "I'm Jo's sister-in-law, *silly*!"

Chloe and I stand at the edge of the black carpet, greeting guests, giving interviews, and everything seems to be going according to plan. Of the 7,000 tickets we sold to the event, about 4,000 guests have arrived already. The party is in full swing.

An enormous black limo pulls up and the crowd parts like the Red Sea. Most of the celebs we invited are already on the step-and-repeat or inside, firmly ensconced in the vaults at the VIP area, so I'm not sure who it could be. Who else could need such pageantry to show up to the Lonely Hearts Club Ball? My mother's already here, so it can't be my parents. And Chloe and I don't have any friends with the sort of money to spend on a limo. Our crowd is more public transportation than private limo, anyway.

I see a long, tan leg make its way out of the car, followed by a long black sequined gown. Then I see a mountain of blonde curls, and I know. I just know. It's Amber Fairchild. Yes, *that* Amber Fairchild.

"What is she doing here?" I say, under my breath to Chloe, as Amber makes her way onto the step-and-repeat. Reporters are practically falling over themselves to talk to her, to get a sound bite. A photograph.

"I don't know," she says. "Why don't you go ask her? If you get into a fight with her, it will make great press."

As I make my way toward Amber, all I can think is how angry Lola's going to be at me—her mom wouldn't let her attend the party since Lola's too young (true), the party's going to run too late (also true), and she felt that the themes of the evening would be too mature for Lola (definitely true). I may have also mentioned to Lola's mom that there were various alcoves and little rooms throughout the venue, old offices, and that who knows what might be going on in them.

"What are you doing here?" I bark at Amber. She's holding a hot-pink evening clutch and I want to scream that the invite specifically said black clothing only. I flash a particularly vicious look Alan Golden's way. He's wearing a black suit with a coordinating hot-pink tie.

But Amber's such a pro. She doesn't even flinch. "Why am I here?" she asks, incredulous, in her husky voice. She puts a perfectly manicured hand onto her chest. "I'm one of your biggest followers!"

The crowd goes wild. Absolutely wild. I grind my teeth and

try to think of something to say about her recent lip-synching scandal.

"Let's hear it for the woman of the hour!" Amber calls out, and grabs my arm. She holds my hand up, as if I just won a boxing match or something. "It's good to see you again," she whispers to me as the cameras are going off.

The worst part is that I know that this is the photo everyone's going to pick up tomorrow. This will be the photo that epitomizes the event.

Amber insists on walking into the ball holding my hand. As if we're sorority sisters or something, off to braid each other's hair. But I can't break away from her. The crowd loves it—that we're together, that we're holding hands, all of it. And there's nothing I love more than to make a crowd happy.

Once inside, Alan whisks Amber off to the VIP section.

"Visit me later, okay?" she calls to me, over her shoulder. I find myself saying okay back, even though I don't mean it. Not really, anyway. Chloe laughs at me, and I find myself looking up, trying to figure out which tiny alcove Max is holding court in. Since we knew we couldn't be seen together, I gave him a bunch of tickets so he could bring his friends and have fun. When I told him about the tiny catwalks and the little alcoves that were scattered around the venue, he decided that he was going to hold court with his friends and make it their own private VIP section. I look up and can see he wasn't the only one with that idea. I see the pale glow from cell phones in various alcoves along the wall. It looks like a million stars lit up in the sky.

"Oh, my God, you're in *US Weekly* already!" Chloe says, and hands me her phone. I take a peek and see that there's a picture on the front page of the app—Amber and me at the step-and-repeat from fifteen minutes ago. "Love, Inc. will be happy," Chloe says. "Amber's head is right next to their logo. Isn't that great?"

"Me and Amber, at the Lonely Hearts Club Ball. Great."

THE DANCE floor is a sea of dirty dancers. People are meeting, bumping into each other, making out…We all may have come in vowing to give up on love, but many of the party guests seem to have forgotten that vow. The band plays a cover of "Love Stinks," and the party guests sing along as they pair off. Love may, in fact, stink, but apparently making out shamelessly with the person directly to the right of you is just fine. I lose Chloe in the crowd, and I figure that she must have found someone of her own to pair off with.

I rush off toward the catwalk to try to find Max. It's dark—almost too dark—on the tiny iron pathway that runs along the side of the bank. The Chalice dates back to the early 1900s—were people smaller back then? In order to pass another party guest on the catwalk, you literally have to brush up against them to get past. Perhaps that's what's leading to the amorous feeling permeating the Lonely Hearts Club Ball? I glance at my watch and see that I've got time. I need to be down by the stage at a little before the clock strikes twelve. That's when I give my grand toast, with just enough time for my band to go on at midnight. For the grand finale of our set, a bunch of actors dressed up as 1920s-era gangsters will come out with fake tommy guns and stage the reenactment of the Valentine's Day massacre that Chloe and I thought up.

I'm glad I switched back to my usual uniform of old concert tee, ripped jeans, and motorcycle boots. Most of the women in stilettos are getting their heels stuck in the catwalk. But me? I'm able to skulk around easily.

I check the first level of alcoves and don't find Max. I climb up a tiny flight of steps to reach the next level. I look down at the view and the party looks amazing. I take out my cell phone to snap a picture. I put it on Instagram with the caption #TheLonelyHeartsClubBall.

I DID it. I really did it. The party is a success. The music's amazing, the alcohol's flowing, and the dance floor's been packed from the second we opened the doors. My mother's having the time of her life, seeing how the crowd is responding to the décor she's designed. (Now, to be clear, the crowd is mainly drunk, but she interprets this as sheer bliss over her design choices. Let her have this one, okay?) Green Day called my father on stage for their final song, so he's in pretty good spirits, as well. (Though he'd never heard of Green Day before. But he still enjoyed himself, regardless.)

It's almost time for the Lonely Hearts Club Band to go on stage, so I take a shot of liquid courage. It's not that I'm nervous, but I haven't been on stage with the band in years, and I wonder if it's possible to go back. To get something back that you once had. I'm not sure if you can, but I certainly will try. Chloe's insisted that I make an announcement, some sort of grand proclamation about the Lonely Hearts movement, so I'm going over my notes. Vodka in one hand, note card in the other.

I feel a set of hands around my waist. Max spins me around and kisses me.

"Someone will see us," I whisper.

"Then let's go hide," he says. We make our way down a catwalk and find an empty alcove. He kisses me and I forget all about the set I'm supposed to do, the speech I'm supposed to give.

"I wanted to do that all night," he says.

"Me too."

We kiss and we kiss and we kiss, and I can't get enough. I can never get enough of Max.

"I love you," he says.

"I love you, too," I say back.

"You're going to kill it tonight," he says.

I kiss him again and I forget all about the set I'm supposed to do. A bright light blinds us, and for a moment I think it's Chloe, taking a picture. Max and I break from our embrace and turn to face the light. Only it's not Chloe. It's a news camera.

"We're here with the founder of the Lonely Hearts Club movement, and it looks like she doesn't have a lonely heart anymore," the reporter says. I can't even see what station he's from, that's how bright the camera light is.

"This isn't what it looks like," I say.

"I'm Kel Kavanagh from Channel 4 News and I've got Jodi Waldman, a girl from Long Island who's reinvented herself into a rocker persona—Jo—and started the Lonely Hearts Club movement. Jodi, what do you have to say to the fans to whom you preach your anti-love message? Would they be surprised to know that you yourself are in love?"

"I'm not in love," I say.

"That certainly looked like love," the reporter says, stifling a laugh. "Young man, what's your name?"

Max doesn't say a word. He's smart enough to know that if he doesn't say a word, doesn't offer a sound bite, Kel's got nothing. No story. Nothing to report. I, on the other hand, am not that smart.

"He's no one," I say. I mean to take the focus off Max, to get him out of this mess I've created, but it comes out sounding like something else entirely. "He means nothing to me. You want me, right? Leave him out of this."

"Just to be clear," Kel says, "you're saying that you're not in love with this guy?"

"I am not in love with this guy," I say. "I barely even know him."

"Then who is he?"

"He's just the rebound guy," I say. "As anyone who follows my blog knows, Jesse was the love of my life and he tore my heart out. Think I'd be dumb enough to fall in love again? I don't think so."

The reporter signals for the cameraman to shut off the light, and finally, I can see again. I turn around to find Max, to explain myself, but it's too late.

He's already gone.

37
I Can't Explain

Chloe's announcing that our band's about to start, so I race back down to the stage. Max is waiting for me, in the wings.

"There you are," I say, out of breath. "I was looking for you."

"What the fuck, Jo?"

"I can explain everything," I say.

"That was the time to come clean," he says. "People are hooking up left and right, clearly everyone's moving on. Everyone but you. Now I get it. That's why you wouldn't sell the site, isn't it? You *do* believe everything you stand for. I thought you meant it when you said you loved me."

"I do love you," I say. "I do."

"I don't know you at all," he says. "Never did. I don't even know your real name."

"And now," Chloe announces from the stage, "the woman you've all been waiting for, the one who created it all—Jo Waldman!"

The crowd erupts in applause, but I'm frozen where I stand. I can't leave until everything's okay with Max and me.

"Your fans want you," he says, and he points to the stage.

"I'm not leaving," I say. "I'm not leaving you until we're okay."

"Jo?" Chloe says into the microphone and the crowd starts chanting my name. My band's already up on stage, waiting to play.

"I've got Jo Waldman for you right here," a voice says from nowhere. It's not Chloe; it's not even coming from the stage. It's like the voice of Oz or something. Then a light shines out— and there I am, kissing Max, on all three stories of the Chalice's concrete wall.

The News 4 reporter has figured out a way to broadcast the footage he just took of me—there's a light shining from one of the alcoves two stories up. I hear Chloe tell security to find them and to turn it off.

"This is who you've been following all this time," he says. "But she's a total and utter fraud. Look at her."

Then the footage cuts to me saying that I'm not in love, that Max doesn't mean a thing to me. Back to Max and me making out. Looking at us, seeing us kiss, there's no mistaking how I feel about him. There's no mistake that I'm a liar. That I'm in love. And then to the big reveal of who I really am—just a plain, regular girl from Long Island. Jodi Waldman, the class outcast. Not Jo Waldman, the cool rocker who inadvertently started a movement. As my high school yearbook photo flashes on the wall, the security team finds the reporter and turns the video off.

But it's too late. The damage has already been done.

PART THREE: THE SHOW MUST GO ON
"Inside my heart is breaking."

38
I Hate Myself for Loving You

'm front-page news. It's all I ever wanted, but not the way I wanted it. *The New York Times* has me headlining the Styles section, and every gossip site has got it on their front page.

LONELY HEARTS CREATOR OUTED AS A FRAUD, the Styles section announces. Page Six puts it a bit differently: NOT-SO-LONELY HEARTS CLUB, they call it. The picture above the fold in the Styles section is the one that appeared on *US Weekly*'s site during the party—the shot of Amber and me holding hands. Best friends forever and all that. But Page Six has got another photograph entirely. Above the fold, they've got a collage of all the bands that played that night—a veritable who's who of punk and rock music. But toward the bottom of the page, so small you'd almost miss it if you weren't looking, is an old photo of my band. An ancient artifact of the Lonely Hearts Club Band. The photo credit reads Chloe Park. Did they contact Chloe to get permission to use the picture?

LONELY HEARTS CLUB TOTAL SHAM, the front page of *New*

York Magazine's online site declares. I click on the article, but can't bring myself to read it. More pictures of Amber and me, more pictures of the bands. For a second, I wonder if they got quotes from any of the bands that played that night. The thought of that is just too awful to bear, so I try not to think about it too much. My favorite bands and my rock idol condemning me would really set me over the edge. And I'm in bad enough shape as it is.

I run downstairs to grab a cup of coffee from my favorite newsstand—some fresh air will do me good—but headlines blare out at me: Lonely Hearts Club Music Festival Ends in Scandal, says *The Observer*. Even *Newsday*, my home paper, gets in on the action: This Girl Is Not Lonely, the headline reads, right over a picture of my face. "Don't let her tell you otherwise."

All this media attention, and my band didn't even get a chance to play.

Next, HGTV gets in on the action. Everyone wants to cash in on my misery. David Bromstad does an interview with my mom (her lifelong dream! To finally be on HGTV!) about the décor of the Lonely Hearts Club Ball. They film on site at the Chalice, and she walks him through her various design choices, how the design complimented the anti-love theme. She even has the posters we commissioned of the anti-love couples hung up behind her as they conduct the interview. I had no idea we'd kept them. But then again, I left the party in such a rush, without even giving my band a chance to play, that I have no clue what happened at the end of the party. I can see from the HGTV special that the cleanup crew Chloe and I hired did not make it to the Chalice.

By 5 P.M., there's a segment on News Channel 4 where Kel Kavanagh interviews people on the street about the Lonely Hearts Club Ball. A few people never heard of it, but most of the people are outraged. They loved me; now they hate me. They trusted me; they poured their hearts out to me. And now it turns out I was just a liar. Just like everyone else they ever loved. Just like everyone else they ever trusted. Just like every other person they ever gave their hearts to.

"What really pisses me off," one guy tells Kel, "is how she pretended she knew how I felt. She made it seem like she was just as lonely as I was. Just as hurt. Those tickets to the Lonely Hearts Club Ball weren't cheap, but I bought one because I believed in Jo. I believed in the Lonely Hearts Club."

"And who's this?" Kel asks. The camera pans out to show the woman who's standing next to our interview subject. The guy's got his arm around her, and she giggles.

"This is Samantha," he says. "We met at the Lonely Hearts Club Ball."

I don't know what I'm more upset about—that I'm being outed as a total and utter fraud, or that all the people interviewed are total hypocrites. Out of one side of their mouths they're saying that they're disappointed in me, but from the other, they explain how it all worked out in the end, since they found someone amazing at the ball or on my site. Don't they realize that makes them total frauds, too?

The Web site traffic's up. But the comments are deadly. I can't take my eyes off them—they rip me apart, calling me a fraud and a fake and a phony, but I can't stop reading. Every time I tell myself to shut my computer, I somehow find myself back on the site, reading about how awful I am.

E-mails start coming in from advertisers—exercising their option to not renew their ads. I guess I'm not the only one reading the comments section. In a week, I'll have no money coming in from the site.

Zilch. Nothing. Nada.

But none of that matters. Everyone's got someone, got

something, except for me. Max won't return my calls, and even Chloe is spending an inordinate amount of time outside of her apartment. It's like she'll do anything to spend less time alone with me.

How do I fix all of this? I decide to start from scratch, just like I did a year ago. I made something out of nothing then, so maybe I can get a little of that fairy dust and make it happen again.

I pick up my cell phone and dial. "I'd like to schedule that meeting," I say. I can't even remember the guy's name, but that doesn't stop him from taking my call.

"About what?" he asks. I can tell he's surprised to hear from me. I'm surprised to be making the call, so that makes two of us.

"I'm interested in selling the Lonely Hearts Club site," I say. I know that the offer's a bit old by now, but maybe it's still on the table. If I can just sell the site, start over again, maybe I can make things right. Make amends with Chloe, start over with my music without any distractions, and get Max back.

"Jo, the site's worthless now," he says. "The time to sell it was before the Lonely Hearts Club Ball. Before the scandal, certainly. The site's over. Everyone's moved on. You should, too. Call me when you come up with your next idea for a Web site. I'd love to be in business with you, and I know you'll come up with something new."

I don't know why I'm disappointed. I knew that no one would want the site now. I knew it was all over. I'm back to where I was last Valentine's Day—no money, no boyfriend, only now I don't have family and friends to help me pick up the pieces.

Amber Fairchild pops on the TV—some second-rate entertainment reporter wants to know what she thinks of the Lonely Hearts Club Ball debacle (their words).

"I thought the party was a big success!" she cries. "I had the time of my life. I danced so much my feet hurt the next day!"

"How can you say that?" the reporter asks. "The founder of the whole thing was outed as a complete and utter fraud."

"That's silly," Amber says. "She threw a great party. High-energy crowd. Amazing bands. Everyone had a blast! In fact, I think lots of folks found love that night. There were lots of people looking very cozy."

Not getting what he wants from her, the reporter ends the interview.

I flip off the TV. At least one person still likes me. Unfortunately, it's the person I hate most in the world, but beggars can't be choosers and all that.

I pick up my guitar and play a few chords. This is what I should have been doing the whole time. This is what I should be focusing on. When did I lose track of that? I lost sight of the one thing that was important, the one thing that always got me through every tough time in my life. My music.

I think about what Jesse said to me right before we broke up—that I haven't written in two years, that I hadn't played in as long. I've been stalled for the last two years. I'm living in the past. He may be an asshole, but he may just be an asshole with a point.

The gift certificate Andrew gave me for my birthday has been burning a hole in my pocket, so I grab it and go.

I sit in the studio for hours, but nothing comes. I have rage coursing through my veins, but I can't seem to channel it. I take out my notepad and try to write an entry for the Lonely Hearts Club blog—I can still write it, even if no one's reading it—but I can't think of anything to say. Nothing that I want to put out there, for all the world to see, anyway. I can't shake the ache of sadness I feel. A constant, nagging ache. I miss having something to work on each day. I miss Chloe. I miss Max.

My eyes start to tear up, but I do what I always do—I stop the tears. Stop the crying. I am not the sort of girl who cries. Crying is weakness, and I need to be strong now. My sound engineer sees me blotting my eyes and asks me if I need a minute.

"I'm fine," I say, and continue to play.

A few hours later, the gift certificate's all used up, and I have nothing to show for it besides a recording of me riffing on chords, doing cover song after cover song. None of it's usable. I've wasted an entire afternoon—the entire gift certificate of expensive studio time—on nothing. That's never happened to me before. I've never gone into the studio and come out empty-handed.

I walk home from the studio, letting the fresh air clear my head. I'm hoping that the exercise will free my mind a little, inspire me to write again, but all I can think about is Max. All I can think about is Chloe. I wonder if Chloe will be there when I get home. I consider texting her to see if she's working late, but then realize if I tell her that I'm on my way home, she'll stay late at the office just to miss me. My only chance of seeing her is by accident.

My thoughts float back to Max. Max. Always Max. I delude myself into this little fantasy that I indulge every evening as I get home to Chloe's apartment—that Max will be waiting for me in the lobby, dozens of roses firmly in hand, ready to tell me that he forgives me, that he knows I truly love him and that he's made a mistake. When the truth is, all I really do night after night is order in Caesar salad and chicken parmesan for myself, sit in front of the TV, and feel guilty for not writing music.

And it's silly to think such a thing would happen. It's a

breakup. They call it that because it's broken. No amount of wishing is going to magically put it back together. That's not how it works. And I should know. I wrote the book on it. Well, the blog, anyway.

And now it's all over.

39
Enjoy the Silence

I show up at the supergood offices a little shy of noon. I figure if Max won't let me come up, I can catch him when he comes down to pick up lunch. He hasn't answered my calls, texts, or e-mails. I try to look like I fit in, like I'm not the stalker that I truly am as I skulk around the lobby. At a little after 1 P.M., it seems clear that Max is not leaving his office for lunch today.

So much for my plan.

I approach the security desk and ask for Max. He picks up the phone and calls the IT department.

"He's not there," the security guard tells me.

"Can you try again?" I plead.

"He's not there," the security guard repeats. Then he looks over my shoulder, his way of saying that he's done with me and he's ready to help the next person waiting in line.

I ask for Chloe. She may be angry, but I know she'll at least let me come up. The security guard begrudgingly makes the call.

"Max won't buzz you up?" she asks, as she picks me up from the security desk moments later.

"Nope," I say, and we ride the rest of the elevator trip in silence.

"This is his floor," she says, and lets me off on the eleventh floor. She doesn't come out onto the eleventh floor with me. She simply gives me a limp wave good-bye and sends me off, out of the elevator by myself. It's only when the elevator doors slam shut that I realize I don't even know where the IT offices are.

For a split second, I rethink my plan to confront Max at his office and turn around to hit the button for the elevator. I hit the DOWN button over and over again, in a vain attempt to get the elevator doors to open a bit faster. But then I stop. After all, the longer I wait, the angrier he's going to get. I need to quash this now, talk to him now. If I can just explain, I know he'll understand.

I walk the hallways of the eleventh floor, trying to look as if I know where I'm going. I pass a string of offices and then the restrooms and then finally at the end of the floor, I see what I'm looking for.

"Max?" I ask to a sea of cubicles, as I enter an enormous open room marked IT DEPARTMENT.

"What are you doing here?" he asks, getting up from his cubicle and rushing me out to the hallway. "I didn't buzz you up."

"Chloe did," I say. "I need to talk to you. I'm sorry. I'm so sorry."

"I don't want to hear it," he says. "And now's not exactly the right time, when I'm supposed to be working."

"You won't answer my calls," I plead. "You won't write back to my texts or e-mails. I even posted a message for you on the Lonely Hearts Club Web site. What else was I supposed to do?"

"Accept that I don't want to see you anymore, Jo," Max says. He places his hand below my elbow and guides me toward the door. "It's over. We're over."

"Give me another chance," I say, turning back to face him. "I'll do anything."

"You're not ready for the sort of relationship that I want," Max says. "I knew it from the beginning, but I let you convince me otherwise. I shouldn't have been surprised. But I let myself believe that things would change."

"They will."

"They won't," Max says. "When it really mattered, you couldn't tell the world the truth. Have you even told your family about us yet?"

"Yes," I say. "Of course I have."

"You're still caught up in being a sellout and hanging on to an old Web site that could have made you a lot of money," he says. "You're not ready to be an adult yet. But I am. So it's best we just go our separate ways."

"I'm ready," I say. "Things are different now."

"Things don't change overnight," Max says. "Which, I guess, is why you couldn't stand up for me when I needed you to. But what I've realized is that I'm looking for a real relationship, a whole relationship. Not something I have to hide. The sneaking around might have been fun at first, but at some point you need to stop. You have to see if the relationship can exist in the real world. And I don't think that ours can. I don't think you even want a real relationship."

"I want a relationship," I say. I can feel tears forming in the corners of my eyes, but I take a deep breath to force them to subside. "I do."

"I think we want different things."

"I want to be with you," I plead. "Don't you want to be with me?"

"No, Jo," Max says. "Not anymore. Not like this."

40
You've Lost That Lovin' Feeling

"Say that again?" I ask my mother.

"I was saying Dominick's at seven," my mother says. "Too early for you? Can you make a six P.M. train?"

"No, not that part," I say carefully. "The part about Barbie not coming because Andrew called off the wedding." Surely my mother knows that's the part that bears repeating.

"Oh yes, that," my mother says, as if she's casually mentioning something inconsequential, like how she broke a nail. "Barbie's not coming. Andrew called off the wedding."

I don't respond for a second. "*And?*"

"And what?" my mother says. There's a slight edge to her voice, a tiny annoyance. As if she's getting bothered by having to relay this information over and over again. How many people has she told already before she thought to mention this to me? "It's off. Over. And your dad is going to fire her this week."

"What happened?" I ask. "What did she do?"

"Nothing in particular, dear," my mother says. "Sometimes these things just don't work out."

"Don't work out?" I ask, laughing even though I think this conversation is the complete opposite of funny. "Sometimes these things just don't work out" applies to trivial things, like when my mother tries to get a last-minute appointment at the hair salon but they're already booked. "Sometimes these things just don't work out" does not apply to the planning of a wedding. Even I know that. "The invitations are supposed to go out next month."

"Well," my mother explains, "now they're not going to."

"Yes," I say. "I figured that part out."

"Did we decide on seven P.M.?" she asks, casually, as if this were the end of the conversation. "I can pick you up at the train at a quarter to."

"I get it," I say. "You're happy. Barbie's mom left you out of the wedding planning, so now you think this whole mess is funny."

"I think nothing of the sort," she says. "My son is in pain, and that's not funny. Not funny at all."

"But you're not going to tell me what happened," I say.

"Nothing happened," she says, exasperated. "Nothing that I know of, anyway. I never really thought Barbie was right for your brother. I guess he finally realized it, too."

"Shouldn't he at least give her another chance?" I ask, desperation creeping into my voice. Whatever happened to giving second chances?

"Sometimes when it's over," my mother says, "it's just over. No sense in going back to try to save something that's not worth saving."

"Oh," I say. I can't process a thought—can't think of much else to say. All I can think is that Max is probably thinking the same thing: Sometimes when it's over, it's just over. That we are not worth saving.

"Sometimes it's just best to move on," my mother says. "Don't you think?"

"I suppose so," I say, and she confirms the timing of the trains for the evening. But I can't shake the feeling that we were having two different conversations. She was telling me that Andrew has moved on from Barbie, and that I should just move on from my band, and from the Web site.

I was talking about Max.

But maybe my mother is right. Moving on is good, it's healthy. Fresh starts and all that.

And I do want to move on. From the band, from Jesse, even from the Web site. But here's the thing: I don't want to move on from Max.

41
The One I Love

BLOG POST FROM JOWALDMAN ON LONELY HEARTS CLUB WEB SITE:

Dear Max,

I'm sorry. I'm so, so sorry. Can't you see that? If you would just answer my calls, I could explain it all to you. This is where everything began, and I'm hoping that it's here we can resolve things.

I know I let you down, but I won't do that again. I want you back. I want what we had back. I love you, and I know you love me, too. Can we try again?

Love,

Jo

BLOG COMMENT FROM STANTHEMAN:

I'm looking for someone, too. Someone I lost. John, if you're out there reading this, I'm sorry. I'm really sorry. Give me another chance?

BLOG COMMENT FROM BLUEBIRD97:

Met a girl on the Lower East Side last night. You said you loved the Sex Pistols. I said I did, too. You were wearing a gray motorcycle jacket and jeans. I was wearing a camo jacket. If you're reading this, meet me tonight at The Bitter End at 10.

TWEET FROM @ALECSAX:

Looking for a lost love? Trying to reconcile with someone you wish were still in your life? Check out the #LonelyHeartsClub

42
Personal Jesus

When I wake up at 8 A.M., Chloe's already left the apartment again in a mad rush. As much as I apologize, Chloe's still angry, still avoiding me as much as she can.

It's time for me to get off her couch. I open my laptop and start searching for apartments before I even make a cup of coffee. Things move fast in New York—I could be out of Chloe's hair by next week. And then we can work on getting our friendship back to where it was before. I know she's angry, but there's something about the friends who have known you since you were five years old. You don't let friends like that go.

Everything's out of my price range. To put it more accurately, I don't really have a price range, since I have no money coming in. The money from the ads stopped the week after the Lonely Hearts Club Ball.

What's a musician in need of money to do? I know what Max would say to that—sell a song. I then run the whole dialogue in my head:

But I don't want to sell out.

It's not selling out.

It is the definition of selling out—selling one of my songs to an artist who's going to tear it apart. Who's going to ruin it.

She might not ruin it.

She will.

You'll be a homeless musician who doesn't sell out. Sell the song.

I don't want to be homeless, but I also don't want my relationship with Chloe to disintegrate any further than it has because I can't leave her couch. I pick up my cell phone and make the call, prepared to be shot down the way Love, Inc.'s parent company did to me about the Web site sale, but to my surprise, Amber Fairchild wants to meet.

"I DIDN'T think you would want to meet with me," I say to Amber. We're at her midtown duplex apartment, on the roof. A person I can only assume to be her assistant is serving us iced green tea with slices of lemon.

"Of course I wanted to meet with you," Amber says. I can never get over the way she speaks. As if she's auditioning for a current adaptation of *Little House on the Prairie*. All wide eyes and big teeth. "I'm a devout Christian."

"Oh," I say. "I'm not Christian."

"I know that, silly," she says, smiling her big-toothed smile. "I meant that I forgive. I'm very forgiving. I forgive you." She says that last bit with prayer hands, like she's about to bow down to me or something.

Green tea almost comes out of my nose. I don't know why I find her earnestness so completely funny. Probably because I know it's all an act. Ten bucks says she'll be cursing and gossiping inside of an hour. Not knowing what else to do, I give the prayer hands back to her, and nod my head down.

"I know that you're not a liar, Jo," she says. "And I forgive you for letting everyone think you hated love when you don't really hate love. You love love, don't you?"

"Do you have any vodka?" I ask. "It might make this green tea a little more palatable."

"Heavens, no," she says. "I don't drink."

"Of course you don't," I mutter under my breath.

"You never asked me my username."

"What?" I ask. I take a sip of my iced green tea and a lemon pit gets wedged in the straw.

"My username," she says again. "On your site. Or do you know all of them already? Do you track those?"

"I definitely do not track them."

"I'm Allsnotfairinloveandmusic," she says. And then she dramatically pauses. Now, I know this is the part where I'm supposed to gasp or faint, or otherwise express extreme shock, but the truth is, at its peak the site had over a million users. I really can't remember any one in particular.

I nod my head in a way that I hope seems knowing.

"I used to write about my husband," she says, *sotto voce*. I still don't know what she's talking about. I wish I had Chloe here with me—she knew so many of the site's users. She'd be able to tell me who Amber was and I could save myself this awkwardness.

"Writing about your husband isn't off limits," I say. "Actually, I started the whole site after a brutal breakup with my ex, Jesse."

"You were married?" she asks.

"No, we just lived together," I say, and then instantly regret saying it. Amber puts her head down and makes those stupid prayer hands again. I guess I shouldn't have mentioned the whole living-in-sin thing?

"Well, I was married," she says when she finally comes up for air.

"That's okay," I say. "That's my point. A lot of people wrote about their spouses. You're not alone in that."

"Well, the problem is," Amber explains, "I don't believe in divorce."

"Does your husband believe in it?" I joke. Amber stays straight-faced. I'm not sure if she doesn't get the joke or if I've inadvertently offended her. Probably not a good way to start a working relationship. "Sorry," I say. "Should we get to the songs?"

"My husband usually chooses my music for me," Amber says quietly. She looks down into her green tea.

"No problem," I say. "Are we waiting for him to get started?"

"He's not home," Amber says. She can't bring her eyes up to meet mine. I don't know much about business negotiations, but I'm thinking that this is not a good sign.

"Oh. Do you want me to come back later? I'm really looking forward to working with you. I can work on whatever time frame is good for you," I say, but in truth, I was hoping to sell at least one song today. I really need the money that Alan had offered me when we first met. I've got my first appointment to look at apartments tomorrow. To sign a lease, I'll need to have first and last month's rent, along with enough for a security deposit. "I know you're going to love what I've picked out. I've got that first song, "When Will Tomorrow Be," that I know you guys really responded to."

I reach down to pick up my guitar—I remember from my supergood days how much better hearing a song played on guitar in the meeting can sell a concept—and when I look up, Amber's crying.

"When I say he's not home, I mean he hasn't been home for two weeks," she says, crying. "No one's seen him, no one's heard from him."

"What do you mean?"

"I mean he's nowhere to be found," Amber cries. "He's gone."

"Does he do that a lot?" I ask.

"Yes," Amber confesses. It's like a tiny whisper that escapes from her lips. From the way she says it, I get the sense that it's the first time she's admitted this out loud. That I'm the first person outside of her camp she's told. "Unfortunately, he does. This time is a little different, though."

"How so?"

"I'm having a slight problem with some of my accounts," Amber says, and then starts crying hysterically again.

"He took your money?" I ask, incredulous. I know I thought it was funny when Amber got stuck with a lip-synching scandal, but this is something entirely different. This is a federal crime.

"All of it," Amber says. "Gone."

"All of it?" I parrot back and Amber nods her head yes.

I don't quite know what to do—part of me thinks I should reach over and give her a hug, but I barely know her. Would a hug from someone you barely know be comforting? I end up putting my hand on top of hers, and she looks up at me and smiles.

"What are you going to do?" I ask. "How are you going to pay for all this?" I look around the rooftop and can't even calculate how much an apartment like this must cost. I can barely afford the rent on a ground-level studio apartment. This gorgeous house in the sky must cost a complete fortune. Not to mention the staff she employs. Payroll alone must run in the five figures.

"My accountant just sold off one of my properties," she says. "So that can hold me over for a while."

"That was smart," I say.

"Alan was the one who encouraged me to invest in real estate," Amber says, and the waterworks start over again.

"That piece of shit," I say, taking a swig of green tea for good measure. Not exactly the same as downing a shot, but I think it has the intended effect.

"Oh, I wish you wouldn't use a cuss word," she says. "He *is* still my husband. We are still bound by God and the law."

"The law?" I say, thinking aloud. "You should have him pronounced dead!"

"Dead?"

"After all, no one's heard from him, right?" I say. "And maybe he really *is* dead! Then maybe you could get your money back."

"I don't want him dead," Amber says. "I don't want anyone dead. Just like I'm sure that you don't want Jesse dead, Jo. You're just cross with him."

"No, I want him dead," I say.

"The Bible tells us..." Amber begins.

As Amber gives me my Bible lesson for the day, I think about what she's said. How could she *not* want him dead? I want the dry cleaners dead when they deliver my clothing a day later than promised. Maybe I could learn a thing or two from Amber. Maybe I could learn to live without the anger. Without the rage.

"Can I confess something to you?" I say.

"Sure."

"I thought it was really funny when you got caught lip-synching," I say. "I really did. But now I feel bad about that. And I'm sorry. I'm really excited to help you get back into the swing of things."

"I thought it was funny, too," she says. "And frankly, I never could understand why they always made me lip-synch at those things. I can sing and dance at the same time, thank you very much."

I can't help but laugh. "I'm sure you can."

"But I'm sure you remember that from *American Star*," she

says, smiling at me. I can't help but smile back. So *the* Amber Fairchild remembered little old me all along. And look at us now.

She sings a few bars of her breakout hit— "I Want You to Keep Me Up All Night (All Right)"—but she does it with just a few chords on the guitar, and plays it slowly, not with the frenetic beat it was recorded with as a pop single.

It's another song entirely.

When I can focus on Amber's voice, and not all of the Auto-Tune electronic sounds, the song takes on another meaning. I can focus on the words, and how beautifully Amber can actually sing, and I love it. I really love it. It's a song about longing, about wanting to be with someone every moment of the day. About how you can never get enough of that person. I connect to it completely—it's how I feel about Max.

"I wrote it about Alan," she says. "When we first met. You know that feeling when you first meet someone wonderful?"

"Yeah," I say. "I do."

I wonder why I don't write songs like that. My songs are usually borne out of anger or rage. About the end of things. Why didn't I ever think to write from a place like that? To write about the beginning? To write about love?

"Do you think maybe we could write a song together?" Amber asks.

"I think that would be great," I say. And I actually mean it.

43
Modern Romance

BLOG COMMENT FROM ROCKBOY1983:
To BrokenHeartontheLES:
I'm so sorry. I know you were waiting for me. I know I was supposed to show. Things have changed, and I couldn't be there. I promise, I'll explain it to you one day. All I can say is sorry. Give me another shot when the timing is right?

BLOG COMMENT FROM VERMONTISFORLOVERS:
You, rushing for the L Train. Me, trying to hold the door open for you, but getting crushed by the doors. I saw you smile at me. We had a moment there, didn't we?

RESPONSE FROM PUNKROCKPRINCESS:
We did. Meet me at the Yellowcard show at Irving Plaza tonight. I'll be waiting outside for you at 8.

44

I Wanna Be Sedated

"Don't forget to breathe," he says to me, pushing down on my back. I know that he thinks he's giving me the "subtle pressure" he warned us about at the beginning of class, but actually, it just feels like torture. "Really breathe your way into this pose, Jo."

Amber told me that whenever she's feeling stressed, she does some yoga. It's done miracles for her moods, she claimed, and has made her more centered and happy all around. I probably should have thought to ask how long, exactly, it would take for me to start feeling more centered, less angry, before I signed up for this class. Because having this ponytailed yogi push down on my back to get me into a most unnatural position is totally pissing me off. So far, we're only fifteen minutes into the class, and already it's had the opposite effect of what was intended.

"I *am* breathing," I say through gritted teeth, as he continues to push.

After what seems like hours, he moves on to his next unsuspecting victim and tells her to breathe. Only she doesn't seem to mind it. In fact, she very much seems to enjoy it.

"Is this right?" she asks him, batting her eyelashes.

"That's just great, Amy," he says, smiling at her. "You're doing great."

"I've really been working on opening up my hips," she says. And then she splays open her legs to show him how loose, in fact, her hips have become.

I'm beginning to think there's an entire subtext to yoga that I'm not privy to.

I look away from the heavy flirting and try to follow Amber's advice—clear my mind and focus on my breath. I listen to the yogi's instructions and try to block out everything else. All the things that are bothering me. All the things that I messed up. All the things I can no longer fix.

The instructor guides us into dead man's pose, which I decide is my favorite yoga pose to do. It basically entails lying flat on your back, with no movement. No engaging your quads, no balancing on your hands, no reaching for the ceiling. You can just lay there. Be still. Be quiet. Be.

As I lie on the ground and listen to the yogi's words, I can actually focus on my breath. I finally get what he's been saying this whole class. I feel my body melting into the ground as I listen to him talk about becoming one with the earth, connecting with it. I feel myself breathing in and out, and I only focus on his words. I don't let any outside noise come in—the constant soundtrack of doubts and regrets flowing through my thoughts—I only listen to what he's saying. For the first time I can remember, I clear my mind.

He then moves us into the sun salutations, and while I'm disappointed that I can't just lay there for the rest of class, I feel more motivated to get into the poses, breathe my way into them. This time, when he comes over to give my back some pressure to guide me farther into my downward dog, I don't get angry, I don't get annoyed.

I go with it.

AFTER CLASS, I feel energized and happy. Calmer than I've felt in a very long time. I immediately text Amber: *Did my first yoga class! Thx for suggesting - loved it.*

She quickly texts back: *Let's go together next time!*

I make my way out of the yoga studio, and the girl who was on the mat next to mine calls out to me.

"I really loved your site," she says. "You're Jo Waldman, right?"

"Yes," I say, and extend my hand. "Nice to meet you."

"I didn't get to go to the Lonely Hearts Club Ball, but I wanted to. Despite everything that happened, I heard it was a really good time."

"Thanks for that," I say.

"I should be thanking you," she says, looking down at her shoes. When she looks back up, she says, "I met my boyfriend on your blog."

"Cool," I say. "That's nice to hear."

"Thank you," she says. "I really wanted to say that to you."

"You're welcome," I say.

"Maybe I'll see you again here next week?" she asks. "Jeremiah is totally the best instructor I've ever had."

I'm surprised when I hear myself say back to her, "Yeah, I think I will."

45
Dancing with Myself

"Table for one."

The hostess looks around the restaurant—it's pretty crowded, especially for a weeknight—and walks me over to a small table by the back. It dawns on me that I've never actually eaten here before, I've only ordered take out. But that doesn't stop it from being my comfort food. It's why I traveled twenty blocks for a Caesar salad and plate of chicken parmesan.

Manager Greg spots me and walks over to my table.

"Is it you?" he asks. I smile back at him. I was hoping to sneak in and eat undetected, but if that was my plan, I probably should have chosen somewhere different to eat. Not the place where the whole Lonely Hearts Club thing started in the first place.

"It's me," I say quietly as Manager Greg sits down next to me. "You probably want me to pay that tab from last year, huh?"

"Hey, everyone!" he yells, popping up from his chair. "Jo Waldman is here!" he announces to the dining room. He throws his arms out and expects a round of applause or something, but no one reacts. No one cares. No one even looks up from their rigatoni à la vodka.

"I don't think I'm quite as popular as I used to be," I explain to Greg.

"Are you all by yourself?" he asks. He sits back down next to me at the table. The way he's sitting, next to me instead of across the table, reminds me of Max. He always used to sit next to me when we went out to eat. He said he liked to be close to me, so he could put his arm around me whenever he wanted.

"Yup," I say. "Just me tonight. I really needed some comfort food."

"Get Jo her regular," Manager Greg says to a passing waiter. "Caesar salad, chicken parm."

"Thanks," I say.

"Of course," Manager Greg says. And then he leans in a bit. "I can't let a local celebrity eat alone."

"I'm okay, really," I explain. "I was actually hoping to be alone."

"I was actually hoping to have dinner with you," Manager Greg says, his cheeks turning a slight shade of red as he says it. He nervously laughs and then looks at me for a response. "Consider it an apology for what happened last year with the inflated Valentine's Day bill."

I do not want to have dinner with Manager Greg. Even now, as I see how handsome he is close up—is he an actor? A model?—it doesn't feel right. How can you start something up with someone else when your heart is broken? When you're still aching for someone else?

But that's how things started with Max, didn't they? I was fresh off a breakup with Jesse, just a few weeks shy of sharing my life with him, when I met Max. I wasn't looking to meet anyone new, but the second he walked into my apartment, there was something about him. I immediately knew there was something special. Something I wanted to know more about. After all, that's why I kept calling him about the site, isn't it? It wasn't because I was so dedicated to the Lonely Hearts Club movement—it was him.

And now I'm alone. But this time it feels different. I don't want to replace Max with someone else. I don't want to rage. I don't want to yell from the rooftops. I just want Max back.

And I really want to eat my Caesar salad and chicken parm in peace.

"I just got my heart broken," I explain to Greg. "Now's not really the best time for me to be dating."

"Does this mean the start of a new Web site?" he asks, the edges of his mouth turning up just the slightest bit.

"No," I say. "This time, I'm going to go about things differently."

46
I Still Haven't Found What I'm Looking For

Armed with the requisite scandal, my mother has found herself with a new show on the design network. Seems after the HGTV special, she and David Bromstad got to talking. She showed him around my dad's office, their house, the spaces she had personally designed herself without any formal training, and he went back to the HGTV bigwigs with a show idea.

The concept of the show is this: My mother gets hired to plan parties with elaborate themes—every week, it's a different theme—and she plans them on a grand scale. Casino night, Las Vegas, Mardi Gras...you get the idea. This week, it's the Wild Wild West. She has on an adorable dress that's made out of bandanas and a pair of red cowboy boots. They've even done up her hair in low pigtails.

She is similarly attired this evening, for the viewing party in honor of the airing of her first show. The invitations looked like a wanted poster, with a picture of her on it. (With her impeccable hair and makeup, she didn't really look like an outlaw, but the invites were adorable nonetheless.) She's decorated the entire house in what she calls "cowboy chic." Elegant red- and white-checked tablecloths over the dining room table, a chandelier made entirely out of antlers, and even an enormous (seriously, it's huge) bison's head hung over the fireplace.

"Congratulations!" I say to my mother. "I'm so happy for you."

"You're not dressed in theme," my mother says, pouting.

"I didn't realize we were all dressing up as cowboys," I say.

"I'm a cow*girl*," my mother corrects. "And it was right there on the invitation. It said: Dress up!"

"I am dressed up."

"You're wearing the same jeans and old T-shirt you wear every day."

"This is my dressy T-shirt."

My mother shakes her head, as if to get the thought that these are my dressy clothes out of her mind. "'Dress up' meant to dress up for the theme."

I pick up a cowboy hat that's hanging on the wall (design tip from Nan: arrange trays or photographs—or even hats!—on the wall in groups of six—makes it a collection!) and perch it onto my head. "Better?" I ask.

"You're destroying my décor," my mother says, taking the hat and placing it back on the wall. "I'll find a bandana for you to put on."

I sit down on the couch next to my dad and he smiles at me.

"Is it just me," I say, pointing to the bison's head, "or does that thing's eyes follow you wherever you go?"

"It's not just you," my father allows.

"I can't believe you let her hang that up."

"Sometimes you do crazy things for the people you love," he

says, looking over at my mom. And then, when he looks back at me: "I'm happy to have the old Jo back."

"This is the old me?"

"I'm thrilled that you're not channeling all of your energy into something so negative," he says. "I didn't think it was good for you."

"Is that why you were posting messages about it, Mr. pianosoundslikeacarnival?"

"You knew that was me?" my dad asks, incredulous.

"Of course I knew it was you," I say. "You didn't exactly try to hide it."

"Were you tracking the usernames?"

"I haven't the first clue how to track a username," I say. "Why is everyone asking me that?"

"So then how did you figure out who I was?"

"You took a lyric from the song 'Piano Man,'" I say. "You've been playing that Billy Joel song for me since before I could talk. It wasn't too hard to figure out."

"Well, I'm sorry," my dad says. "But someone had to talk about how you were channeling your energy into all that rage. All that anger. It wasn't healthy. It wasn't good for you. I know you're upset, Jo, but I'm happy that the Web site is over. Nothing good could come out of something so negative."

"But it helped me find Max."

"Maybe it wasn't the right time for you and Max," he says. "Because of the negativity, the hiding. If he's the right one for you, it'll work out. Those things always do."

"He's not speaking to me, Dad."

"You'd be surprised what a little time can do," he says.

"Does that mean that time's made you realize you should give me the loft as a gift after all?"

He laughs. "No. But now that you and your brother are single, maybe you could spend some more time together. Maybe even rent an apartment together."

Exactly what I was looking for—more time with my brother, Andrew. Sure, I'm glad that Barbie's out of our lives (and my dad's office), but I'm not exactly looking to spend more time alone with Andrew. And anyway, what are we going to do? Paint each other's nails? Go out on the town together? Double date? Though I would like to know why he and Barbie abruptly broke off the engagement without even the tiniest of explanations.

"Can I at least come back to work for you?" I ask. "With Barbie gone, you must need a few extra hands. And I could use the cash."

"No, Pumpkin, I want you to break out on your own. Make your own success. You still think you can conquer the world, don't you?"

"Yes, Dad," I dutifully reply. "I do."

"Atta' girl."

ONCE MY mother's show is over and the champagne is all gone, I make my way back into the city. Andrew offers to drive me in, but I take the train. I hit the C Note around midnight, ready to see one of the bands Chloe and I used to follow around the city. They sent out a text blast at ten, announcing the surprise show.

Chloe's sitting at our old table.

"Fancy seeing you here," I say. I don't sit down. I'm pretty sure Chloe doesn't want me to.

"Have a seat," she says, and motions for a server to come over and take my drink order.

"I don't want to cramp your style," I say, still standing. "I just wanted to say hello."

"Don't be an ass," she says. "Sit."

"I got the feeling you were avoiding me."

"I *am* avoiding you," she says. "I'm so mad at you. You hurt me so badly."

"I know, Chlo," I say. "I'm sorry."

"Sorry?" she practically spits. "You hid something from me for months. Months! And when I did try to call you out on it, you lied. Right to my face. We've never lied to each other before."

"I know," I say. "I'm sorry."

"I wouldn't have judged you," she says. "I don't judge you."

"I don't judge you, either."

Chloe responds with a look. And then: "My flavors of the week? That's not judgmental?"

"That's just the truth," I say, laughing. Chloe does not laugh back. "I'm sorry. I'm sorry. You're totally right. I'm totally wrong. Will you accept my apology?"

"I'm so mad," Chloe says. "So, so mad."

"Maybe you should write a blog about how mad you are," I say. "I hear there's a real market for that sort of thing."

Chloe can't help but laugh. She mutters something to the effect of "I should write a blog about you," but the club's getting a bit louder since the band's about to come onstage.

"What can I say?" I ask. "I'm so sorry. Do you think you could ever forgive me?"

"Sure," Chloe says. "Forgiven. But I think the real question is: How can I ever trust you again?"

"I promise, Chlo," I say. "I will gain your trust back. Just give me a chance."

Chloe leans over and hugs me. I hug her back tightly. I don't let go until she breaks away from my grasp.

"Enough," Chloe says. "I get it. You're sorry. Okay, enough of the pity party. You're never going to guess who's coming here tonight."

Max, I think. *Max, Max, Max.*

"Who?" I ask. Already, the edges of my mouth are turning up. I feel my pulse race, my entire body heat up—I can barely stay in my seat. He's here. It's happening. I'm going to get him back.

"Rockboy1983," Chloe says, and I try to hide my disappointment. But Chloe knows. Chloe always knows. "Who did you think it would— Oh, Jo."

"No! No one! In fact, that's exactly what I thought." I say. "I'm so excited you're finally meeting your rocker boy."

"He's not a rocker boy," Chloe says. "Turns out, he's a rock climber."

"He climbs rocks?" I ask. "I never understood how that was an actual sport. Football, basketball, these are sports I can understand. But climbing rocks? Why would anyone want to do that?"

But then I remember someone who *does* like to do that. Someone I know very well. And then I remember who Rockboy1983 is: engaged to a woman only because she recently announced she was pregnant.

"So," I say, "if you're meeting him, I guess this means that he broke off his engagement?"

"Yeah," Chloe says. "It's actually pretty awful. She found out she wasn't really pregnant a full three months before she told him about it. That was the first time we were supposed to meet. But then she begged him for another chance, so he gave it to her since they were already engaged and everything. I guess he felt bad, since her mother had already booked a venue for the wedding, already put a deposit down on a wedding gown."

"What happened?"

"He could never forgive her for lying," she said. "He never

got over the fact that she lied and didn't come clean for so long. I mean, can you blame the guy?"

"No," I say. "I can't." And I can't help but think of Max. Will he ever forgive me for all the lies I've told? The way I hid our relationship from my friends? From my family?

"This isn't the same as you and Max," Chloe says, reading my mind.

"Isn't it?"

"No," she says. "He knew what was happening all along. He helped you build the Web site, for God's sake! And the night of that first interview, he was the one who went along with the ruse that you two weren't together. He was complicit in the whole thing. I think he just needs a little time to realize that this whole thing isn't as bad as it seems."

"Do you really think so?" I ask, but Chloe's already glancing toward the front of the bar. I turn around to look at what she's seeing.

"What is your brother doing here?" she asks, but I already know. It takes Chloe a second to get there. Rockboy1983—the guy who got engaged to a girl only because she thought she was pregnant—is my brother. And that's why he got engaged to, and then broke it off with, Barbie. Not only was she not pregnant, but she actually let Andrew believe that she still was pregnant for three whole months while she planned her dream wedding.

"Chloe?" my brother asks as he approaches our table.

"Andrew?"

"Why are you wearing a Runaways T-shirt?" he asks.

"The same reason you're wearing one," Chloe says. "You're Rockboy1983."

"And you're BrokenHeartontheLES," Andrew says.

I excuse myself as they sort things out. I find a tiny corner by the front door and dial a familiar number on my cell.

"Max," I say to his voice mail. "I'm sorry. I messed up. I took you for granted—I took us for granted, and I never should have done that. If you give us another chance, I promise things will be different. I'll appreciate what we have the next time around. Let's just try this again, okay?"

The band comes on to play, so I walk back to Chloe's table to see how she and Andrew are doing—I'm ready to deflect the situation if things have gotten beyond awkward. But when I get there, I see that I'm not needed. They're up from their seats and on the dance floor. Dancing very, very close. A little too close for my eyes to take right now, but I'm sure I'll adjust to my best friend and my brother hanging out, right?

Right?

I immediately head to the bar to start drinking shots.

47
Only the Lonely

BLOG COMMENT FROM **TEDTHEARCHITECT:**
We met at Rodeo Bar and you gave me your number. But then my jacket got stolen at a downtown after-hours club. You said your favorite movie was *Say Anything* and I told you that you weren't old enough to have seen that movie. Meet me at the Rodeo Bar this Thursday at 8?

BLOG COMMENT FROM DARKNIGHTRISES:
Give me another chance, Angie, and I promise I'll do better. I'll put you first. There won't be any excuses. I know you still love me.

FACEBOOK COMMENT FROM REDYELLOWANDBLUE:
Is there anyone out there who still believes in love at first sight? Anyone secretly wish Jo was planning another party?

48
Runnin' Around

"Don't I know you from somewhere?" the real estate broker asks me.

"Probably," I say. He's showing me a studio apartment in a prewar building down in the 20s. It's the third place we've seen today. The other two weren't right—one was in a brand-new glassy building, and it was so sterile I could practically feel the white walls closing in on me. And the other was on the Upper East Side—a tiny ground-floor studio in a brownstone that would have been perfect, but for the fact I'm not ready to move so far uptown just yet. I may be turning into a responsible adult who pays rent on her own apartment, but I'm still taking baby steps. Moving to a neighborhood where everyone's got a job, a husband, and a baby is just way too fast for me. So he took me to the 20s. Not quite Gramercy, not quite Chelsea, but somewhere between the two, it's in my price range because it doesn't have a fancy address. Or even a name for the neighborhood. (I'm sure at some point, it will be christened Chelmercy and the rents will go through the roof, but for now, I can afford it.)

I kind of love the apartment, but I don't want him to know that. I've never had to negotiate something like this before, but I'd imagine gushing about how much you love the place as soon as you walk in wouldn't do much for your bargaining power.

I asked my father to come with me to help haggle today, but he turned me down. Another speech about how he'd coddled me for too long, and it's time I do things like this on my own. I was pretty proud of myself that I didn't then ask my mother, who can never say no to me. (And is also a very good negotiator.)

"You're that Lonely Hearts girl," he says. "I saw you on the news!"

"Yeah," I say. "Do you think they can do any better on the rent? My Web site kind of died and I'm pretty tight with funds."

"No," he says. "Rent is firm. Need me to show you something else? Something more in your price range?"

This is not how it happens in the movies. Isn't there supposed to be some sort of back and forth here? Shouldn't I be using my charm and moxie to get what I want? But then I think about how I negotiated all of the ads for the Lonely Hearts Club Web site. I didn't hesitate—I just told the advertisers what I wanted, and they all fell in line. I can do this.

"Listen," I say. "I like it, but you're going to have to cut the rent by about a third. And I'll give you the first and last month's as security, but I want two months free rent. I know that's the going rate in the market now."

For the record, I do not know what the going rate in the market is right now.

"You can have a quarter off," the broker says. "No one's doing a third. And I'll give you the first month for free. But that's the final offer."

"I'll take it," I say.

"Congratulations," he says. "You're going to love it here."

"Thanks," I say. "I really think I am."

49
Waiting on a Friend

"Keep it, sell it," Amber says. "Sell it. Sell it. Let's wait a bit for that one."

I'm at Amber's place—we're supposed to be writing songs, but her assistant had an idea about how to raise some short-term cash for Amber: sell off more of her stuff. So far, she's agreed to sell two of her cars, her beachfront property in Miami, and most of her jewelry. Money's been trickling in from the sales, so she's been able to keep her place in Manhattan so far.

"I may be moving in with you soon if some more money doesn't come in," she jokes. "How big is that studio, anyway?"

"Four hundred square feet," I say.

"Well, that's plenty," Amber says. "Before I move in, I'll probably have to sell my shoe collection, anyway."

"The pocketbooks would never fit," I say, remembering the tour of the apartment I got last time I was here.

"Good point," she says. "We'll just have to write a song today that sells millions."

"That sounds like an excellent plan," I say.

"I had an idea about recording 'When Will Tomorrow Be.'"

"What's that?" I ask.

"My sound engineer wasn't too happy about it," she says. "So maybe it wouldn't work, after all."

"Don't keep me in suspense," I say. "Spill."

"I was thinking of going back to my roots, of doing an acoustic version," she says. "Like the way you originally sang it."

"That sounds great," I say. "Obviously, I arranged it that way, so I think that's what works best for the song. What was the problem?"

"My sound engineer doesn't want me to do it that way," she says. "He thinks we shouldn't mess with what's been working for me."

"Then maybe you need a new sound engineer," I say. "I have a great one I've worked with."

"Do you think it's a good idea to mess with what's been working for me?" she asks. "Part of me wants to do something new, now that I don't have to do what Alan always wants me to do, but part of me thinks that's crazy. Why mess with a good formula?"

I'm not sure how to respond. What I wanted to say—what was on the tip of my tongue—was this: Because it's a formula. Because it's disposable pop. It has no heft, no meaning. It's nothing. And you're better than that. You've let them convince you that all you are is a mess of big blonde hair and some hip gyrations, but you're more than that. You can sing. You can play. You can write. You're better than what they've made you.

But instead, I ask, "What's your gut telling you?"

"That this apartment ain't cheap," she says and laughs.

"What if you downsize?" I say.

"It's not just me," she says. "I support my whole family back home. Extended family, too, all the way out to cousins thrice removed. Without me, they'd have nothing. They can barely make ends meet even with my financial support."

"Then you stick with what's working," I say.

"But that's the thing," Amber says. "I don't want to anymore. I want to do something different."

"I have an idea," I say. "Why don't you do both? Let's record both—our version with my sound engineer and their version with your sound engineer. We let the one you like better drop first, and if it doesn't catch on, we have the other one to fall back on."

"That's not a bad idea," Amber says. "Sort of like insurance."

"Exactly," I say.

"Thanks, Jo," Amber says. "I really appreciate the help."

"No problem," I say. "Now, should we get to writing your next big hit?"

"Definitely," she says.

So we do.

50
Sympathy for the Devil

"When it's true love, you just know," Jesse says. And there it is. True love. "Yeah, man, you just know."

I can't believe what I'm hearing, but there's Jesse, live on MTV, telling a seventeen-year-old VJ that he has found true love. He proceeds to tell the VJ, a pretentious poser loser wearing an oxford shirt with a collared polo shirt over it, how he met Cassie, his true love, because he was arranging for me to sing onstage with her band.

"Your ex, huh?" the VJ says, making a self-conscious grimace before continuing: "Does she sing as well as Cassie?"

The crowd erupts into a round of ohs and ahs—*MTV poser loser VJ, you're so bad*. He makes another grimace that is even more self-aware than the first and thrusts the mike into Jesse's face.

"No one can sing as well as Cassie, man," he says sheepishly.

Bullshit, I think as I turn the television off. *I can sing better than Cassie.*

I call the studio and book the next slot of time they've got free—Saturday morning. Then I call Amber and Chloe to see if they can meet me there. Having my newest friend and my oldest friend in the world there will give me some perspective. And hopefully motivate me to not waste another expensive session in the recording studio. Though I do have a bit of a nest egg going after selling "When Will Tomorrow Be" to Amber. She's already recorded it, and it drops in four days. Which is perfect timing, since it turns out the only thing more expensive than renting an apartment in Manhattan is furnishing an apartment in Manhattan. I'll be needing that first royalty check when it comes.

The buzzer rings and I've forgotten that my parents were coming in to the city for lunch. I buzz them up and then set about straightening up the apartment. The nice thing about living in a tiny studio is that it doesn't take very long to clean up. I can practically make the bed, wipe down the kitchen counter, and tidy the bathroom all at the same time.

My mother walks in and starts telling my father where to put stuff. She has a bunch of my old vinyl records and a roll of double-sided tape. Before I have a chance to tell her that most of those records are collectors' items, she's creating a little vignette of vinyl on the wall. And I have to admit, it looks pretty kick-ass.

"Your music," my father says. "Right there on the wall. Pretty clever, huh?"

"Yup," I say.

"I thought you'd be more excited about it?"

"I'm having a little love-hate thing with my music right now," I say. "It has nothing to do with the records. Though some of those were collectors' items, you know."

"I know," my father says. "I thought the same thing, too, at first. But you wouldn't want albums that weren't great on the walls, would you?"

"Good point."

"What's the love-hate?"

"I'm afraid I've become the sort of person I hate most," I say.

"Do I even want to know?" my father asks.

"A person who would sell out her music," I explain. "Don't get me wrong—you're right. It feels good to do things on my own, to make my own money, make my own decisions. But I guess I'm just questioning how I got here. I'm not sure I feel good about selling that song to Amber."

"Was that the first song you ever wrote?" my father asks.

"No," I say. "Of course it wasn't. You know that."

"And will it be your last?"

"No," I say. "It won't."

"Then I don't see what the problem is," he says. "And I don't see why selling a song makes you a sellout. It wasn't the first song you ever wrote, and it won't be the last. Anyway, the song was about Jesse, a man who was a tiny blip on the radar of your life. Who really cares about it?"

"I guess," I say.

"And if selling that song enables you to do what you want to do—create more music—then it was the greatest thing in the world. Most people don't get to do that."

"You're right," I say. "I guess I just envisioned all of it going down so differently. I saw myself as a performer, not a person who writes things for other performers."

"And you still may be," he says. "Your path isn't yet written. You're still on it. But you made a really smart choice."

"What if the song becomes a runaway hit and it would have been *my* runaway hit? What if that was my chance and I sold it?" I ask.

"Even if it becomes the biggest hit in the world, there's no telling if it would have been the biggest hit in the world for you. But by selling it, you've guaranteed it was a success for you. It gave you the freedom to pursue your dream."

"Thanks, Dad," I say.

"I'm proud of you," he says. "I don't think that you're a sellout at all."

"Why isn't anyone asking me what I think?" my mother asks. She puts down her hot-glue gun and regards both my father and me.

"Mom," I ask, "do you think I'm a sellout because I sold that song to Amber?"

"No, honey," she says. "I think you're the most brilliant musician in the world. I beam proudly any time I watch you play. No matter who's in the lineup, you're always the best out of everyone. If it takes the world a little more time to figure that out, well, then you've made a really smart decision that ensures you can financially support yourself until it's time for you to enter the big time. Brilliant. You're just brilliant."

"Thanks, Mom," I say, and as much as I hate to admit it, I can feel myself blushing. She reaches out and gives me a big hug.

"My greatest hope for you," my father says, "is that you can finally be comfortable in your own skin."

"I'm trying to get there."

Tears well up in my eyes and I start to cry. Finally. And this time, I don't stop myself like I usually do. I don't think about how crying makes me weak. I don't think about how crying is manipulative. I don't think about it at all. I just let go. I let myself cry and I let my mom and my dad hug me tight. Because no matter who you are, sometimes you just need a hug from your parents.

AFTER THE tears, I feel so much better. It's like I can breathe again, only I didn't know I was holding my breath. I feel lighter, calmer, happier, like I don't have anything to cry about at all. I can't believe how cathartic that cry was. I don't know why I never allowed myself to do that. Why I thought it would be weak to give myself a little release every now and then.

My mother passes me a tissue and I blow my nose and wipe my eyes. I splash some water onto my face, and I realize that even a tough girl can cry. And what's more—I can already feel the lyrics to a new song forming in my head.

51
See You Again

BLOG COMMENT FROM SANTAFESUMMERS:
John, I know I messed up. I know it. I'm sorry.

BLOG COMMENT FROM ROYALTENNENBAUM:
We met on the line for Shake Shack. You were with a gaggle of girls. I was there with a gaggle of guys. But I saw you see me. Didn't you?

RESPONSE FROM GOODGOLLYMISSMOLLY:
Were you the one in the bright yellow sports jacket?

RESPONSE FROM ROYALTENNENBAUM:
Yes, and you were the one in the polka-dot dress. Meet me at Shake Shack again tonight?

RESPONSE FROM GOODGOLLYMISSMOLLY:
7 P.M.

52
We Gotta Get Out of This Place

"You didn't have to move out, you know," Chloe says, as she looks around my new digs. Since the whole place is sort of tiny, it doesn't take that long to give her the grand tour. You just sort of stand at the front door and point: bed, couch, kitchen, bathroom.

"Yes, I did," I say. "But thank you for letting me stay with you. Even after you came back from California. I appreciate it so much."

The truth is, I loved staying with Chloe. Even when she got back from California and things were cramped, to say the least, it was great having my best friend around. To get to know the minutia of her every day. Sure, we call, text, and e-mail all day long, but there's something about living with someone, sharing a space, that lets you get to know them even more intimately.

"You could have stayed," Chloe says.

"No, I needed to move out," I say. "It was time for me to stand on my own feet. My dad was right."

"Admitting your father was right?" Chloe asks. "It's like you're growing up right before my very eyes!"

"Oh, stop it," I say. But I secretly like being teased by Chloe. Having our relationship strained, even though only for a few weeks, was hard. I don't want that to ever happen again. Ever.

"I wasn't kicking you out," she says.

"You were just avoiding me," I say, with a sly little smile on my lips. It's okay to tease her back, isn't it? If I have to deal with watching her date my big brother, the least I can do is tease her mercilessly every now and then.

"But I didn't kick you out," she says. "I want that on the record."

"Noted," I say.

"Good," she says. "And you can come back anytime you want, you know. You can keep that set of keys. Just in case."

I had that set of keys before I moved in—it was the emergency set she kept at my place—but I don't say that. I get what she's trying to say to me. And it's good to have the option. Good to know Chloe's always got my back, no matter what.

"I don't want to be around when my brother comes over," I think but don't say. Or rather, don't mean to say but blurt out. I see the expression on Chloe's face, so I say more gently, "How are things going with you two?"

Chloe smiles uncontrollably, and I have my answer. I can see it on her face. She's happy. She's really happy with Andrew.

It's a look I've seen before—it's how she was with Billy. That relationship may have ended in tragedy, but falling in love is always a good thing. And Chloe is, without question, in love. I'm happy Chloe is able to fall in love again. I didn't know if she ever could. If she ever would.

"Things are okay, I guess," Chloe says, trying for nonchalant, but her bright eyes and smile betray her. "It's whatever, you know."

"Yeah, whatever," I say.

"These records are very cool," Chloe says, looking at the collection my mother created on the wall. "That was a great idea to hang them on the wall like this."

"It was my mother's idea," I say.

"I had a feeling," she says. "You're not the type to damage a record."

"They're more than just records," I say. "They're history."

Out of the corner of my eye, I see Chloe roll her eyes.

"What?" I say. "Music is important."

"It is," Chloe says. "That's why you should be making more of it."

53
Sing

"That sounded good, Jo," Amber says, and I see my engineer nod his head in agreement.

"Let's play it back!" Chloe says, and I can see the engineer fighting a frown. He does not want to play it back. Chloe has asked for a playback on just about every track I've recorded today. She's excited to be in the studio, but we've been here for three hours straight already, and it's definitely time for a break.

"I think maybe we'll record that one," I say to my engineer. And then to Chloe, "And we can give all the tracks a listen later over dinner."

"Speaking of food," the engineer says, "ready for a lunch break? We've got a great Thai place around the corner."

I smile in agreement, careful not to let my expression betray me, but I can't help feel a stab of sadness. Thai food reminds me of Max. I keep my vibe upbeat as we all place our orders, but all I can think about is Max. But then again, everything reminds me of Max. Having pepperoni pizza with red wine, going to a rooftop at a downtown club, hearing Daft Punk's new single on the radio.

"How can we turn that frown upside down?" Amber asks me, touching her index finger to my nose.

"I wasn't frowning."

"You were doing that thing with your face," Chloe chimes in.

"I don't do a thing with my face," I say.

"Are you unhappy with the tracks?" Amber asks. "We can do them over after lunch if you're not happy. I thought they were great, but if you're not feeling good about them, let's do them again."

"That's not what the face is," Chloe says. "I know that face."

"Can everyone please stop talking about my face?"

"You're still thinking about Max," Chloe says.

"No, I'm not," I say, but then I instantly wonder why I'm trying to hide my heartache from my friends. After I finally cried, I felt so much better. Maybe if I confess my feelings about Max, I'll feel better, too? "Okay, I *am* thinking about Max. In fact, he's all I think about. I can't stop thinking about him, wishing we'd get back together."

"Then why don't you call him?" Amber asks, as if this simple solution will solve all of my problems.

"I've already called him a million times," I say.

"And texted," Chloe says. "And e-mailed, and blogged. Anything I'm leaving out? Did you try Instagram yet? We can post a picture of that frowny face you keep making."

"I didn't tweet," I say. "Maybe I should send a tweet?"

"You definitely should not tweet," Amber says. "Maybe you could accidentally-on-purpose bump into him somehow?"

"I tried talking in person," I say. "That didn't go so well. Is there some form of communication I'm not thinking of?"

"Smoke signals," Chloe says.

"An old-fashioned letter?" Amber suggests.

"That's actually a good idea," Chloe says. "Letter writing is so romantic."

As Chloe and Amber wax philosophical about the lost art of letter writing, it dawns on me. There *is* another method of communication. It's just a matter of getting access to it.

"I just thought something," I say. "I've gotta go."

"What about lunch?" Chloe asks.

But I'm already out the door.

54
Coming Clean

"I'm pleasantly surprised that you called," Kel says. "I didn't think I'd ever hear from you again."

He's in the hair and makeup chair, with a little tissue tucked into his collar, getting ready for the 12 P.M. live broadcast of *Saturday, New York*. Nothing like a dainty little tissue tucked into the collar to make a man a whole lot less formidable and scary. A man with a prim tissue tucked into his shirt can't hurt you. He's not a lion; he's a lamb.

This is just what I needed. Just the thing to give me the strength to do what I need to do.

"Thanks for making this happen," I say. It's exciting to be at the News 4 offices. The newsroom is a tornado of energy and excitement. I can feel it pulsing through my body. I'm ready. Ready to apologize to Max on air, ready to admit everything to the world (or at least the viewers watching News Channel 4). Ready to admit that I am a total, utter, and complete fraud—I'm going to tell everyone that I really do believe in love and that I'm in love with Max. Kel couldn't get me on the air fast enough.

"Do you want a touch-up?" Kel's makeup artist asks me.

"I think I'm okay the way I am," I say. I look into the mirror to take a peek at my appearance, and I decide that I don't want to change a thing.

"How about some hair?" she asks.

"Nope," I say, finding my hand subconsciously brushing the hair off my shoulder. "I'm going to go on like this. Just be myself. Kel, is that okay with you?"

"No problem at all," Kel says, as his makeup artist goes back to applying a thick layer of foundation to his head, neck, and face. Then his hairdresser gets in on the action, forcing his hair into a helmet with an enormous bottle of hair spray.

"Are you ready?" Kel's station manager asks me.

"Yes," I say. "Let's rock."

"We're here with Jo Waldman," Kel begins, "founder of the recently defunct Lonely Hearts Club movement."

"Thanks, Kel," I say. I'm hoping my words sound even, that my voice doesn't tell the world how I really feel inside: scared, terrified really, and a little bit overenergized. I'm going for steady, smart, strong, except I'm sure I sound anything but. "I just want to thank everyone who was a part of this thing. The people who believed in it, the people who contributed to it, the people to whom it really meant something.

"And I also want to apologize to those people, too. Because the truth is, I'm a fraud. Kel was right when he outed me the night of the Lonely Hearts Club Ball. I'm a liar. And I deceived all of you.

"I am madly, completely, head over heels in love with someone. His name is Max and he's the person who helped me design the Lonely Hearts Club site in the first place. We met the night after my first post, when my computer crashed from all the traffic, and from the second he walked through my door, I knew. I just knew. I fought it at first, because I'd sworn off love, and encouraged the rest of you to do the same thing, but the truth is, I love him.

"I do believe in love. So, there you have it. There it is. What else can I say? I believe in love.

"But I also believe in hating love, in raging, in telling the world exactly how you feel. Sometimes you need to experience that. Maybe it's a good thing to get all of the negativity out—to scream it at the top of your lungs. Because you've got to get rid of it. You can't let it fester, can't let it stay with you. You cannot keep it inside. Because you don't need it. What you need is to move on.

"Love *is* important. And not just romantic love. All types of love. The love you have for your family, the love you give to your friends, and the love and attention you give to making your dreams come true. It's all important. It all needs to be nurtured.

"I'm sorry to anyone who I hurt throughout this whole crazy ride. I truly am—I hope you can all see that. And to the one person I hurt the most, I want you to know: I love you. I love you so much. If you give me another chance, I promise you, things will be different this time."

Kel smiles back at me and nods his head. "Well done, Jo," he says.

"How did I do?" I ask.

"We'll find out after our next segment. I'll give you some time to get yourself ready and then you'll find out for yourself," he says, as the window shades open to reveal an entire plaza filled with people. "That's the power of live TV."

55
We Can Work It Out

TWEET FROM @ALLYMARGOLIS:
Hey, lonely hearts, check out Jo Waldman on Saturday, New York talking about the Lonely Hearts Club Ball. Turns out, she's in love! #notsolonelyhearts

TWEET FROM @ ALLSNOTFAIRINLOVEANDMUSIC:
Hey, @madmax, if you're not watching @NewsChannel4 right now, you need to tune in.

TWEET FROM @LONDONCALLING:
Did you see Jo Waldman pour her heart out on Saturday, New York? Watch it here: http://tinyurl.com/mlovbyu
How I wish I were @madmax at this very moment. #notsolonelyhearts

**E-MAIL FROM CHLOE@
SUPERGOODADVERTISING.COM TO MAX@
SUPERGOODADVERTISING.COM:**

You need to get your ass to the Channel 4 studios ASAP. Seriously, dude. I know you're spending the day at the Ziegfeld for that Star Wars marathon. Let me help you out—Vader is Luke's dad.

You're only 6 blocks away. Run, do not walk. You've got 10 minutes.

56
Let's Stay Together

Twenty minutes later, I walk out of the studio and it's a sea of people. The entire plaza is filled with fans of Kel's show, and it seems they've all just watched it on enormous screens that are strategically placed around the Channel 4 building. A camera's followed me out—Kel said he wanted me to go out in the crowd, gauge their reactions, and when I stop to take it all in, absorb how many people are there, people who just witnessed my grand confession, the cameraman doesn't realize I've stopped and walks right into the back of my head.

"Sorry, Jo," he says, as he dislodges his camera from my mess of hair. "This will work better if you actually walk out there."

"There are just so many people," I say.

"This is a fraction of the people who were on your site," he says. "The Plaza only holds about a thousand people. Didn't you have over a million on your site? You can do this."

I take a deep breath and walk right out. There are gates set up, so that I have to approach the crowd if I want to interact. They can't all rush in and grab me. I walk into the tiny circle of space they've created and the cameraman motions for me to talk.

"Hi," I say, unsure of what to say next. "I'm Jo Waldman. Thanks for watching me on News 4."

"Say something more, Waldman," I hear in my ear. Kel's on the earpiece they gave me on my way out. "*Do* something."

"Thanks for giving me the chance to set the record straight," I say. "Anyone have anything to add?" I ask the crowd.

The whole crowd clamors for a chance to speak. I have no I idea who to talk to, who to give their due. But then I hear a voice. A familiar voice. I spin on my heel and see Max.

"I have something to add," Max says. I rush over to him. He's holding his phone, which is playing a clip of the interview I just did. I was hoping he'd see it. I have no idea how he knew it was on, or how he got here so fast, but I don't care. I'm just happy he's here.

We don't say a word. We come together and kiss. I throw my arms around his body and he's got his around mine. We kiss and we kiss and we kiss. I can barely breathe, but I don't care.

"I missed you so much," he says.

"I love you."

"I love you, too," he says. And then he kisses me again.

I can feel the light of a camera on me but I don't care. We kiss and we kiss and we kiss, like it's the end of the world.

But it's not. It's just the beginning.

57
Start Me Up

"Well, what did they say exactly?" Max asks. We're at my apartment—my new apartment—and we're eating Thai takeout on the floor, drinking Riesling out of the new glasses I bought earlier at the flea market across the street.

"I don't know, really," I say, trying to recall my conversation from earlier today. "Something about getting the site back to its former glory. I wasn't really paying attention to that part. I kind of got stuck on the whole we-may-be-interested-in-buying-your-site thing. That was the important part, right?"

"Are you going to get something in writing, something that guarantees they'll buy the site?" Max asks. "We don't want to lose out on this again."

"We have a meeting set up next week," I say. "But I thought it would be a good idea to reconfigure things now, so that the site's up and ready to go with the new format before our meeting. Let them see what it can do. Get that bid up as high as we can get it."

"Get that bid up?" Max asks. "Who are you right now?"

"Still me," I say and smile. I take a bite of pad thai, and then put a forkful up for Max to try.

"What if they want a total redesign?" Max asks.

"Then," I explain, "I'll tell them to hire you to do a total redesign."

I can tell Max is the tiniest bit annoyed—after all, I got little to no details from Love, Inc.'s parent company about the terms of selling my site to them. But I got the gist: They're interested in the new direction that the site is taking. Since the Lonely Hearts Club Ball fiasco, the site has become a place where people try to find other lonely hearts. It started when I began posting open letters to Max, begging him to take me back. It wasn't long before others followed suit, and then still others posted messages looking for people they'd missed—people they met at clubs but didn't exchange numbers with, people they passed on the street, and even people they worked with who they were afraid to confess their true feelings to.

I love the new direction the site's taken—the focus is no longer rage and anger, it's love. Finding love, getting love back, and looking for love wherever you can. Sure, there's still rage and anger in there, there's always bound to be some when there's a breakup, but the negative is all focused on a place of letting that go and getting back to the positive part. Chloe even suggested we throw another Lonely Hearts Club Ball next year, but with a slightly different theme. This time, it will be about people who are alone on Valentine's Day, but looking for connections with other people. Looking for real relationships.

Is it any wonder that Love, Inc.'s parent company wanted a piece of it? The meeting's next week, but this time I'm taking Max's advice. I will take the meeting seriously—no more hanging onto the past for me, thank you very much. I even let my mother take me shopping for a new dress to wear to the meeting.

I've been in touch with my old band. It was fun rehearsing and trying to get the band back together, but the truth is, that chapter of my life is over. It died when Billy died. It just took me a while to figure that part out. Frankie thinks I should try to break out as a solo act. He's all for helping me when I need it, but he's really focused on teaching and being a good dad. (Stacey delivered a healthy baby boy. I sent them a toy guitar as a baby gift.)

"What do you want it to look like?" Max asks. "I'm assuming we're going with the old color scheme?"

"No," I say. "I'd like to add some color."

"You want pink?" he asks. "Who are you and what have you done with my girlfriend, Jo?"

I love it when Max calls me his girlfriend.

"I don't necessarily want pink," I say. "I don't want it to look like the Love, Inc. site. It needs to have its own stamp. Chloe suggested these blues and these greens. She worked some salmon in, and I think it looks great." I hold up the sketches Chloe did of a sample new home page for the site.

"So, pink."

"It's not pink," I explain. "It's salmon."

"Salmon is pink."

"It's not pink!" I insist. "You know I hate pink. Salmon is totally different. Chloe said it was elegant and subtle."

"Chloe's lying to you," Max says.

"It's salmon!" I say and swat at Max's shoulder. "Stop teasing me!"

"Oh, I'm not going to stop teasing you," Max says, as he pulls me to him. "What would be the fun in that?"

We kiss, and he puts his hand to my cheek. Before I know it, a tiny peck has become a full on make-out session—his hands are in my hair, my arms are around him, drawing him closer. As we lean back onto the floor, I hear the tiny clink of a wineglass going over, probably spilling wine all over the floor, but I don't care. All I care about is Max, and how now that I have him, I'm never letting go again.

He plants kisses all along my neck and I can't help it—a tiny little murmur escapes my lips.

"More of that, then?" he whispers in my ear.

"More of everything," I say.

His lips trace the line of my neck and then continue downward. He lifts my shirt up to kiss my belly and then lets his hands lazily travel down my body. His touch sets my entire body on fire, and I tell him so. He doesn't answer me. He just lets his hands stay where they are, driving me crazy, making me lose my breath.

I can't rip his clothes off fast enough. I'm kissing his chest, I'm kissing his stomach, and then he lifts my chin up to kiss his lips. We kiss slowly, deliberately, and it's such a good kiss that all other thoughts are erased from my mind. It's a kiss that leaves me thinking just one thought, one thing over and over again: Max.

Max, Max, Max.

And then he's all over me, inside of me, and it feels like the first time we were ever together. Every time with Max feels like the first time. His body fits so perfectly with mine—like we were made for each other. Like we were destined to find each other.

"I love you," I whisper, and he whispers it back.

As we lay on the floor afterward, I feel something wet tickling my toes. The wine. I make a mental note to clean it up later—there's no way I'm leaving Max's arms anytime soon. I know it will create a sticky mess, and I know that part of being a grown-up is having your own space and then actually cleaning up after yourself, but surely there's an exception for times like this?

"We have got to make it to the bed one of these days," Max

says.

I smile back at him.

"I mean, it's not even that far away," he says, motioning to the bed that we're leaning up against.

I think about how lucky I am to have Max back in my life. Why is it that you sometimes have to lose something to realize how much you needed it? I don't know the answer to that one. Does anyone, really?

I guess I'll have to write a song about it.

58
Future Love Paradise

It's an entirely different backstage scene than the one I'm used
to. For starters, Amber Fairchild's here, and I'm happy about
it. "When Will Tomorrow Be" was a huge hit for her—she
recorded the whole thing acoustically, and the rest of the world
responded the same way I did the day when I heard her play her
guitar and sing. It's the start of a new phase of her career, and
I already got my first royalty check. It will cover my next two
months' rent, so I can focus on my music. But Chloe's boss also
called me about a possible freelance gig coming up in a month,
so I'm excited to do that, too.

Lola's sitting next to Amber, sipping a Shirley Temple. They
are both wearing leopard-print ballet flats with a hot-pink
grosgrain ribbon bow on top, and I can tell they are getting along
just as well as Lola always dreamed they would.

"Are you going to ditch me for Amber as your Big Sister?" I
ask Lola. Amber recently cut all of her hair off (Alan would never
let her do it when he was managing her career), and Lola has just
announced that she wants a short bob cut, too.

"Totally," Lola says. "Amber, would you be my new Big Sister?"

"I think you can have two Big Sisters," Amber says, smiling. "I'll come along the next time you two meet."

Amber's people hired a detective to get Alan back (and her money) and found him at the Four Seasons in Dubai, surrounded by prostitutes and a huge spread of lobsters, champagne, and cocaine. They may not have been able to extradite him back to the United States, but they were able to get back a big chunk of Amber's money. And alert the authorities about the prostitutes and drugs. Amber doesn't believe in divorce, so she was somehow able to sweet-talk a judge into letting her annul her seven-year marriage based on the fact that she "never really knew him at all, now, did she?"

"Thank you, Jo," Lola's mom says to me, and I'm not sure what she's thanking me for: the Amber thing, or the fact that my dad hired her as a nurse now that Barbie's gone. But it doesn't really matter. It makes me happy to see that good things are happening to good people. As much as I hate to admit it, my dad may be onto something with all this talk about channeling your energy into positivity, as opposed to negativity.

I look over at Max, working on the sound and lighting for tonight on his computer, and I can't help but smile. But then I look over at Chloe and Andrew—my best friend and my brother—cozying up at a corner booth, and I can't help but cringe. When, exactly, will it get less vomit inducing to see my brother and best friend as an item?

"Do you think I'll be planning a wedding soon?" my mother asks.

"Oh, God, I hope not," I say, eyes still on Chloe and Andrew. "Give me a little time to get used to the idea first, would you?"

"I meant you," my mother says. "Max is such a nice young man."

"Mom!" I say. "I just turned twenty-three years old. I'm way too young to be married."

"By the time I was twenty-three, I already had you and your brother."

I have no words for this.

THE SET goes perfectly. I invite Amber up on the stage and we do an impromptu duet of "When Will Tomorrow Be." The crowd loves it. And by crowd, I mean my parents, brother, best friend, Little Sister, and her mom. But they all totally love it, just the same.

I do a few more songs and then it's time to close out the set. For my last song, I do something I've never done before—I invite my dad to come up on stage and play with me. He showboats for a few minutes ("Let me get all warmed up here," he says as he runs his fingers along the keys, hitting each note perfectly), and then we get ready to do a duet on his favorite song, "Piano Man."

"I'm so glad I have my father up here with me to perform one of his all-time favorite songs," I say. "I'd like to dedicate this next song to all those lonely hearts out there. I hope that you, too, find love like I have."

And then I play.

Acknowledgments

Thank you to my lovely and talented agent, Mollie Glick. I can never thank you enough for taking a chance on me, all those years ago. I am so very lucky to have you in my corner.

Big, big thanks go to my editor and the founder of Polis Books, the smart and all-around amazing Jason Pinter: I'm so incredibly excited to be working with you on this book, and my first two books as well. I'm so happy to be here at the launch of Polis Books—and I'm honored to be among the few who can say we were there when it all started.

As always, an enormous thank-you to my family: Bernard and Sherry Janowitz, Judy Luxenberg, Sammy and Stephanie Janowitz, Jen and Lee Mattes, and Stacey and Jon Faber.

Shawn Morris, Jennifer Moss, Danielle Schmelkin, and Tandy O'Donoghue: my best (and fastest) readers, my best friends. Sometimes you just need the friends you've had since you were eighteen years old.

And to my readers. Always to my readers. Thank you.

The biggest thank you goes out to Douglas Luxenberg. I may be a writer, but I can never find the exact words to tell you how much you mean to me. And to Ben and Davey, the lights of my life. You make it all worthwhile.

About The Author

A native New Yorker, Brenda Janowitz has had a flair for all things dramatic since she played the title role in her third grade production of Really Rosie. When asked by her grandmother if the experience made her want tobe an actress when she grew up, Brenda responded, "An actress? No. A writer, maybe."

Brenda attended Cornell University, earning a Bachelor of Science in Human Service Studies, with a Concentration in Race and Discrimination. After graduating from Cornell, she attended Hofstra Law School, where she was a member of the Law Review and won the Law Review Writing Competition. Upon graduation from Hofstra, she went to work for the law firm Kaye Scholer, LLP, where she was an associate in the Intellectual Property group, handling cases in the areas of trademark, anti-trust, Internet, and false advertising. Brenda later left Kaye Scholer to pursue a federal clerkship with the Honorable Marilyn Dolan Go, United States Magistrate Judge for the Eastern District of New York.

Brenda is the author of *Jack With A Twist* and *Scot On The Rocks*, featuring Manhattan attorney Brooke Miller, both of which are available from Polis Books. Her third novel, *Recipe For A Happy Life*, was published by St. Martin's Press. Her work has also appeared in the *New York Post* and *Publisher's Weekly*. You can find Brenda on Facebook or on Twitter at @BrendaJanowitz.

Enjoy even more Brenda Janowitz!

Hollywood Punch

A Novella

To Ben and Davey

Chapter One

You know that feeling you get when everything seems to be right with the world? When the planets seem to be in alignment? One of those days when you're actually running on time, your apartment is (relatively) clean, and you haven't gotten into an argument with your mother/ best friend/ boss/ therapist in at least a week? That's exactly how I feel today.

And why not? Last spring, I survived my ex-boyfriend's wedding with my dignity ever so slightly intact, and now I'm engaged to a man I love, and working at a job that I don't hate. Which, as a lawyer in New York City, is really the most you can hope for.

Well, okay, so going to my ex-boyfriend's wedding last spring wasn't really as easy as I'm making it sound. Sure, I survived with my dignity ever so slightly intact, but only barely. You see, mere days before the wedding, my gorgeous Scottish boyfriend, Douglas, broke up with me and announced that he was getting engaged to someone else, but that was all right. I had a plan—I simply took my friend Jack as my date instead. Okay, okay, I actually forced my best friend Jack to *pretend* to be Douglas, thus helping me to keep my dignity ever so slightly intact for the whole of Trip's wedding, but it was really just a harmless little lie, you know? Who would ever be the wiser? Certainly not my ex, Trip, and definitely not my more recent ex, Douglas (wow, I have so many ex-boyfriends that I'm confusing even myself....). And Jack was such a good friend that he really didn't mind one bit. Not even a little. Anyway, how hard could it be to pretend to be Douglas?

Okay, okay, so Douglas was obsessively Scottish and planning to wear a kilt to my ex-boyfriend's wedding, all of which I had warned said ex-boyfriend of in advance, so this little charade took slightly more than a name change, but how hard could it really be for Jack to don a kilt and a fake accent, right?

Well, it wasn't easy, but Jack was a trooper and we managed to go to Trip's wedding, have a great time, and then, as an added bonus, fall madly in love. And now we are a bona fide couple, on our way towards marching down the aisle. See, sometimes the cliché is right—every cloud *does* have a silver lining.

Which is why this morning I didn't have a care in world about what I would wear for dinner tonight. Even though it's a dinner with Trip, my ex-boyfriend. And his beautiful movie star wife, Ava Huang. Yes, *that* Ava Huang. The perfect Hollywood "It" girl, Ava Huang. Who has an Academy Award nomination. And a royal title.

Not like I'm jealous of her or anything.

I mean, what's to be jealous of? My fiancé, Jack, recently made partner at a large law firm in Manhattan. In many ways, I think that's harder to do than to get an Oscar nod. To get her nomination, all Ava had to do was play an autistic transvestite who was sexually abused as a child and grew up to cure cancer. And everyone knows that when a gorgeous actress does a role where she gets to look ugly, she gets an Oscar nod. Whereas Jack had to work twelve to fourteen hour days for nine years before they even *considered* him for partner. And, I mean, to be born royal, you only have to... well... be born, so working your butt off to make partner for years is certainly more impressive than that.

When I woke up and got dressed for work today, I didn't really give a second thought to what I'd wear to dinner with my ex and his movie star wife. I mean, I'm engaged now, so what does it really matter what I'm wearing? Soon, I'll be a married woman myself and I'll be much too busy being the normal well-adjusted wife that I am to worry about the little insecurities that I entertained when I was single.

I mean, when you're an engaged woman, does it really matter what you wear for a weeknight after-work dinner? What do you have to prove, really? This is just like any other casual dinner with friends. Even if one is an ex-boyfriend and the other is his Oscar-nominated wife. In fact, I specifically *didn't* think twice about what I would wear tonight because I'm so above such petty jealousies.

And now, as I sit here at my desk, mere hours away from tonight's dinner, only one thing pops to mind: what the hell was I thinking? Clearly, this morning I was delusional. I'm having dinner with a movie star, for the love of God! I must go home immediately and change.

From: "Brooke Miller" <brooke.miller@sgr.com>
To: "Jack Solomon" <jsolomon@gilsonhecht.com>
Subject: Re: tonight

running home to change before dinner. want to look cute for you! pick me up at the apartment instead of the office tonight? love you.

Brooke Miller
Sent from my wireless handheld

I race out of my office and hop into a taxi cab. As I give the driver my address, my BlackBerry begins to buzz.

From:"Jack Solomon" <jsolomon@gilsonhecht.com>
To:"Brooke Miller" <brooke.miller@sgr.com>
Subject:Re: Re: tonight

Love you, too.

Jack Solomon
Gilson, Hecht and Trattner
425 Park Avenue
11th Floor
New York, New York 10022

*****CONFIDENTIALITY NOTICE*****
The information contained in this e-mail message is confidential and is intended only for the use of the individual or entity named above. If you are not the intended recipient, we would request you delete this communication without reading it or any attachment, not forward or otherwise distribute it, and kindly advise Gilson, Hecht & Trattner by return email to the sender or a telephone call to 1 (800) GILSON. Thank you in advance.

I can barely contain my smile as the cab lurches uptown and

we arrive at my apartment building. I just know that the second Jack picks me up in a cab, he'll flash his baby blue eyes at me and say, "I am the luckiest man in the world. Never leave me, Brooke, for without you, I would surely die," or something as equally heartfelt and romantic.

I rush up to my apartment, turn on the radio and march into the bathroom. That's it—freshening up with a little "getting ready" music will put me in a good mood. The radio begins to blast an old Madonna song from the 80s and I dance around the bathroom, mood lightening. After all, when Madonna tells you to "get up and dance and sing," you listen.

Throwing my head upside down, I give it a few good shakes. Flipping my hair back and standing upright, I look at my reflection in the mirror. Ever since I cut eight and a half inches off of my signature locks, I've also taken to wearing my hair with more of its natural curl in it. This past summer, I even let it dry naturally on days that I wasn't appearing in court (for those days, I resorted to my old tried and true classic bun), and with the Indian Summer we were having this September, I'm still doing the same.

I pull out the bathroom mirrors so that I can see myself in 3-D. *I look okay,* I tell myself. *I look fine.* After all, it's just a casual dinner at a local French restaurant with some friends. One of whom happens to be one of the biggest movie stars in the world. Who is married to my ex-boyfriend.

I must go get my hair blown out. Letting my hair dry naturally and frizz ever so slightly is okay for an evening at home with my fiancé who already gave me a ring and asked my father for permission and all that—he's already stuck with me—but it just won't cut it for dinner at Pastis with a real, live movie star.

What if the paparazzi is there? I wouldn't want to embarrass my friends and family by being photographed with frizzy hair. I really am a very considerate girl.

And anyway, it's really not all that uncommon to get your hair professionally done. I heard once that Marilyn Monroe used to wash and set her hair up to three times day when she was on a movie set. I mean, if Marilyn Monroe in her *heyday* had to constantly wash and set her hair, what hope do we normal gals have, anyway?

Oh please! As if *you* wouldn't get your hair washed and blown out if you were going out to dinner with your ex-boyfriend and his movie star wife!

From:"Brooke Miller" <brooke.miller@sgr.com>
To:"Jack Solomon" <jsolomon@gilsonhecht.com>
Subject:Re: Re: Re: tonight

on second thought, why dont you pick me up at
the cheap hair place on the corner of lex and 62nd?
i want to get gorgeous for you....

Brooke Miller
Sent from my wireless handheld

From:"Jack Solomon" <jsolomon@gilsonhecht.com>
To:"Brooke Miller" <brooke.miller@sgr.com>
Subject:Re: Re: Re: Re: tonight

of course you do.

Jack Solomon
Gilson, Hecht and Trattner
425 Park Avenue

11th Floor

New York, New York 10022

*****CONFIDENTIALITY NOTICE*****

The information contained in this e-mail message is confidential and is intended only for the use of the individual or entity named above. If you are not the intended recipient, we would request you delete this communication without reading it or any attachment, not forward or otherwise distribute it, and kindly advise Gilson, Hecht & Trattner by return email to the sender or a telephone call to 1 (800) GILSON. Thank you in advance.

Perfect! I have just enough time to change into my newest little black dress, get to the hair place and get my hair washed and blown out straight. And, maybe if there's time I can get a manicure. And have my make-up done, too. But, only if there's time.

What? I wouldn't want to keep the paparazzi waiting.

Chapter Two

"You had your make-up done, too?" my fiancé Jack asks as I slide into the town car. "How much did getting ready for this dinner set you back?"

"I just wanted to look beautiful for you," I say, giving him a peck on the lips.

"Well," he says, "I'm just glad to see that this has nothing to do with the fact that we're having dinner with your ex-boyfriend and his movie star wife."

"No," I say, laughing, "of *course* not!"

"Yes," he says, putting his hand on my leg, "of course."

Fifteen minutes later, we're down in the Meatpacking District, pulling up to Pastis. Ah, Pastis—a restaurant which *would* be considered a casual French bistro, but for the fact that it is a huge celebrity hangout and has a three month waiting list for a reservation. The second my foot hits the cobblestone street, I hear my ex-boyfriend, Trip, call out my name. He and his wife, Ava, are already ensconced at one of the outside tables. Getting a reservation at Pastis is hard enough, but getting an outside table is nearly impossible. Of course, within the first five minutes of conversation, Trip drops the fact that this is their regular table.

You know those celebrities who go out to restaurants at odd hours and take tables in the corner, facing inside, desperate not to be seen or recognized? Trip and Ava are not those kind of celebrities.

"So, I said to DiCaprio," Trip says, making no effort at all to lower his voice, reveling in the fact that this causes all of the nearby tables to turn and look at him, "if you don't do it, you're insane!" To which he and Ava laugh hysterically and Jack and I merely smile politely.

Eating with Trip and Ava is incredibly difficult. Every so often, you see the flash of a bulb go off and you just know that a papparrazo somewhere out there has just taken your picture. You feel the constant glare of camera phones on you as you try to take a bite of your steak sandwich. I'm desperately trying to eat in an attractive way, which is no easy feat, I assure you.

I guess this is why Ava is so thin.

"That crazy DiCaprio," Jack says in a Scottish accent. Now, I suppose I should mention here that Jack isn't actually Scottish. But, yes, you read that correctly. Yes, tonight Jack is speaking with a Scottish accent. There really is a very logical reason for all of this.

You see, it's your typical girl-gets-invited-to-her-ex-boyfriend's-wedding-only-to-be-broken-up-with-by-her-awful-cad-of-a-Scottish-boyfriend-mere-minutes-before-the-wedding-forcing-girl-to-drag-her-best-friend-Jack-in-his-place-and-make-him-wear-a-kilt-and-speak-with-a-Scottish-accent-in-a-desperate-attempt-to-keep-her-dignity-ever-so-slightly-intact sort of story. Kind of story you hear about all the time, right? This is also the story of why Trip and Ava are calling Jack "Douglas."

Okay, so I understand that most women don't get invited to

their ex-boyfriend's weddings. And I realize that most women don't RSVP 'yes' to their ex-boyfriend's weddings because they are dating gorgeous hunky Scotsmen and they want to show up their exes. And, okay, most women, when then broken up with by their hunky Scotsmen, don't recruit their friends to take his place and pretend to be him. And pretend to be engaged to said faux-Scotsman. But, then again, I'm not most girls.

And therein lies my charm. I think. I'm pretty sure Jack told me that once. Or at least I think he did. Didn't he? Anyway, the point is, I'm not most girls. And Jack, luckily for me, is not most guys.

And I'm lucky that he's not. Since going to Trip's wedding as a fake couple, Jack and I have actually become a real couple. Which was an easy transition since we were the best of friends before the wedding. It just took a trip to LA and seeing Jack in a kilt for me to realize that he was the one for me. And now that I have, I have no intention of ever going back to being just friends again. Because Jack is amazing. As evidenced by the fact that he's dressed up as a Scotsman once again, phony accent and all, just to save my pride. And he even remembered to bring me the fake engagement ring I wore to Trip's wedding, which I swapped out for my real one when Jack picked me up in the cab.

Now, I know what you're thinking. How can she go on like this? And really, it's easy. You see, I don't plan to see Trip and Ava ever again after tonight. And, I'm sure, after having to feign a Scottish accent for an entire evening, by tomorrow, Jack will be of a similar mind. Maybe even later tonight. We're only here in the first place to be polite (that, and the fact that I was unsuccessful in dodging Trip's calls. He had his assistant call me seven times. Yes, seven! I wonder how many times he had to call Leo to get *him* on the phone....).

Trip's assistant assured me that there was something that Trip just *had* to tell me. And I just had to know what it was. Trip and I always had a very competitive relationship, even back when we were an item in law school, but now I can't imagine there's much left for him to say to me. Still, curiosity got the best of me. But, really, what could he possibly be here to announce? I mean, he's won, hasn't he? He was married first and to an Oscar nominated star, at that. It's really not much of a contest. I get it.

Why am I at this dinner again?

"So, did he say yes?" I ask. I don't want to ask, but Trip so clearly wants me to ask more about his silly little Leonardo DiCaprio story. The man is so starved for attention. Trip, I mean. Not Leonardo DiCaprio. I've never met Leonardo DiCaprio, but I'm sure that he's very well adjusted and nice. Although he *was* a child star (who didn't love him on Growing Pains?!), so maybe he's not as nice as he seems, even though he *does* feel passionate about the environment. But I digress....

"As a matter of fact, Brooke," he said, "he did. Leo's going to be starring in Ava's next picture." It drives me insane that Trip calls movies 'pictures' as if he's Orson Welles or something. He's not even her director. He's just her agent. Isn't there some sort of confidentiality thing he's violating here? Note to self: write a note to the bar association to determine confidentiality implications of an agent being romantically involved with the actress he's representing.

"Great," Jack says, "Jolly good." I don't think that Scots say things like 'jolly good,' but I let it slide since Jack's being so great by pretending to be a Scotsman on a weeknight. Anyway, the industry talk is probably the only saving grace for Jack this evening. Jack always wanted to be an actor but never really made a go of it. Jack's like a lot of litigators—frustrated thespians who use their dramatic flair in the courtroom instead of on the stage.

"And Ava will be playing the lead, " Trip continues, as the

waiter begins clearing out plates. I say a tiny prayer that Trip and Ava won't want to order dessert and that Jack and I can get out of here. "DiCaprio will be the ex-boyfriend, whose wedding Ava attends."

Suddenly, time begins moving in slow motion.

"Excuse me?" I ask. Surely, I must have misheard Trip.

"Oh, did I forget to mention that?" Trip asks, a tiny smirk creeping onto his lips. "The picture is about a woman who goes to her ex-boyfriend's wedding."

This story is beginning to sound alarmingly familiar.

"Let me get this straight," I say, "Ava's next movie is about a girl who goes to her ex-boyfriend's wedding?"

"Yeah," Trip says with a laugh. "You inspired me to write it!"

"*You* wrote it?" I ask. Back in law school, Trip couldn't write to save his life. Or his GPA, as the case may be.

"Well," he says, "I'm in the process of writing it. But we already have a deal in place. And now, we've got our stars attached!"

"Who's going to play Jack?" Jack asks, Scottish accent all but gone.

"Who's Jack?" Trip asks.

"Douglas," I say, correcting Jack. "He means Douglas. Who's going to play Douglas?"

"It's hard to find someone who can do a convincing Scottish accent," Ava says. "That's the real obstacle we're having now."

"You really just need someone who can *fake* a Scottish accent," Jack offers and I grab at his knee under the table. Unfortunately for me, this does not have the intended effect. He thinks I'm flirting, and so he grabs at my waist.

Sometimes it's a real curse to be so darned irresistible.

"Is the point of this dinner to ask me if you can make a movie about me?" I ask. "Because, you can't. I mean, I'd prefer it if you didn't do that." After all, I know my rights. And the second I get home, I will log onto my computer to find out just exactly what they are.

"I don't have to ask your permission to write a movie about you," Trip says. "Remember, I went to law school, too, and so I know that I don't have to ask your permission for this. You're not famous."

Thank you, Trip, for reminding me of that very, very obvious fact.

"Well, how do you know I won't sue you?" I ask.

"You're not going to sue me," he says, laughing at the mere thought of it, "but anyway, even if you do, the studio has a team of lawyers."

"Well, that's good to know," I say. "Because it sounds like you could have a lawsuit or two on your hands."

"Well, I thank you for your concern, Brooke," Trip says. "But what I'd really love to do is to interview you. Get some more background information for the script. Whaddya say? For old times sake?"

"Um," I eek out. "No, thank you."

And really, I don't want to do it. And it's not just because Trip is my ex-boyfriend. And it's not just because Trip doesn't know the whole story behind my attendance at his wedding. Actually, those are pretty good reasons in of themselves, aren't they? Yes, they definitely are….

But, more importantly, it's because he's writing a movie about my life. And not about the good parts, either. I'm sure he doesn't have a scene about all of the charity work I do here in the city. Well, okay, fine, I don't have a ton of time for charity since I work fourteen hour days regularly, but I do attend my fair share of Black Tie charity events, so that should count. Or, say, he could write a scene about the time I helped that blind lady cross Lexington that day at lunch. That would be nice. But, I just know that that's not the kind of movie he'll be writing. No, he's going to be writing a movie about a sad single girl in New York City. Instead of scenes that showcase her fabulousness, he'll be writing scenes where she obsesses endlessly about going to her ex-boyfriend's wedding. Instead of scenes that show how hard she works at her big-time law firm, there will be scenes where she does silly thing after silly thing in a fruitless attempt to keep her dignity ever so slightly intact, and instead ends up looking like a fool. No, thank you!

And, also, when I think about what I spent this evening on hair and make-up alone, I just cannot afford having to see Trip on a day to day basis. Case closed.

I don't really know what's said for the rest of the dinner. It barely registers who paid the bill or if we even paid the bill at all. I'm in a daze for the rest of the time and all I can think is: my ex-boyfriend is making a movie about me.

Jack shuttles me into a cab and I open the window to get a gust of cool air as we head uptown.

"So," Jack says, turning to face me, "do you think they'll offer me a part?"

Chapter Three

"Wow," my best friend Vanessa says.

"I know."

"Wow."

"I *know*," I repeat.

"Wow."

"Okay, you're going to need to say something other than 'wow.'"

"I can't think of anything else to say," she says, and sinks into her chair. We're at Bernard's Gourmet on Third Avenue for lunch. I needed to convene a special counsel to discuss the fact that my ex-boyfriend is making a movie about my life. And that it's starring his gorgeous movie star wife. You'd really think that a big-time Hollywood agent and his movie star wife would have better things to do with their time than to ruin my life.

But, no.

"Maybe I should be flattered," I say, taking a bite of my Cobb salad. "I mean, clearly, my life is so interesting that Trip thinks the entire movie-going public of America wants to know about it."

"Don't forget Europe," Vanessa says, her gorgeous mocha skin looking pristine, despite the heat outside. "American movies play overseas, too." She takes a bite out of her hamburger and I silently curse her for the fact that she can eat whatever she wants and I gain weight if I even *look* at a hamburger. Maybe this is owing to the fact that she's five foot eight, and a marathon runner who religiously runs 6 miles a day, but still. And more important than the fact that she's thin, she's so gorgeous that if *her* ex-boyfriend made a movie about her life, they'd probably be asking her if she'd consider playing herself.

Yes, Vanessa is tall and gorgeous and thin. I have no idea why I'm friends with her.

"And Asia," she adds. "Don't forget about Asia."

"Okay, I won't. So, my ex-boyfriend is making a movie out of the single most humiliating moment of my life." I say. "No big deal, right? I'm sure that this is the sort of thing that happens to *lots* of women out there every day."

"I'm sure it happens all the time," she says. I can tell she's lying by the way she self-consciously smoothes her hand over her short hair, but I don't care. It still makes me feel better.

"And being friendly with an ex really isn't that big of a deal, is it?" I ask, taking a bite of my salad, only allowing myself the tiniest bit of dressing. I mean, so what?"

"So what, indeed," she says and dips one of her French fries into the ketchup.

"I mean, so what if my ex decides to take the most embarrassing moment of my life and turn it into a major motion picture starring his new wife?" I say, taking another bite of salad, this time abandoning the dressing altogether. "And, so what if said new wife has to gain twenty pounds just to play me? I mean, so what?"

"So what!" Vanessa says, slamming her fist down on the table, and I can practically hear a choir rising up in the background.

"Just because I'm not married and I'm not royalty and I'm not an Academy Award nominated actress, I'm still fabulous anyway, right?"

Oh please. As if *you* wouldn't be fishing for compliments the day after you found out that your ex boyfriend was making a movie out of your life.

"Fabulous enough for them to make a movie all about you and your crazy adventures," Vanessa says, motioning to the waiter for refills on our diet iced teas.

"Yes," I say. "That's right. I'm fabulous." I smile at Vanessa. Sometimes I forget just how truly fabulous I am.

"Did you convince yourself on that one?" she asks.

"No," I say, looking down at my Cobb salad and then scooping up a forkful of bacon. I silently decide that you don't have to stay on your diet on the day after you find out your ex-boyfriend is making a movie out of how pathetic your life is. "Did I convince you?"

"Nope," she says, and goes back to her fries. "But, one good thing to come out of this is the fact that Trip knows everything about you going to his wedding. It's all out in the open, so you don't have to hide any secrets anymore."

The secret. I'd nearly forgotten about that. You'd think that once your ex is making a movie about your life, it can't get worse.

But, you'd be wrong.

"Right," I say, grabbing at a stray napkin that's on the table. I tear it into two pieces and then into four. Vanessa regards me.

"Oh, no," she says.

"What?" I ask, tearing the napkin in my hand into eight pieces.

"So, he doesn't know?" she asks and I keep my eyes firmly

planted on the floor. "You haven't told him that you actually brought a fake date to his wedding?"

"About that..."

"That Douglas broke up with you on the eve of his wedding, so you brought Jack instead and made him wear a kilt and speak with a Scottish accent?"

"I was there," I say, "you don't have to remind me what happened."

"But Trip doesn't know any of that?" she asks, staring at me with such intensity that I can feel her eyes burning into my head.

"No idea," I say, without bringing my eyes up to meet Vanessa's.

"Then what the hell is the movie about?"

"A girl who goes to her ex-boyfriend's wedding," I say, taking a sip of my iced tea. "Apparently, that's interesting enough in of itself to turn into a movie. You don't even *need* the fake kilt part."

"Brooke," she says, employing the same tone she'd use in speaking to a small child.

"Well, I don't see why I should have to say anything," I say, scooping more bacon onto my fork and dipping it into the dressing. Then I take another bite and pile bacon onto blue cheese and dip *that* into the dressing.

"I don't see why you wouldn't tell Trip," she says, shrugging her shoulders. Um, is she kidding me?!

"You don't see why I wouldn't?" I cry out, my voice an octave higher than I intend it to be. "Well, for starters, it makes me look like a huge loser—"

"But you have Jack now," Vanessa says, cutting me off. "Nothing matters anymore now that you have Jack. He's what's important. Not some silly semblance of your pride that you're trying to protect."

And she's right. When I think about Jack and how lucky I am

to have finally found love, I can't help but feel silly that I'm still obsessing over the fact that my ex got married before me. The first thing that I'm going to do tomorrow is to call Trip and tell him everything. That Douglas broke up with me right before his wedding, so I brought Jack instead. And that, in order to keep my dignity ever so slightly intact, I made Jack pretend to be Douglas, which meant that he had to don a kilt and a fake Scottish accent and I had to wear a fake engagement ring, but that none of that matters anymore since Jack and I are together for real and it's wonderful and it's everything I always wanted but never realized was right in front of me because I was too busy thinking that all the wrong things were important. But, now I've got my head screwed on straight, and I'm engaged to an amazing guy. I will call Trip immediately and tell him all of these things.

But first, I'm going to steal some of Vanessa's French fries and order myself a hamburger.

Chapter Four

"Well, this is unexpected," I say, as Trip saunters into my office. I think, but don't say: *and unwelcome.* First, I silently curse Trip for showing up unannounced. Then, I silently curse my assistant, for not announcing that he'd arrived.

You see, today's the day I'm supposed to be coming clean to Trip about the fact that I brought a fake date to his wedding—the wedding that he's making a major motion picture about—but he's shown up unexpectedly and I'm not really mentally prepared to tell him the truth just yet.

Maybe I should ask him to come back on a day where I've had time to go to the spa to get a massage, manicure and pedicure? Maybe even a facial. Or even a scrub. Yes, I'm sure a scrub would do the trick. Surely then I'd be more relaxed and more prepared to admit the fact that I was too embarrassed to tell him that Douglas broke up with me on the eve of his wedding, so I made Jack dress up as a Scotsman and pretend to be Douglas? But I ask you: is there ever a good time to tell your ex-boyfriend that your man broke up with you on the eve of his wedding, so you made your best friend dress up as him and come with you to the wedding?

Wine. I was going to need some wine before I do this.

"Is now a good time?" Trip asks, settling into one of my leather visitor chairs, his stance indicating that he didn't actually care whether or not it was, in fact, a good time for me. I slip off my real engagement ring and reach into my pocketbook to try to find the fake ring I wore to Trip's wedding. "I thought we could bat around some ideas for the screenplay."

The fake ring is nowhere to be found. I decide to forgo wearing any ring at all. After all, no ring would be better than wearing a different ring he's seen before, right? Although wouldn't it be great if you could have more than one engagement ring and then just wear whichever one matched your mood? Maybe I could get that started as a trend…. Focus, Brooke!

"You mean the screenplay you're writing about my life," I say, looking him dead in the eyes.

"I mean the screenplay about my wedding and how I invited my ex-girlfriend," he says, returning my gaze. "See, Brooke, it's really my story to tell."

"Isn't Ava the star of the movie, not Leo?"

"Well, yes," he says, picking at an imaginary piece of lint on his jacket.

"So, then, it's really her story to tell," I say, folding my arms across my chest. "It's the ex-girlfriend's story." I couldn't help but smile at my little victory. I always *was* a better litigator than Trip.

"Look, Brooke. I just need something more to really make the story solid," Trip says. "So, help me out, would you? It'll be just like in law school when we used to collaborate all the time together."

What he means to say is: *it'll be just like law school, where we were dating, so I made you do all the work for me.* Only his charm has worn off now, and the only thing I'll be helping him to do is to leave my office.

"Where's your engagement ring?" he asks, doing a half-stand out of his chair to get a closer look at my hand. Which has the effect of making me immediately cover my left hand with the right.

"Oh," I say. "That. Yes, well. It's at the cleaners. I mean, the ring cleaners. You know, the jewelers. You know what I meant. Since when are you so interested in jewelry?"

Must get the ex-boyfriend out of my office, stat!

"So, were there any other complications in being an unmarried girl going to your ex-boyfriend's wedding? Anything else you haven't told me?"

"No," I say, with a clipped tone, turning to my computer. I begin to check my email, hoping that he'll think that I'm too busy to talk to him and just leave.

An email pops up on my screen:

From:"Vanessa Taylor" <vtaylor@gilsonhecht.com >
To:"Brooke Miller" <brooke.miller@sgr.com>
Subject:Do it!

Did you fess up to Trip yet???

Vanessa Taylor
Gilson, Hecht and Trattner
425 Park Avenue
11th Floor
New York, New York 10022

*****CONFIDENTIALITY NOTICE*****

The information contained in this e-mail message is confidential and is intended only for the use of the individual or entity named above. If you are not the intended recipient, we would request you delete this communication without reading it or any attachment, not forward or otherwise distribute it, and kindly advise Gilson, Hecht & Trattner by return email to the sender or a telephone call to 1 (800) GILSON. Thank you in advance.

That girl's timing is uncanny. I look over to Trip, sitting on my visitor's chair like a sad little puppy, his pad out, ready to jot down any words of wisdom I may spew out.

"I just feel like I'm missing something here," Trip says, tapping his pen against the side of the pad. "What the script really needs is something to bring it all together. It needs more comedy. More of a love story."

"How's this," I say, throwing him a bone. "I *did* lose my luggage at LAX when we flew in for your wedding. I didn't have a dress to wear, so we had to spend the whole day shopping, trying to find a replacement. Use that."

"Right on, right on," Trip says. Even though he's originally from Connecticut, he certainly has adapted to being a left-coaster. If he says 'bitchin' I'm kicking him out of my office.

"Okay, so great," I say, standing up. "If I think of anything else, I'll call you!"

Trip stays planted in his seat.

"I'm sorry," he says. "I don't mean to be bugging you. It's just that there is so much pressure on me to make this thing great. It just needs a little oomph. Something to make it stand out from all of those other romantic comedies out there. This means a lot to me. And to Ava."

And just like that, I begin to soften. I was so busy trying to one-up Trip that I forgot that there are things that I actually like about him. His determination. His stick-to-it-ness. For a moment, I remember how devoted he could be to something he believed in. Which is probably what makes him such a great agent. Seeing him work so hard at something really makes me feel like I want to help.

I try to formulate the words—how exactly do you tell your ex that you brought a fake date to his wedding?—and just as I am about to tell him the truth, the thing that will make his movie truly great, he says:

"That's it. I just figured it out."

"What?" I ask, curious to hear what fabulous plot point he's come up with. See, Trip was right—collaborating *can* be fun!

"Why you're not wearing your ring," he says. "That's it. I've figured it out."

"Figured what out?" I say back very quickly, suddenly squirming in my office chair. This will be so much more embarrassing if he's figured out what I've done before I get to fess up to him and maintain at least one tiny shred of dignity.

"You're pregnant!" he says, jumping up from his chair and running around my desk to give me a hug. "That's why you're not wearing your ring! I knew you looked a bit bloated today. But, you're pregnant, aren't you? Aren't you?!? You can tell me."

Note to self: Must go home immediately and burn this entire outfit. And then murder my ex-boyfriend.

"I. Am. Not. Pregnant."

"Oh, man," he says, arms falling down to his sides as he releases his grip on me. "Are you sure?"

"Oh yes," I say. "I'm sure. Not pregnant, just bloated."

"I don't know what to say, Brooke."

And with that, those old feelings are gone.

"Get out," I say, and Trip finally leaves my office.

Chapter Five

"What's great about this film is that I don't have to lose weight for the part," Ava says to Nancy O'Dell. "In fact, they're encouraging me to gain more!"

Nancy O'Dell nods back knowingly. I can just picture the two of them out to dinner now—*I can have even more edamame?! And I can actually leave the rice on my sushi rolls?! Oh, happy day!*

"Now, that sounds like my kind of shoot!" Nancy says and she and Ava break out in giggles.

My ex-boyfriend's wife is on *Entertainment Tonight* today to talk about the new movie she's starring in. That my ex-boyfriend wrote. About my life. Yes, my ex-boyfriend has taken the single most humiliating moment of my life, attending his wedding, and is turning it into a major motion picture, set for release next summer.

You can catch it when it comes out on the big screen, but please just do me a favor and don't tell me if you go.

Oh, please. As if you're not *dying* to go and see it now that I've told you all about it.

I roll my eyes at my best friend, Vanessa. She rolls back and takes a handful of popcorn. We both rushed home from work tonight to watch Ava's appearance together. We're at her apartment in comfy sweatpants, with a huge bowl of popcorn between us and a pitcher of margaritas to help wash it down. The pain, that is. Not the popcorn. (But it works on the popcorn, too.)

"Obviously they're not talking about you," Vanessa says. "They probably just want Ava to look more like a real woman. Not the stick figure that she is."

Since Vanessa is a bit of a stick figure herself, this is not exactly a compelling argument from her. Now, it's true: Vanessa stays thin because she's five foot eight and runs six miles a day, but still, it's annoying.

But Vanessa's right. It's not actually all about me, since Trip doesn't know the whole story involved with my coming to his wedding. He thinks it's just your normal girl-goes-to-her-ex-boyfriend's-wedding kind of situation. Thankfully, he doesn't know about the part where Douglas broke up with me mere minutes before the wedding, forcing me to drag my friend Jack in his place. Since Douglas was a Scot, I made Jack dress in a kilt and speak with a faux Scottish accent for the whole evening. I even wore a fake engagement ring to really sell it.

"Thanks," I say to Vanessa and we both look at the television. I take a big swig of my margarita. Maybe we should have cut to the chase and just had shots of tequila before watching this?

"So," Nancy says, putting on a serious expression, "tell us more about the film."

"Well," Ava says. "It's the story of a woman who goes to her ex-boyfriend's wedding."

"Wow," Nancy says, "that sure sounds like quite a story!"

"It is, Nancy," Ava says, leaning in to Nancy as if they're sorority sisters or something. "It is. And lots of single women everywhere can relate to it."

"I don't know about that," Nancy says with a laugh. "You couldn't pay me enough to go to an ex's wedding."

"It's going to be a funny movie," Ava says. "I can personally guarantee lots of laughs. And maybe even a tear or two."

"They're going to be lining up in droves to see this movie!" Nancy says.

And she's probably right. Why couldn't they be making a small art house film about my life that no one would ever see? Why must it be the movie that's slated to be the biggest blockbuster of the summer? Why oh why must my life be so darned interesting that a major motion picture studio has greenlit a production about it?

"Is it a concern," Nancy says, putting a grave expression onto her face, "that people won't think that the story is believable? I mean, what woman in her right mind would actually go to her ex-boyfriend's wedding?"

"That's the great thing, Nancy," Ava says, eyes sparkling, clearly ready for this question to have been asked. "It really *did* happen! To my husband's ex-girlfriend."

"You mean to tell me that your husband's ex-girlfriend actually came to your wedding?" Nancy says and gives the camera a look of shock. Oh please. As if this whole interview wasn't pre-rehearsed. Who does she think she's kidding?

"Yes!" Ava says. "She's actually an attorney right here in Manhattan. And she's very nice."

"Nice or not, I can't believe you let one of your husband's exes come to your wedding!" Nancy says, still doing the shocked expression thing. I mean, doesn't Nancy have any other expressions in her arsenal? What does she do when she interviews someone who actually reveals shocking things? I guess this is why they pre-record all of their shows.

Ava nods in response. *Yes, I am so wonderful that I allowed my husband's ex to come to our wedding. I also do all sorts of other types of charity work.*

"They're making me sound like a stalker," I say to Vanessa and she shhhes me. I finish my margarita and lean over to the pitcher to re-fill my glass.

"But," Nancy quickly says, "it's not as if a woman like you has to worry about any sort of competition. What man would ever choose another woman over you?"

"Oh, God," I say, "is that what everyone's going to be saying at the premiere? Why would he want to be with *her* when he could be with Ava?"

"Oh, don't be silly, sweetie," Vanessa says, looking at me. "We're not going to be invited to the premiere."

"My husband, Trip, was so inspired by the story of his ex coming to the wedding that he decided that it would make a great movie." That Ava doesn't answer Nancy's question and begins posturing makes me think that maybe Trip gave her a script for this interview. "She came with her gorgeous Scottish fiancé, so everything worked out in the end. It's a story about love and friendship. And life's special moments."

"This is beginning to sound like a tampon commercial," Vanessa says, taking a ladylike sip of her margarita. She's still on her first of the night. I'm already pouring number three.

"This is so humiliating," I say, "I can never leave my apartment again."

"No one's even going to see the stupid movie," Vanessa says, "don't be ridiculous. This whole thing will blow over in minutes."

"Maybe the movie will be bad," I say. "Maybe no one will see it!"

"I'm sure no one will," she says, and clicks the television off. "And it will be forgotten before you can even say 'straight to VOD.'"

"Really?" I ask. "You really think that?"

"Sure," Vanessa says, filling up my margarita glass. "Of course I do."

"I guess I should be looking on the bright side," I say, taking a handful of popcorn. "My one saving grace is that Douglas hasn't found out. It's bad enough that I've been humiliated in front of Jack. In fact, this whole thing has actually been a test of how much he truly loves me."

"And he still wants to marry you after all this. He passed," Vanessa says. "With flying colors."

"True," I say. "But if Douglas found out about this whole mess…. Well, let's just say that Douglas doesn't have as good of a sense of humor about things. He would really torture me about this."

"You don't have to remind me about how awful Douglas was," Vanessa says. "I remember."

"Well, then, can I remind you about how wonderful Jack is?"

"Let's just make a toast," Vanessa says, and raises her margarita glass. "To Douglas never finding out about all of this."

"Here, here," I say.

So, now all I need is for Douglas to never watch *Entertainment Tonight* or deign to go see a chick flick. Piece of cake, right?

Chapter Six

"Excuse me, miss, but do I know you?" a handsome man asks me just as I'm about to enter my office building.

"No, I don't think so," I say with a smile. Normally, New Yorkers don't talk to each other on the street, but I wouldn't want to be rude. And it's not just because he's good looking; I'm not superficial like that. You see, I would speak to a stranger even if he *wasn't* attractive. I just so happen to be the exception to that New York rule. Well, okay, I wouldn't speak to a stranger if he looked like he was deranged or something. I mean, that could be dangerous. But a stranger who was average looking? Yes, I would definitely talk to that stranger. If he was handsome and wearing a great suit and had a really really really nice smile, well, that would just be a bonus. A big, gorgeous well-dressed bonus. But, I digress.

"Are you sure I don't know you?" he asks and I can't help but laugh, as I continue walking into the building.

"Sorry," I say, pushing through the big double doors of my laws firm's office building, "but I'm engaged."

How much do I love saying that?! But, how typical is this? The second you're attached, you've got random hotties approaching you in the street. And since you're already involved, you can't do a thing about it. When I was single, this sort of thing never happened to me. Life can be so unfair sometimes.

"Aren't you Brooke Miller?" the hottie says to me as he follows me into the building. Did he just call me by my name? Um, how does he know my name?! Okay, so, now I've got random hotties *stalking* me in the street. I'm strangely conflicted about this.

"How do you know my name?" I ask, edging my way towards the security desk. In a split second, I formulate a positively brilliant plan for getting away from hottie/stalker, should things go awry. I will simply throw my briefcase at his chest and distract him momentarily so that I can run to the safety of the security guard. I don't think that the guards are real cops or anything, but they're still pretty darn imposing. Especially Margie Ann. That woman will put the fear of God into you with just one look. Now, if hottie/stalker actually *catches* my briefcase instead of getting distracted by it, my plan was pretty much blown. But none of that mattered in the end anyhow:

"Yes, I thought it was you. Brooke Miller," he says, reaching into his briefcase. "You've been served."

"I DON'T get it," my ex-boyfriend Trip says, walking into my office unannounced (it's like there's just no point in actually having an assistant in the first place). "I thought that Douglas was cool with all of this. He seemed fine when I told him the other night about the movie we were making about a girl who goes to her ex-boyfriend's wedding. We had that great dinner all together at Pastis, but now, this."

"You mean the movie you're making about my life," I said.

"No," he says with a nervous laugh. "I thought we already established this. It's my story about getting married and then inviting my ex-girlfriend to come to the wedding."

"You say tomato," I say, under my breath as I roll my eyes at Trip. Then, in my sensible lawyerly voice, without the eye roll: "I don't get it, either. Let me give him a call and I'll call you as soon as I hear back from him."

Trip settles into one of my visitor chairs, clearly ready to watch as I make my phone call, which confuses me. If he thinks that I'm about to call my fiancé to ask him why he's suing me, does he really think that I want my ex-boyfriend here to watch? Trip can be such a moron sometimes. Which reminds me....

"Trip, I thought you told me that I couldn't sue you for making a movie out of my life?" I ask.

"Didn't you get a A in torts?" Trip asks. "I got a C, but I still remembered that a private citizen can sue for their rights of privacy."

"I knew you were wrong!" I said. "I just had too much wine and got confused."

"Or maybe it's just that," he says. "After all, you're just not really a better lawyer than me."

I think but don't say: "No. I still am."

"That's why I took you guys out to Pastis that night," he says, leaning back in his chair. "I thought I had your consent. And Douglas's, too."

"I never consented to anything," I say, my hand involuntarily flying up to my chest. "But, I *thought* it was strange that you were hounding me to go out for dinner."

"It was my assistant who called you," Trip points out.

"Whatever," I say under my breath.

"The strange thing here," Trip says, "is that you're a named party in this lawsuit, too. Which means that your fiancé has just served you a lawsuit."

"I know," I say, trying to formulate a reason why my fiancé might be suing me. Maybe it has to do with the fact that the real Douglas wasn't actually at that dinner. It was Jack. Pretending to be Douglas. "So, why don't you let me call him?"

"Yes," he says, leaning back in his chair and putting his hands behind his head. "Please do."

"Okay," I say, nodding my head towards the door. Trip doesn't take the hint. "Okay, so I'll call you later after I've had a chance to sort all of this out."

Trip nods enthusiastically, still not getting the hint.

"So," I say, "you should leave now."

"Oh, yes," he says, "of course."

Trip finally leaves my office and I prepare to call "Douglas."

Instead, I call Jack.

"Ohmigod! Douglas is suing me!"

"Who is this?" Jack says. I'm pretty sure I can tell that he's smiling broadly on the other end of the line.

"Can you please be serious for a second?" I say, jumping up from my desk and closing my office door shut with my foot. "I'm being *sued*!"

"Well, first of all," Jack says. "For a lawyer, you don't react very well to conflict. Or to potential litigation. Where's the fight in you, Brooke?"

"Jack, I am being serious here. What am I going to do? I've never been sued before!"

"But you've been involved in tons of lawsuits before. So, you know that most lawsuits end up settling. He must be looking for money. How much is he suing for?"

"Two million dollars."

"Jesus Christ," Jack says letting out a huge sigh.

"Um, okay, not helping."

"I can give you a really big discount on my fees if you want me to represent you," Jack says, still smiling. Okay, I know I can't see if he's smiling, but I just know.

"Still not helping."

"Well, you're going to need a lawyer," Jack says. "Actually, should I be billing you right now?"

"Not! Helping!"

"Okay," he says. "Then, how's this: Let me make a few calls and try to find you a lawyer—one who's not actually involved in this whole thing—and in the meantime, maybe you should go speak to Douglas. Maybe if you tell him what happened, he'll drop the lawsuit."

"You've met Douglas," I say, "haven't you? He's not exactly the kind understanding type."

"Well," Jack says, "then the other option would be to go and tell Trip the truth. That you and Douglas broke up on the eve of his wedding so you brought me instead and made me wear a kilt and speak with a Scottish accent in an effort to pretend I was Douglas. Actually, now that I'm thinking about it, maybe that would be best. If you explain it to him now, he'll realize this whole thing was just a big misunderstanding. And ultimately, if you can get him on your side instead of Douglas's, it'll make Trip a lot less likely to countersue you for making misrepresentations to him. If you and Trip can stay aligned, you have a much better chance of fighting Douglas. Just call Trip."

"Okay," I say.

"Okay, you're going to talk to Trip? That was easy."

"What?" I ask, beginning to shut my computer down. "Oh, God, no. I'm going to go and yell at Douglas."

Chapter Seven

"Well, this is unexpected," my ex-boyfriend Douglas says, and he's right. The last time we saw each other, I told him in no uncertain terms that I didn't want to marry him and that I never wanted to see him again. So, under normal circumstances, it would be curious that I'm here. But under normal circumstances, I wouldn't *have* to be here. Up until one day ago, I was 100% sure that I'd be keeping my promise; I had no intention of ever seeing Douglas again.

"How is this unexpected?" I ask through gritted teeth. "You're suing me!" He doesn't get up from his desk, like he normally would when a lady enters a room. He stays planted behind it, using it as a shield.

The coward.

"You broke up with me and refused to talk to me," Douglas says, matter-of-factly, picking a pen up from his desk and then examining it. He's calm, cool. Which has the effect of making me even more angry than I was when I marched in. (And, yes, you read that correctly, I didn't walk in, I marched.)

"No, *you* broke up with *me* by getting engaged to another woman!" I say, voice rising higher and higher with each word that comes out of my mouth. "It was only after you tried to humiliate me at my ex-boyfriend's wedding that you even wanted me back."

"That's not true," he says. "That's not true at all. I realized that you were the one and so I came to the wedding as a romantic gesture."

"If only that were true," I say. "After I said 'no,' did you get back together with Beryl?"

Yes, Douglas broke up with me and got engaged to a woman named Beryl. I don't know what's worse. The fact that he was cheating on me or the fact that it was with a woman named Beryl.

"Right," he says.

"Right," I say back.

"Right."

"Right," I say, but then realize I have no idea what we're even saying 'right' to anymore. In fact, I think that he's saying 'right' to something completely different than what I'm saying 'right' to. And clearly, you want your 'rights' to be right. Right? "Wait? What are we even talking about here? Why are you suing me?!"

"Because you're writing a movie about my life," he says, hands folded neatly on top of his desk. Then, looking me dead in the eye he says: "What, you didn't think I'd find out?"

And, no, the truth is: I didn't think he'd find out. A tiny little part of me (the very, very stupid and naïve part, I'm now figuring out) thought that Trip and his wife could just make their little movie about my life quietly and no one would ever be the wiser. Not Douglas, and certainly not Trip.

But the more I think about it, I realize that this is all because of that clip on *Entertainment Tonight*. If Ava hadn't gone on *Entertainment Tonight* to announce plans of this film, none of this would have happened! Douglas wouldn't have found out that my ex-boyfriend was making a movie out of my life and he would never have sued me. This is all Nancy O'Dell's fault! Damn you, Nancy O'Dell! Why do you have to be so damned perky and report the entertainment news so well?! That's it—from now on, I am boycotting that show. Yes, from now on, I will only watch *Access Hollywood*! But, I digress.

"*I'm* not doing anything. How would I write a movie and get it produced? Why would I write a movie? I'm a lawyer," I say. "It's Trip. My ex-boyfriend Trip is writing the movie as a star vehicle for his wife, Ava. Remember Trip? If you'd just come with me to his wedding last spring, none of this would have ever happened."

"Well," he says, "according to *Entertainment Tonight*, it seems that I *did* come with you."

"About that—" I start to say, only to be cut off by Douglas.

"I knew it! Trip still doesn't know, does he?" Douglas asks. "He actually thinks that that silly American colleague of yours is me?" Douglas throws his head back and laughs with a deep throaty thunder, as if this concept is the most ridiculous thing he's ever heard. Which is ridiculous in of itself. You see, Douglas is laughing because he thinks that Jack is no match to impersonate him—that he, himself, is so fabulous that Jack isn't fit to shine his shoes, much less pretend to be in them. When in reality, the opposite is true. Jack is the best thing to ever happen to me. Douglas, as it turned out in the end, was the worst. And Jack was my best friend through all of it. Through the fights and the heartbreak, Jack was always there for me. I'm just lucky, that after all these years, Jack and I finally ended up together.

"Jack," I say to Douglas. "His name is Jack."

"Well, whatever," Douglas says, a sly smile creeping onto his lips. "I wonder what Trip will say when he finds out that Jack's not me?"

"If you drop your lawsuit, I promise that I'll tell Trip," I say, and Douglas's sly smile becomes a full blown grin.

"Well, I was hoping to get to court at least one time to see you in one of your cute outfits," he says. Even though I never figured out exactly what it was that Douglas did for a living, he always found a way to diminish what I did for a living. Cute outfits for court? I'm a big time lawyer, for God's sakes! Sometimes being so devoted to fashion really has its drawbacks.

"I'm leaving," I say, getting up out of my chair.

"Wait," Douglas says. "Sit down. Are you really going to tell Trip everything?"

"Is that what you want? To humiliate me once again? Dumping me mere minutes before my ex-boyfriend's wedding wasn't enough for you? Now you want me to confess to my ex that I was so desperate to keep my dignity ever so slightly intact that I made my best friend dress up and pretend to be you?"

"Well, yes, actually," he says, leaning back in his chair. "That's exactly what I want."

Hmm…. Risk public humiliation at the hands of my ex-boyfriend or face a two million dollar lawsuit? The sort of quandary single girls everywhere must face on a daily basis.

"Fine," I say, trying to plaster a fake smile onto my face. "If I tell Trip everything and completely humiliate myself, will you then drop the lawsuit?"

"Sure, Brooke," he says, putting his hands behind his head. "Sure I will."

"Shake on it?" I ask, thrusting my hand out for him to shake.

"I have a better idea," Douglas says, and pulls my hand so that my body goes flying across his desk. I fall on top of his desk and try to use my other hand to get back up. "Now, this is more like it," he says, leaning over me. "*This* is what I call a negotiation."

"You disgust me," I say, pulling away and struggling to stand upright. I straighten my suit and spin on my heel.

"You'll come back, Brooke," Douglas says as I walk out of his office. "You always do."

Chapter Eight

"Trip," I say to my ex-boyfriend, "we need to talk."

We're on the set of his latest film. You know, the one that's starring his movie star wife about a woman who goes to her ex-boyfriend's wedding? Yes, that's the one. The one that's all about my life.

Long story.

"I don't have time to talk, Brooke," he says, ever the uber-agent to the stars. "If you haven't noticed, we're trying to make a movie here."

"About that," I say. "There's something you need to know."

"Oh no," Trip says, "has the screenplay been leaked on the internet?"

"No," I say. "Trip, listen to me. It's about Douglas. Well, not Douglas, but…. Okay, let me start over. Douglas—I mean, the person who you think is Douglas—isn't Douglas. That's why the real Douglas suing us."

"What are you talking about, Brooke?" Trip says, putting down his clipboard and giving me his full attention.

"Well, there *was* a Douglas. A Scottish guy I was living with. But we weren't engaged when I told you we were—in fact, we were never engaged—and he broke up with me just seconds before your wedding. I didn't know what to do. I had nowhere to live—thank goodness for Vanessa—and my life was turned upside down. You see, I thought that I had to go to your wedding with some gorgeous Scottish guy just to show you up, but now I realize that none of it really matters."

"But you *did* bring a Scottish guy to my wedding," Trip says, furrowing his brow. "You mean to tell me that you were able to find *another* Scottish guy to come with you to my wedding?"

"Right," I say, "about that. That was Jack, a friend of mine from work. He faked the accent. And the Scottish back story. And we rented the kilt. We even bought a fake engagement ring at a costume shop."

"You're kidding me, right?" Trip says. "This has got to be a joke."

"It's not," I say, wishing that it was, in fact, a joke. "I brought Jack and Jack pretended to be Douglas. Everything worked out in the end, because Jack and I ended up getting together and now we're engaged for real, but that's why Douglas is suing us. All of us."

"You're serious about all this?" Trip says.

"Yes," I say slowly. "And now you know everything."

"Okay," he says back just as slowly. "but, what I don't understand is why you did it? Why couldn't you just tell me that you and Douglas broke up? I would have let you bring Jack to the wedding anyway if you wanted to."

"Well, we *have* always had a competitive relationship," I say.

"No, we didn't, Brooke," he says, grabbing my hand. "You could never really compete with me."

"Yes, well, anyway," I continue, releasing my hand from his

grasp. "The point is, I was trying to keep my dignity ever so slightly intact. I felt humiliated. And I thought that if I showed up alone, I'd be even more humiliated. Do you understand?"

"Yes, of course I understand," Trip says and throws a compassionate arm around my shoulder. "I would never want you to feel humiliated or like a loser."

"Just humiliated," I say. "I said I'd be humiliated. I didn't say loser."

"The point is," Trip says, "you know I love you, Brooke, and I would never do anything to embarrass you or hurt you."

"Really?" I say. "That's so sweet of you."

"Really, Brooke."

"That's great to hear," I say. "So, then the movie's off?"

"Oh, hell no," Trip says and my mouth drops to the ground. "Are you kidding me? I finally have my hook. We're going to make this thing a hilarious romantic comedy. I'm going to have my people put a call into Sandler."

"What?" I ask.

"Adam Sandler in a kilt," Trip says. "Non-stop hilarity!"

"You're still making the movie?" I say. "After everything you just said?"

"Of course I am, Brooke."

"But what about not humiliating me?" I ask. "About never doing anything to hurt me?"

"Well, Brooke," Trip says, furrowing his brow as if he's on an after school special and is about to tell me the lesson I should have learned. "My grandfather always said that the only person who can embarrass you is you."

"Your grandfather was wrong," I say.

"Now that I know everything," Trip explains, "the movie finally has what it needs! So, it doesn't even matter that there's a massive lawsuit against us. It's okay, because now I have a killer plot. And since this thing is going to be a huge blockbuster, the production company's lawyers will even represent you, since you gave us all of this great material."

The lawsuit. I'd totally forgotten. In addition to the fact that I've been totally humiliated, there's also a two million dollar lawsuit hanging over my head.

I walk away from Trip and call Douglas from my cell phone.

"I told him," I say in the place of 'hello.' "I told Trip everything, so now you can call off the lawsuit, just like you promised."

"You finally came clean?" Douglas asks. "Well, fuck me, I didn't think you had the backbone to do it."

"Well, I did," I say. "So, now it's time for you to hold up your end of the bargain and call off your lawsuit. I want it called off against Trip, the movie studio, and me. Just drop the whole thing."

"Well, darling," he says, "it's not really that simple."

"Yes, Douglas," I say. "It is. You simply call your lawyers and tell them to drop it. Then, they simply call the judge and it's over. Simple."

"Well, I'm not going to drop it," he says.

"What do you mean?" I ask. "You promised."

"Well, I've had a change of heart," he says. "The suit stays on."

"Then, I'll sue *you* for breach of contract," I say. "You made me an oral promise. I then acted in reasonable reliance on that promise and did something that I wouldn't do otherwise. That makes what you promised me a legally binding contract."

See, I told you I was a good lawyer.

"Save the legal mumbo jumbo, Brooke," Douglas says. "I really couldn't care less. And, anyway, I'm sure Trip will be delighted that the lawsuit's still on. After all, it will be great publicity for the film."

I hang up the phone without saying goodbye and run over to the hair and make-up trailer to go find Jack and Vanessa.

Walking through a film set is a surreal experience. And it's not just because they have a mock-up of a New York City street right next to a mock-up of an elegant Los Angeles hotel. It's because this film set is my life. Right across from the hotel, they've got my old office at Gilson, Hecht and Trattner (which is accurate down to the little stress ball that was always perched at the edge of my desk), and the Soho apartment I used to share with Douglas. How different my life is now. I'm sure that by tomorrow, they'll be constructing a set of Vanessa's Upper East Side apartment now that Trip knows the truth about what happened between Douglas and me, and how I had to move in with Vanessa after he kicked me out of our apartment.

I walk through the wardrobe department and see that they have a vintage Halston dress, one that's exactly like the one that I wore to Trip and Ava's wedding, just waiting to be worn. They also have a wedding dress hanging, ready for the actress who will be playing the bride. I walk over to the dress to get a closer look. It looks nothing like the actual dress that Ava wore to her wedding, but it's beautiful all the same. The bodice has intricate double embroidered lace, covered in little pearls and tiny crystals. As I reach out to touch it, Vanessa calls out my name.

"We're going to find you a wedding dress that will be even more beautiful than this," Vanessa says.

And I know we will—Vanessa and my mom are taking me dress shopping next week and I can hardly wait.

"Trip is still making the movie," I say, "and Douglas isn't dropping the lawsuit like he promised."

"Oh, who cares? Let Trip make his stupid movie and let Douglas have his stupid lawsuit. Your life will go on," she says, and I actually believe her. For the first time since this mess began, I realize, my life has nothing to do with this movie or the lawsuit. My life is about the people who love and support me most. The people who think that I'm fabulous no matter what. The people I feel the same way about. Vanessa motions to the hair and make-up trailer. "Let's go."

"Hey," Jack says, as he sits in a director's chair, getting make-up airbrushed onto his face. Yes, after all he's been through, I managed to wrangle him a little cameo in the movie. He's playing wedding guest #5 and I must say, he's looking rather dashing today in his tuxedo. The one bright spot in the fact that Trip's still making the movie.

"Hey yourself," I say, as Jack leans in for a kiss.

He reaches into his pocket and pulls out a box. "I think you forgot something."

I open the box and see that Jack's brought me my engagement ring. Not the fake one I wore to Trip's wedding, but the real one. The ring that his grandfather gave to his grandmother when he came back from World War II.

An ascher cut diamond with regal trillions flanking it on either side and channel set diamonds around the rest of the platinum band, I've never seen anything more beautiful in my whole life. I slip my ring back onto my finger. Where it belongs. And as I do, I realize that I never should have taken it off in the first place. And I never will again.

"Are you sure that you want to marry a girl who's going to be publicly humiliated next summer when *Scot On The Rocks* hits a theater near you?" I ask Jack and he smiles back at me.

"I wouldn't have it any other way."

POLIS BOOKS